TOURIST TRAP

"Now for the Grand Tour," Therion said to Paul.

They passed beyond the wall, where the creature waited, its canine face peering into an enclosure where a multitude of creatures struggled to escape. Most had the bodies of humans; some wore the scaly skins of fish. Heaped in the corner where the scrambling feet had scuffled them were the remains of a feast: fruit rinds, shards of pottery, bread crusts and human hands and feet . . .

FAITH OF TAROT
The third adventure on
the miracle planet TAROT
PIERS ANTHONY

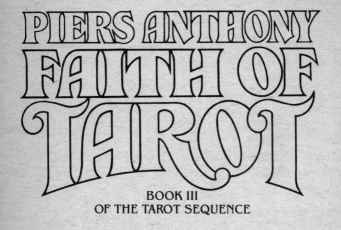

PIERS ANTHONY
FAITH OF TAROT

BOOK III
OF THE TAROT SEQUENCE

A BERKLEY BOOK
published by
BERKLEY PUBLISHING CORPORATION

FAITH OF TAROT

A Berkley Book / published by arrangement with
the author

PRINTING HISTORY
Berkley edition / February 1980

ISBN: 0-425-04443-2

A BERKLEY BOOK® TM 757,375
PRINTED IN THE UNITED STATES OF AMERICA

**Dedicated to
the Holy Order of Vision**

Acknowledgments

A HISTORY OF THE BIBLE, copyright © 1959 by Fred Gladstone Bratton. Published by Beacon Press. Used by permission of the publisher.

THE HISTORY OF THE DEVIL AND THE IDEA OF EVIL, copyright © 1974 by Paul Carus. Published by Crown Publishers. Used by permission of the publisher.

NO LAUGHING MATTER: RATIONALE OF THE DIRTY JOKE (Second Series), copyright © 1975 by G. Legman. Distributed by Breaking Point, Inc. Used by permission of the author.

The author wishes to thank J. W. Drought for the passage reproduced here from his novel, THE SECRET, published by Skylight Press, Norwalk, Connecticut, 1963.

Author's Note:

This is the concluding volume in the three-part novel of Tarot. The first volume, *God of Tarot*, presented the challenge of finding God, and developed the character of the protagonist, Brother Paul of the Holy Order of Vision. The second volume, *Vision of Tarot*, explained the religious background of the quest, including the graphic reenactment of the crucifixion of Jesus Christ. Though the present volume is a unified tour of Hell, the novel should be more intelligible and meaningful if the reader goes through the prior two volumes. For those who are unable or unwilling to do so, here is a summary of the salient aspects:

Brother Paul is sent to Planet Tarot by his superior, the Reverend Mother Mary, to discover whether the Deity manifesting there is or is not God. He finds numerous schismatic religions there who also need to know the truth, so that they can unite and survive the rigors of colony life. He is the guest of the Reverend Siltz of the Second Church Communist, whose son wishes to marry Jeanette, a Scientologist; Siltz is strongly opposed. Brother Paul encounters the lovely woman Amaranth, who worships the snake-footed god Abraxas and seeks constantly to seduce Brother Paul. He is befriended by the Mormon Lee and the devil-worshiper Therion, who become his Good and Bad

Companions in the visions, leading him respectively toward improvement or mischief. He discovers he has a daughter, Carolyn, as yet unborn but whom he loves deeply. All parts are played by Planet Tarot colonists. They encounter the monster Bigfoot, and participate in a series of playlike scenes, seeking truth yet failing to resolve the issue. Brother Paul concludes that only by knowing himself, putting himself to the ultimate test, can he find God. He decides to visit his own, personal Hell—and his companions elect to accompany him, even there.

Volume III, *Faith of Tarot*, commences with the group's descent. Portions of this narrative may be objectionable to some readers. Hell is not a nice place.

FAITH OF TAROT
TABLE OF CONTENTS

I

Violence: 20

When Jesus Christ was crucified, Governor Pontius
Pilate assigned Roman soldiers to stand guard. One of
these soldiers, named Longinus, had a malady of the
eyes. When Jesus died, Longinus took a spear and
pierced his side, verifying his death. Blood ran down the
shaft of the spear, and a drop of it got on the soldier's
eyes. Immediately they were healed. This, combined
with certain other signs occurring at the time of Jesus'
death—the darkening of the sun and quaking of the
earth—caused Longinus to be convinced that Jesus was
indeed the Son of God, and the soldier was converted to
the Christian faith. He gave up the military life, studied
with the Apostles, and became a monk. Many years
later he was brought before the Governor because he
refused to sacrifice to idols. He was subjected to torture; his tongue was cut off and his teeth torn out. But
Longinus took an axe and smashed the idols, his brazen
act calculated, as though to say "If these be gods, let
them show themselves!" Demons came out of the idols
and took over the bodies of the Governor and his aids,
and the Governor became blind. He then had Longinus
beheaded. But after, he fell down before the corpse, and
wept, and did penance. His sight returned. Thereafter,
he did good works.

They stood in a hollow in the ground ringed by hugely twisted oaks. The full moon illuminated the tops but hardly penetrated to the ground. It was a beautiful but hauntingly evil setting.

"There were these two devils," Therion remarked. "And the little one said 'I'm *tired* of being the lesser of two evils!' " No one laughed.

Slowly an opacity formed from the shadow, and this shaped into the walls of a building—a single large room with bench pews at one end and an ornate stone altar at the other. A church.

But what a church! The cross on the altar was upside down, and crooked at that, with a crack traversing it. The stained glass windows seemed to be smeared with drying blood and formed pictures of obscene sexual acts involving satyrs, plump women, and pigs. Beyond the altar was a sculpture of the Virgin Mary, one breast dangling tubularly, masturbating the infant Jesus. A monstrous pentacle enclosed the altar and a goodly portion of the floor, including several of the pews. It was a five pointed star, the extremities symbolizing the five projections of the human body, the five senses of man, and the five elements of nature. Everything was wrong, profane, or disgusting—calculated to be the reverse of normal religious procedure. As it had to be. For this was to be the Black Mass, the infernal ceremony through which they would summon Satan.

Brother Paul felt a shiver go down the outsides of his arms. Did he really want to go through with this? No question about it: he did *not*! He had known what he thought was ultimate horror in his first Animation, the horror of personal degradation—only to suffer worse horror in the second. This was the third, and it would surely be the worst if he survived it at all. Yet—he had to do it not only for the sake of his mission, but, ironically, for his personal satisfaction. He had to know himself—whatever that self might be. Only then could he hope to know God.

He wore a black cape embroidered with Satanic symbols and serpents, hanging open in front to expose his genitals, for he wore no underclothing. The congregation was grotesquely masked with some individuals being in complete animal costumes. The acolytes were naked young men whose lingering glances tended to rest on each other's posteriors: blatant sodomists. They swung censers that reeked of marijuana, opium, and worse.

The high priest stepped up to the altar. His robe, like Brother Paul's was open; unlike Brother Paul, he had an erection augmented by Animation to inhuman magnitude. It was of course Therion. Under his direction, members of the congregation lifted a mattress to the top of the altar, covering it with a dirty black drape.

"Let the ceremony begin," Priest Therion said sonorously. "Virgin—dispose thyself."

Amaranth came forward, diffidently. The animal congregation began a chant whose words were indistinguishable—because the litany was being recited backward. She wore a fetching gown similar in respects to the nightgown she had used as Sister Beth: the material was sheer and tended to fall open at key locations, exposing portions of her lush anatomy. Brother Paul was no longer so naive as to suppose such offerings were accidental; she liked to put her torso on display. And he, male that he was, liked to see it thus. Now she did a little dance, removing films of material from here and there and flinging them away in the manner of a cheap strip-tease artist. Slowly her bouncing breasts came into full view and her flexing thighs.

"I would rather have made a try for Heaven," Lee muttered beside him.

Brother Paul knew what he meant. But imperfect man had no chance to achieve Heaven directly; first he had to settle with Hell. On this they more or less agreed. Brother Paul had gone to Lee's Hell to fetch him out; now Lee was coming to Brother Paul's Hell to help in whatever way he could. This was the nature of friendship.

Amaranth disposed of the last item of apparel and danced naked. She was such a splendid figure of a woman with her generally slender body blessed by full breasts and buttocks that Brother Paul had trouble with his posture. If only he had more concealment for his crotch!

"Marvelously protean flesh," Lee said, and Brother Paul realized that this was Antares' thought. The amoebic alien naturally appreciated flexibility, tubular elongations, and jellylike quiverings of anatomy.

The congregation acknowledged her beauty with a medley of snorts, growls, grunts, groans, and animalistic howls. Several males rubbed their crotches suggestively, making bucking motions with their hips, while the females tittered rudely.

Brother Paul felt his temper rising. How was he to stand here and tolerate this indignity to the woman he loved? (*Loved*? How had *that* term entered his mind! He might be tempted by her, but not. . . .) Yet she was doing it voluntarily—and doing it to assist his own mission. For this was the way, according to Therion, to find Satan most swiftly and surely—and Therion was the expert in such matters. If this were the worst of the indignities he, Brother Paul, had to suffer here, he was well off.

Amaranth walked languorously to the altar and picked up two burning candles there. Brother Paul knew they were made from human fat. Holding one candle in each hand, she carefully seated herself up on the altar, then leaned slowly back to lie upon it, face up. Her head rested on a pillow inscribed with Satanic designs, and her arms spread wide to either side to support the guttering candles. They gave off an odor like cooking meat, making Brother Paul's stomach roil unpleasantly. Her legs spread wide, dangling off the edge of mattress and altar so that her vagina lay open to public view. Brother Paul tried to keep his eyes away from the moist aperture, but they strayed back. He bit his tongue, fighting off the reaction that his open robe would advertise to the entire congregation.

The acolytes brought sacramental wafers stolen from a legitimate church, and sour wine that looked distressingly like diluted blood. The Priest held the wafers above Amaranth's body and pronounced a ringingly profane curse upon them. He handed them back for distribution to the congregation, then bent down and kissed the girl resoundingly between her legs.

Brother Paul started forward, but Lee restrained him. "It is the ritual," he cautioned. "It is an abomination—yet the road to Hell is paved with abominations, as we well knew before we made this compact."

"And the angel of Hell enjoys every one of them!" Brother Paul pronounced through gritted teeth. But his friend was right: this had to be suffered. Had he expected an easy route to the Infernal Region?

The congregation accepted the wafers and wine, but neither ate nor drank. They threw the wafers down on the floor, trampled on them, and poured the wine on top. "Jesus Christ eats shit!" someone yelled, and Brother Paul flinched, remembering the terrible crucifixions of the Savior. "Fuck the Virgin Mary!"

"Words mean little—either of worship or condemnation," Lee murmured. "The Satanists overrate the significance of external expressions. Neither Jesus nor his mother can be touched by the likes of these."

And that of course was correct. This infernal ceremony was valid only to the extent Brother Paul allowed it to touch him, like Voodoo magic. Let the demons curse; they were only advertising their own powerlessness.

Priest Therion raised a benign right hand, very like the Hierophant he once had been. His left hand fingered his penis. Brother Paul was reminded of the Spanish obscenity: "You irritate my penis!" in lieu of the English "You are a pain in the ass!" Evidently Therion irritated his own penis. "All in good time," Therion said, responding to the cries of the congregation.

"They shall pay—in good time," Lee murmured in a deadly low tone. It was evident that despite his encouragement to Brother Paul, he could not avoid being moved himself.

Now the members of the congregation opened their costumes and urinated on the mash of wafers and wine.

"Piss in the mouth of God!" one bawled, then jumped as the woman behind him gave him a playful one-fingered goose in the rectum.

The Priest bestowed another juicy kiss on the Virgin's vagina, then rose, smacking his lips. "Fill the Grail," he said.

The acolytes scraped up a mound of urine-wafer mash and dumped it into a huge dirty chalice. Therion took this chamber pot of a Grail, gestured obscenely over it, and lo! it was a human baby. "Celebrant, come forward," he cried.

"That's me," Brother Paul said glumly. "Last time I traveled his road, I regretted it. . . . "

"It is only ritual," Lee reminded him. "Profanity, nudity, urine—these can harm you only if you yield to them. Keep your mind pure, your intent honorable, and all the fiendish powers of Satan are futile."

Good advice! Brother Paul stepped forward.

Therion held the baby out to him. "Place this innocent infant on the belly of the Virgin, slit its throat, and catch the blood in the chalice," he instructed. "Here is the sacrificial knife; here is the cup. You must do it well, or Satan will not come." And he gave his standing penis another jerk with one hand momentarily freed for the purpose to show that there was also a sexual connotation to his statement. When Satan came, he came.

Brother Paul froze, appalled despite his preparation. "I can't do that!" he cried. "I can't kill—"

Therion frowned, looking truly demoniac. "Oh, come on, Paul," he said under his breath. "It's not *really* a baby, you know; it's a puppy. An animal. A living sacrifice for Satan. See?" And for a moment Brother Paul glimpsed the little beast, its tail curled tightly between its legs. "Don't be a fool. Go along with the gag."

The shape of the baby reappeared. So it was illusion! He should have anticipated that. After all, he had seen it change from chalice to infant. But was it right to kill a dog?

"Come on," Therion urged. "You're holding up the

show. Do you think it's any worse than butchering a swine for bacon?''

Was it any worse? How many times had Brother Paul eaten of the flesh of animals? A thousand? Ten thousand? For each such meal, some animal, somewhere, had had to die. He would be a hypocrite to balk now.

He took the baby and set it on the soft white tummy of the Virgin. Virgin? How *could* she be after his liaison with her in the Castle of the Seven Cups two Animations ago? Yet he could not be *sure* about that, since Therion had—

He shook off the ugly thought, as he always did, and accepted the knife and chalice. This was horrible, but it represented his rite of passage. If he could eat the flesh of an animal killed *for* him, he should be able to kill an animal himself.

"Daddy." Brother Paul paused, thinking he had heard someone speak. But the screaming encouragement of the congregation drowned out all else. He must have imagined it. He hefted the knife, seeing a shaft of pale moonlight glint from its cruel blade.

The baby opened its eyes and looked at him. And abruptly Brother Paul recognized it. "Carolyn!" he breathed.

No—that was impossible. She was at least ten years old by this time, assuming the Animations progressed chronologically. No baby! And as a colonist she was twelve, verging on nubility. So this had to be a false identification, perhaps a figment of his own balking mind.

He gripped the knife with sweaty fingers and raised it to the tiny throat. It wasn't really *her* throat, but that of a puppydog. Merely illusion—

He froze again. Illusion? If Therion could make a puppy resemble a human baby, why couldn't he make a baby resemble a puppy? Or a young girl resemble a baby?

Whose throat was he cutting?

Again he remembered that episode at the Castle when he had grabbed the naked Amaranth—and later looked in the window and seen Therion standing where the girl had supposedly been. Had Therion made himself resemble Amaranth, and—

"Get *on* with it!" Therion said through gritted teeth. "The natives are getting restive. Do you want to ruin everything?"

Brother Paul had gone along before—and regretted it profoundly ever since. Was he so much the fool that he could be destroyed twice by the same magic? How much worse a deed was he being guided to this time by the Evil Companion?

"Now! Therion cried, his desperation such that even his penis lost elevation.

Now Brother Paul was sure. He dropped the knife and lifted his daughter from the stomach of the Virgin. "What in Hell are you trying to do?" he demanded with no profanity.

"Fool!" Therion cried. "It is too late to stop it now. Satan is coming!" He snatched at the baby, but Brother Paul drew aside, using his judo balance, and stepped out of the way with her in his arms.

Now the congregation, balked of its expectation, became a ravening mob. With an animal roar it charged forward.

Brother Paul set the child down behind him and braced himself for devastating action. He had in his hands the skill to maim and kill, rapidly, and if that was what this horde really wanted—

"No, Paul!" Lee cried.

And Brother Paul understood. Lee was not concerned for the welfare of the mob; he was cautioning Brother Paul. Once before he had yielded to Temptation—by doing its will in the name of opposing it. That had been the path to ruin. Instead, his model had to be Jesus Christ: to preserve his own values regardless of the threat.

He stood firm, his arm about the child—and it was as if an aura surrounded him, a shining light, impervious. The rabble broke against this shield and was rebuffed.

"Damnation!" Therion cried. "Satan is coming; He

must have His blood! There is only one chance remaining—and I'll have to do it myself!" He grimaced as
though contemplating an act so horrible that even *he*
had to nerve himself for it.

Therion stalked up to the altar, a hand on his phallus.
The Virgin still lay there, holding the two burning
candles. Therion positioned himself between her legs
and lowered his boom, orienting on her exposed vagina.
"I hate this," he said. "I'd rather crap on her face. But
this has to be according to form."

Brother Paul started forward—but again Lee
cautioned him. "You have won—don't throw it away
now! What means most to you?"

And Brother Paul realized: the life of his daughter
was more important than the virginity of his girlfriend.
He stood firm.

Therion closed his eyes, bared his teeth as though
before a firing squad, then steeled himself with a hearty
oath and rammed his member home. Amaranth gave
out a gasp of amazement and dropped the candles;
evidently she had anticipated only another genital kiss.
But it was too late for any meaningful protest on her
part; she had already been speared. There was a spray of
blood: her maidenhead, its rupture augmented by
Animation.

The mob went wild again. It dissolved into a swearing
scramble of bodies. Clothing was ripped off. Men for-
nicated frantically with women, genitally, orally and
anally, and those who could not get hold of female
anatomy rapidly enough plunged with equal fervor into
the orifices of whatever was within range. It was an incredible orgy of lust, imperative and insatiable. One
woman came up from the heap with something bloody
dangling from her mouth: a bitten-off penis. Some of
the congregation, it now developed, really *were* animals;
a billy goat was mounting a sprawled woman while two
men attempted to penetrate the animal's rectum
simultaneously.

The whole demoniac church shuddered. Smoke issued
from vents around the perimeter of the pentacle. But the

mob paid no attention. Every person was too busy slaking his, her, or its drug-loosed, beastly passion. All except Brother Paul, Lee, and Carolyn.

Therion was still performing his sacrifice at the altar, shoving ex-Virgin and mattress askew in his grim determination to complete the ritual properly. "Disgusting!" he muttered. "But I can't let it faze me! I must ejaculate the Offering though the Gorgon petrify me!" And he strove ever harder against the impotence that threatened him.

Amaranth was trying to scramble to her feet, but could not get them under her before he left off his efforts. "What the Hell are you talking about?" she demanded, her surprise, confusion, and pain turning to anger as she began to comprehend exactly what he was talking about.

Therion stiffened with a climactic effort, then slowly relaxed in place. Then, in an amazed afterthought: "I *did* it! I really did it! I conquered the gaping monster! I prevailed over Manifest Castration itself! Only Satan could have brought me through that horror!"

"That *horror!*" Amaranth exclaimed, furious. "Get away from me, you fairy!"

And Brother Paul understood also. To certain homosexuals, the female genital region was the terrifying proof of the reality of castration, for where there should be a penis and testicles was only a slash like that left by a knife. The awful Sword had removed everything! Such people had constantly to reassure themselves by dealing only with those who remained unmutilated: other males. Homosexuality was Hell.

"But do you know," Therion added with even greater amazement, "I think I liked it!" The man had, in his fashion, just been tested as crucially as Lee had been in Dante's Hell—and profited as much. He had discovered heterosexuality.

The smoke gave way to thin fire, jetting up like blowtorch flames on each of the ten sides of the pentacle, outlining the five points of the star in flame. The entire congregation was within this outline. The fire rose up in sheets, forming a new enclosure, shutting out the obscene church. The floor shuddered again as though subject to an earthquake.

"Satan approaches," Lee said tersely. "The Priest's act summoned—"

"No—I suspect we are going to the Inferno," Brother Paul said. "The Priest only greased the channel, as it were. The mountain seldom comes to Mahomet."

"Daddy, put me down," Carolyn said. Brother Paul discovered that he was holding her so close her feet were off the floor. She was no infant any more; she had swiftly and subtly grown to her colonist size. If he wielded the knife, catering to Therion's supposed hate for all the distaff sex—no! He eased up so as to let her slide to the floor. He had already come far closer to Hell than he liked!

The whole surface of the pentacle jumped with a rending clang like that of metal on concrete. Steam hissed up in great clouds, stifling the fire. Ozone fumes suffused the air. The ex-Virgin fell off the altar, carrying the Priest with her; in a tangle of limbs they were separated at last.

"Daddy, pick me up!" Carolyn cried.

Instead, he squeezed her thin shoulders gently but firmly, holding her steady. "We're going to Hell, honey," he told her. "Don't be frightened."

She turned her startled gaze upon him. Suddenly he realized the incongruity of what he had said. They both burst out laughing.

Lee looked at them disapprovingly. "Mirth— hallmark of the Devil," he muttered.

The air became close as the steam-vapor surrounded them. The rampaging congregation at last become aware of the changing situation. There were sounds of coughing and hacking as the smog coalesced into soot that coated everything. Brother Paul found a handkerchief and gave it to Carolyn to breathe through. She insisted on sharing it with him, so he stooped down to put his mouth to one end. It did seem to help filter out the choking gas and dust.

The bottom dropped out. The entire pentacle plummeted into a bottomless hole in the earth like an elevator whose cable and safety brakes were broken. Down, down, in free fall, stomachs floating. "Even so did I plunge into the abyss!" Therion said from somewhere, reviewing his recent performance, his supreme act of courage.

There was wretching among the congregation. But Brother Paul, Carolyn, and Lee stood firm. Therion slid free of Amaranth's legs, and she scrambled to her feet, virtually floating free of the blood-spattered altar mattress. Brother Paul tried again to keep his eyes averted from her and from Therion's now-dangling member, but was not entirely successful. Somehow he felt she had betrayed him, though obviously she had neither anticipated nor cooperated in—what had happened. And of course he shared responsibility, for he had balked at sacrificing the baby, necessitating Therion's alternate procedure. So Amaranth had been sacrificed instead of Carolyn—and therein lay the key to his basic values. Now, looking at the naked woman, with his arm about the child, he could not second guess his decision. He *did* love his daughter more.

Air screamed past the plummeting platform. Air—another hallmark of the Devil! The mixed vapors shot upward, their discolorations seeming to writhe like serpents. The velocity of the pentacle was now so great that the wind actually whistled. Strange creatures, all fang and wing, passed by, peering momentarily into the pentacle as though it were a feeding dish. But after the first gut-wrenching shock of falling, equilibrium was returning, making the platform seem stationary. The congregation, some in tatters and some naked, stood in frightened huddles looking out. The approaching Animation of Hell was evidently more than these people had bargained for!

Even in this awful descent, Brother Paul found himself musing on the technical aspects of the production. The Animations could make things appear to be other than they were and convert mirages to reality—but these were matters of perception. The actual mind was not affected directly. So how could there be a sensation of falling and of violent motion? But the answer came as he phrased the mental question: there were many more senses than the proverbial five, and the perceptions of balance, motion, and muscle tension were part of the Animation whole. The most intense Animations covered the full spate of senses; there was no way other than pure reasoning and memory to know any part of the objective situation. And even memory was subject in part to Animation as he knew from his vivid flashbacks.

The fact was that the greater part of what made up individual awareness was controlled by the Animation effect. Perhaps forty percent of Brother Paul's faculties affirmed that reality was a visit to a colony planet by a novice of a minor Order whose purpose was to ascertain whether Deity sponsored any part of the Animation effect. Sixty per cent of him said he was going to Hell.

"We are going to Hell," he repeated softly, and this time he was not laughing at all.

With a jolt that sent people sprawling, the platform changed course. Brother Paul staggered, trying to prevent Carolyn from falling. Lee reached out and caught her arm, stabilizing her and, through her, Brother Paul. "Thanks," Brother Paul gasped.

"You steadied me," Lee said. "You showed me the error of my philosophy and brought me to unity with Jesus Christ." Now Lee was a tower of strength, able to contemplate Hell itself with an approximation of equanimity because his soul was pure.

"But what of mine?" Brother Paul asked himself. "My soul is a nest of scorpions that I thought had been safely buried—and now they will surely be loosed!"

The platform was now traveling to the side. The congregation scrambled for the pews, seating themselves and holding on tightly. Therion held on to the altar which was near the front point of the pentacle. "Get over here!" he called. "Want to get knocked off?"

Lee looked out at the slanting colors beyond the rim. The mists were thinning, showing an awesome chasm below, through which bright tongues of fire leaped. "And where would we fall to," he asked, "that we are not already bound for?"

Good point! Except for one qualification. "If we stay on the platform," Brother Paul said, "we visit Hell alive and perhaps return from it. If we fall off the platform, we may die and never return."

Carolyn looked too. The maelstrom of fire seemed to intensify, forming an amorphous demon face glaring up hungrily. "Oooh, I feel dizzy!" she exclaimed, teetering. Brother Paul jumped to fetch her in again, but Lee's hand was already on her arm, securing her.

Yet with the angling, lurching, and acceleration of the pentacle, all of them were being nudged toward the dread abyss. The congregation was secure because the pews seemed to be well anchored to the floor; some people even lay on the tapering points of the star and hooked their fingers over the forward edges so they could peer down raptly into Hell. But here at the front section there was nothing to cling to except the altar.

Brother Paul was loath to touch that altar whose cover and mattress had been dislodged and now rested on the floor near the rim. But he felt increasingly nervous at their precarious footholds. This was like standing on the wing of an airplane—and the intentions of the pilot were uncertain. Condensed slime coated the floor, making the footing treacherous. Any sudden shift—

It happened. The pentacle lurched, sending the three of them sliding. The mattress fell off the edge. There was a spurt of flame from below as it ignited.

Now it was Therion who extended a hand. He caught hold of Brother Paul's flailing arm and with demoniac strength hauled him and Carolyn and Lee in a human chain to the altar. "We are going home," Therion said with grisly satisfaction. "I shall see that you don't get lost on the way. My Master would be angry."

And he was the agent of Satan. Well, what had they expected? In the Infernal Region, the truly evil man was lord.

They stood by the altar, fingers hooked over its stone edges, and peered forward. There were rails ahead, resembling railroad tracks—shining ribs of steel curving into darkness. So that was how this platform was being guided!

"A roller-coaster ride!" Carolyn exclaimed.

Brother Paul exchanged glances with Lee. "Out of the mouths of babes . . ." the latter murmured. Could Hell itself be no more than a scary ride?

A tunnel appeared ahead: a black hole in a boundless wall. The tracks led straight into it.

The pentacle whipped straight into the hole—but abruptly it became apparent that the vehicle was too large for the aperture. At the last moment there was a scream of terror as the people at the star points on either side realized the threat. Then a crash—and those two points were sheered off cleanly by the tunnel walls. The people on them—were gone.

Brother Paul suffered a mental picture of bodies flattened against the wall like squashed flies, sticking there for a while before dropping into the flames below. Hell was cruel—but again, what had he expected? He hoped Carolyn did not realize the implications.

"Daddy, they weren't very nice people," she said. "But still—"

He drew her close against him again, and she laid her head against his shoulder and cried silently. She had a way of doing that when her sensitivities were hurt, in contrast to her more open crying for normal problems.

The platform was no longer a full pentacle. It was an arrowhead, arrowing through the blackness along its track.

Suddenly a monster loomed at one side. It had glaring yellow eyes, bloody red teeth, and talons fifteen centimeters long. "HOO-HAH-HAH-HAH!" it laughed with horrendous volume, keeping pace with the platform.

"It's a horror-house image," Brother Paul told Carolyn reassuringly as she cringed. If only she could have been spared this journey to Hell; he had thought she was safely out of this Animation . . . until Therion brought her in for the sacrifice. *Damn* Therion! At times the man had seemed decent, but always some new door opened on his charactor that made him seem worse than before. That sacrifice—could any but a truly evil mind have organized that? Tricking a man into slitting the throat of his daughter-figure? "It's *meant* to be scary—but it isn't real."

"It sure *looks* real," she said, taking heart.

The monster reached down with its two awful arms and caught up two people. They screamed—and so did Carolyn. Brother Paul started back toward the action, but both Lee and Therion restrained him. An odd situation when these two natural antagonists acted in accord! "They are already damned," Lee said. "No one can help them or change the manner of their departure from this frame."

The monster carried the victims up toward its gaping mouth. Carolyn hid her face. Therion laughed. But the monster drifted back and out of sight before consuming its prey. The fading sound of the screams of the two unfortunates were all that remained of them.

The remaining members of the congregation, once so violently eager to summon Satan, cowered in their places. But the next apparition was a tremendous octopus with a cruel, gnarled beak who blithely wrapped eight tentacles around eight more people and hauled them screaming and kicking into obscurity.

"Do not be concerned," Therion said in an offhand manner. "All who touch the sacred altar are safe from bestial molestation."

Because they were being saved for a worse fate? Brother Paul's misgivings mounted.

Amaranth looked up. "*I* wasn't saved!" she cried. "I was right *on* the altar when—" But she didn't bother to finish.

The remaining congregation hid itself under the benches. There was an internecine struggle for position, and two people were shoved off one edge to disappear with the usual screams—that cut off abruptly in a great crunching sound. *What lay below?*

Lights appeared, each like a gleaming eye—a line along the sides like the lamps of a subway tunnel. If these images were drawn from his subconscious mind, that mind's imagination lacked a really original thrust. But Therion seemed to be the dominant character in this

Animation so far. Hell was his province; it could be as
unoriginal as he wished.

The vehicle accelerated. The lights became a blur.
Then the tracks curved, and they were flung to the right
as it swept into a tightening spiral. Down, down, in a
whirlpool vortex, tighter and tighter—and now the platform spun like a gyroscope, adding torque to
revolution. They clung to the altar for dear life—and
what was so dear about it now?—their fingers sliding
across the slimy stone.

The marker lights funneled into an aperture too
narrow for the remaining platform. The points snagged
on projections and tore off. Again the despairing
screams of the congregation were heard as people were
hurled into the darkness outside the spiral, and under
the wheels of the platform *inside* the spiral, to be sliced
into pieces. Sections of arms and legs flew up, bounced
off the platform, and skidded back into the gloom. One
whole head glared momentarily as it rolled, leaving a
dotted line of blood splotches. "They took no heed for
their souls," Therion remarked without pity. "They
were unprepared to meet their Master."

"And are *we* prepared?" Brother Paul inquired,
holding his fingers over Carolyn's eyes in a futile effort
to conceal the horror from her. "To meet their
Master—or our own?" He knew that the congregation
was composed of phastasms rather than real people;
throwaways being thrown away. That was why they had
not been able to touch him when they had attacked him
earlier; they were merely part of the scenery. The
nucleus of five real people was here about the altar.
Why hadn't he thought to explain that to Carolyn?

The platform was now a pentagon—five sides, no star
points. A dozen Devil worshipers clung to the sole
remaining pew. The pentagon spun down through the
nether eye of the vortex and plumped with a loud
smacking splash into dark water.

Lee looked disapprovingly about. "This is Hell?" he
inquired.

"Merely the sticks," Brother Paul murmured.

"Oh, the River Styx," Lee repeated, not catching the pun.

"Hell has not yet begun to manifest," Therion assured them with gusto.

So all this had been but the prelude. The warm-up show. Brother Paul felt an ugly chill. What would Hell produce when Hell got serious?

The pentagon bobbled on the gentle swell, moving with unseen power and guidance across the river. There was a moderately stiff headwind that carried the stench of rot, and it chilled them despite its warmth. Other boats were afloat, more conveniently shaped; this one was really a raft. Oddly, as many boats were going back as forward and were fully loaded. People *leaving* Hell?

Therion looked forward, baring his irregular teeth in a savage smile. Amaranth kept her head down upon the altar; *her* hell had begun at the outset of this descent. She had been so eager to give her samples; had that all been pretense? Or was it simply that Therion was the wrong man? The fact that she had actually been a virgin argued for the pretense theory. There were women like that, Brother Paul knew. All show and no substance. Well, she had substance now!

Carolyn's horror had abated, for she was young; now she glanced about, intrigued by the scene. Lee stood with eyes closed in seeming meditation. Brother Paul decided not to attempt to engage any of them in conversation. Actually, this was probably about as peaceful as Hell could get.

"Shall I tell a joke to pass the time?" Therion inquired. "There was this time when God got horny and went to Earth and knocked up this Jewish girl, and as a result—"

"Christianity," Lee said. "Why don't you try to be original for a change?"

A boat cruised by on a parallel course but traveling faster. Ripples rocked the raft. Therion frowned. "Watch where you're slogging, duffer!" he yelled.

"Go soak your snout!" someone yelled from the boat.

Therion swelled up with delighted indignation.

"Osculate my posterior!" he cried. "Your waves are slopping my gunwales."

"Yeah? Try *these* waves, peckerhead!" the other bawled. The boat looped about, accelerating to an unholy velocity. Now the ripples became rolling waves. They overlapped the raft's rim, sliding across to soak the feet of the five standing people and the bodies of those still lying under the benches. The latter got up hastily, cursing, for the water was not crystal clear; it was gray with pollution and it stank. Brother Paul observed that there were objects in it that resembled—yes, they *were* fecal matter.

Therion reached down, scooped up a dripping chunk, and hurled it at the boat. His aim and force were excellent; the turd scored a direct hit on the shoulder of one of the passengers.

There was an undecipherable roar of rage from the boat. The passengers stooped to scoop out their own ammunition. In a moment a small barrage of feces scored on the raft.

"Of course you realize this means war," Therion said, grinning with the sheer joy of battle. He squatted beside the altar, not hiding but rather straining to produce fresh ammunition. Brother Paul turned away in disgust; Therion was very much the fecal personality, and this was manifesting more openly as Hell drew near.

Others on both crafts were quick to follow Therion's example. Why should they seine the murky water for used shot, when superior grade and personalized material was so readily available? Soon the air was filled with stinking blobs. One person after another was hopelessly spattered in brown.

Amaranth straightened up, becoming interested in the proceedings. "Oh, shit!" she said. She spoke the truth: a mass of the stuff had scored directly between her breasts, breaking up and dribbling down her white torso.

Carolyn went around the altar to her. "I'll help you," the child said.

Surprised, Amaranth just looked at her, neither moving nor speaking. Carolyn scraped off the main mass with her fingers. She turned half about, holding it, looking across to the boat.

"Uh-*uh!*" Brother Paul warned her.

Reluctantly, Carolyn dropped the mass into the water, then stooped to rinse her hands. Then she scooped up a double handful of water and held it up for Amaranth to use to cleanse herself somewhat. "You dear child," Amaranth murmured. Then, choked, she did not speak again, but splashed the water on her front.

Why hadn't *he* helped? Brother Paul asked himself. And answered: because Amaranth had suffered herself to be defiled in his eyes. She had lain with the shit-conscious apostle of Satan. And if that had been unplanned, it was only the alternative to the far worse crime she *had* known about: the execution of this same child who now was helping her.

Carolyn, in her blessed childlike naivete, had forgiven Amaranth. Brother Paul had not.

Something massive but soft struck him on the back of the head. He knew what it was before he scraped it off. Once before he had acted immorally—and had had his soul rubbed in shit for it. This time he had passed what might have been an unfair judgment and been similarly punished.

Now only Lee remained untouched by fecal matter. He stood in meditation, eyes closed, proof against all incursions. Even on the border of Hell, there was that of Divine grace about him.

The two craft separated and the battle died out. No one had gained by it; they all were going to Hell anyway. Perhaps this was merely part of the initiation: a necessary degradation, immersion in filth. As if physical soiling could set the scene for spiritual soiling. As perhaps it could. "Dirt thou art," Brother Paul murmured. "To dirt thou returneth." Was Hell the grand compost for filthy souls?

The bank of the river arrived. But there was no need to disembark at the landing; tracks led out of the water, and the roller coaster ride resumed.

"Now for the grand tour," Therion said contentedly.

"We cannot do justice to all the aspects of Hell in these few minutes, but we can glimpse a fraction in passing." He smiled, and it was not a nice expression. "Don't forget that Satan and His minions are themselves deities whose only crime was to lose out in palace politics. For a long time the Horned God was worshiped in His own right—and some remain true to that faith to this day." Meaning himself.

The platform swept into an exotic gallery reminiscent of the bowels of the Great Pyramid. Ancient Egyptian pictures and pictographs decorated the walls, and there were large, grim statues guarding every alcove: griffins, hippopotami, crocodiles, pigs, tortoises, and serpents. Human-headed birds perched on stone branches near the ceiling.

A line of people stood, each in a short skirt and head-dress, waiting for assignment. The demon in charge had the body of a man but the head of a strange beast with an elongated snout. "That is Set," Therion explained. "He has the head of an Oryx. He is the God of War, brute force, destruction and death. Even the Hyksos invaders feared him; they tried to placate him, calling him Yahveh, but in Egypt he was finally dethroned and called Satan." He shook his head. "A sad conclusion for such a noble God."

The craft shot through the wall and into a new chamber. Here there was a huge bird-footed, four-winged monster, standing on his hind feet. His front claws were hooked over a wall, and his canine face peered into the enclosure where a multitude of creatures struggled to escape. Most had the bodies of human beings and the heads of animals: lion, dog, bear, sheep, horse, eagle, snake. Some wore the scaly skins of fish. Heaped in the corners where the scrambling feet had scuffled them, were the remnants of a feast: shards of pottery, fruit rinds, bread crusts and human hands and feet. "The God of the Chaldeans laughs at man's puny efforts to escape his fate," Therion remarked. "Laugh, Anu, laugh!" And awful sounds of mirth filled the chamber. "The Sumerians, Accadians, Assyrians, Babylonians and the like had well-developed religious mythologies from which the Hebrews plagiarized freely. The Creation, Eden, the Tree of Life, the Deluge, the Tower of Babel, the destruction of cities by fire, Sargon-in-the-Bulrushes, the twelve signs of the Zodiac, the symbols of the Cherubim—all recorded on tablets before the Bible was written. Even the Holy Trinity of Ea, Bel and Ishtar, with the Goddess represented as a dove—"

But the carriage plunged through another wall. Suddenly the hot air was filled with huge buzzing flies. "Ah, this must be the abode of the Phoenician God, Baal Zebub, Lord of the Flies," Therion said happily. "Later corrupted to 'Beelzebub,' and changed into a devil in the time honored practice of losers. But he was actually no worse than—"

They went past another wall and into a room dominated by a giant erect phallus. "The lingam of the Brahman God Siva, part of the Trinity of India," Therion exclaimed with joyful recognition. "Symbol and instrument of the creative faculty and the all-devouring fire, evolved into the rod, staff, scepter, and Crozier. Maybe we'll catch a glimpse of Siva's consort, the multi-armed Goddess Kali, the Power of Nature and the ruthless cruelty of Nature's laws. In her honor the Thuggees killed thousands of—"

But again the scene changed. "Oh, come on," Therion protested, annoyed at last. "Each of these fine Hells deserves a lifetime of attention, and we are getting bare seconds. Stop, stop—let's look at one more carefully!"

The platform screeched to a halt, almost throwing them off. They were in a long, narrow cavern, with room only for the tracks and a footpath littered with obstructions: rocks, bodies, jagged fissures from which noxious fumes drifted. A line of bedraggled people marched slowly down this path, harassed by demons. "Hm—not sure I recognize this one," Therion admitted. "Must be a convoy, a transfer of personnel from one unit to another."

The platform moved along at walking speed, pacing the depressed marchers. The demons ran up and down the line on either side, screaming at the humans, kicking them, beating them with whips and clubs.

Carolyn stared wide-eyed, her mouth half open in dismay. Amaranth's reaction was more specific. "Stop it!" she cried. "Leave those poor people alone!"

"This is Hell," Therion said. "Sinners are *supposed* to suffer."

Brother Paul and Lee were silent, knowing it was not their place to interfere. Hell would indeed be a failure if it were pleasant. This was one of thousands, perhaps millions of similar punishments, yet it was hard to tolerate.

A child stumbled over a sharp projection and almost fell into a fissure. The woman behind him grabbed his arm to steady him. "Get your hand off!" a demon cried, whacking her across the head with his club. She staggered and fell half into the crevice herself, one leg rasping across the sharp edge. Blood flowed. The demon laughed.

Then another demon came. He caught the woman's arm and steadied her, helping her across the crevice. "I'll get a doctor if there's one available," he told her. "I can't promise, but I'll try."

"Fool," the first demon said. "This is Hell! You'll fry yourself if you don't shape up."

The second demon turned his back and went about his business. The first demon returned to *his* business, kicking at lagging people, shouting insults at them, and in general expressing his nature.

"Strange," Brother Paul observed. "Even among demons there are human differences."

The path rounded a corner and ended at a double door. The condemned souls were herded through the right door; Brother Paul could see an escalator beyond it going down. The demons, their tour of duty complete, passed through the left door. The tracks paralleled this one; he now witnessed the fate of the demons.

Lo—the demons stripped off their uniforms. Their forked red tails were part of the costume, and inside their cloven-hoofed shoes were human feet. They pulled away masks, and the horns came off. They were human beings.

A genuine demon sat on a minor throne. As each pseudo-demon came before him, he gestured thumbs up or thumbs down. The thumb-ups were wafted gently through an aperture in the ceiling from which colored lights and jazzy music leaked; the thumb-downs were dropped through a trap door in the floor.

The demon who had clubbed the woman was a thumbs-up; the one who had helped her was a thumbs-down. "See," Therion said as both disappeared. "When in Hell, you'd better do as the demons do—or pay the penalty."

Brother Paul felt sick at heart.

But now the track looped about to pick up the people who had been marching. They too were stripping away costumes—and lo! they were demons in disguise!

Carolyn could contain herself no longer. "Miss Demon," she called to the woman who had been struck, now a healthy female demon with cute hoofs and horns and tail. "If you're not *really* a person, why did you—I mean, the man who helped you, he—"

"He was found unfit for Hell," the lady demon answered. "That trap door goes straight to Heaven."

All the people on the platform stared. "But—" Therion began.

"If you act like a demon just because you think you are in Hell," the lady demon informed him, her pointed teeth showing in a knowing sneer, "you will surely soon *be* in Hell. But if you are a misfit, we have no use for you. That man who helped me obviously had no idea what Hell was all about."

Brother Paul exchanged glances with Lee as the vehicle resumed speed. What an infernal test of character!

Therion seemed shaken. "I didn't know that *anyone* escaped once he got in this far," he said.

"I suspect Satan is more discriminating than we know," Lee said.

They passed through a dizzying array of Hells. They saw people being boiled in oil, hung by their tongues, buried headfirst in burning sand, caged in boxes of immortal scorpions, disemboweled among flesh-consuming worms, thrown off high cliffs, wasted by terrible diseases, and suffering all the torments diabolical minds could imagine. They saw the Hell of the early Christian Gnostics, contained by a huge dragon with its tail in its mouth, with twelve dungeons ruled by demons with the faces of a crocodile, cat, dog, serpent, bull, boar, bear, vulture, basilisk, seven dragons' heads, seven cats' heads, and seven dogs' heads. The condemned souls were sometimes thrown with pitchforks into the open mouth of the dragon or stuffed into the dragon's rectum. They saw King Ixion, who had lusted after the wife of the Greek God Zeus and in punishment was spread eagled on a fiery wheel, his limbs and head forming its five living spokes. They saw Hades, Sheol, Gehenna Tophet, the Hindu Naraka with its twenty-eight divisions, the Moslem Fire with its seven regions each containing seventy thousand mountains of fire, each mountain enclosing 70,000 valleys, each valley 70,000 cities, each city 70,000 towers, each tower 70,000 houses, each house 70,000 benches, and each bench 70,000 types of torture. Brother Paul brought out his calculator to figure out the total number of tortures this progression represented, but got distracted by new visions of Hell and had to give it up.

At one place two grotesque demons investigated each soul. Carolyn called them "Monkey" and "Naked," mishearing the proper names Therion provided. If the person had lived a good life, his soul was drawn gently and painlessly from his body and wafted upward; but if he had lived a bad life, the demons ripped out his soul with terrible brutality. Further along they saw the Norse Goddess Hel, daughter of Loki, in her domain beneath the roots of the Great World Tree. Now it was clear to Brother Paul how heavily Dante had borrowed from Norse mythology to fashion his vision of the Christian Hell. Indeed, it was evident that Christianity itself had incorporated great chunks of Teutonic legend. They heard the enumeration of the myriad Princes of Hell: Lucifer, Beelzebub, Leviathan, Asmodee, Belial,

Ashtaroth, Magot, and on interminably. All the Gods
that past peoples had ever worshiped had become
Christian devils, and it was obvious that contemporary
Hell was extremely well staffed and could handle any
emergency.

At last the impressive, horrible tour was over. Brother
Paul's head was spinning, and his companions looked
dazed. Only Carolyn had adjusted moderately well; she
was still close enough to the fantasy realms of childhood
to accept more of the same. They had set out to see Hell;
it was more than they had bargained on. Which,
Brother Paul reflected, was about par for the course.

Now at last their vehicle rolled up to the dread gates
of the Devil's residence. A horrible clamor swelled in
volume: screams of terror, disgust, anguish, and shock.
The air was close and hot, and the odor of ozone
became strong.

They rounded a turn—and there was Satan Himself.
He was huge, seven or eight meters tall, and His hands
and feet were claws, and every joint of His arms and
legs was the face of a monster from whose wide-open
mouth the extension of the limb continued. He had a
two-meter long phallus in proud erection, great bat-like
wings, and long twisted horns. Snakes curled around
each arm, and when He picked up a struggling naked
person, the viper bit that victim in the crotch. He was
carrying people up to His grotesquely tusked mouth and
chewing them up alive. Simultaneously, He squatted
part way, and from his meter-wide anus were extruded
the shit-slimed, partially digested people He had consumed. As each dropped headfirst, being born again in
Hell as it were, a minor demon snatched his brown-
coated body and bore him down into the bottomless
flame.

"Master!" Therion cried. "Here they are!" He
smiled triumphantly. "Now reward me with this one for
myself!" He hauled on Amaranth's arm.

Brother Paul stared. So that was it! Therion, having
finally conquered his horror of women, now wanted to
possess Amaranth permanently and was making his deal
for her. For this he had betrayed them all!

Satan glared down. Beams of brilliant light speared from his eyes to bathe the couple, even as Brother Paul's stunned awareness came.

"And does the bitch want *you*?" Satan inquired. His voice reverberated as though from a great distance. "Will she buy her freedom by going with you?"

"Sure she will!" Therion cried. "She likes getting screwed!" And Amaranth, terrified by the presence of Satan, did not protest.

Satan laughed. His two claws swept down and forward and snatched the two of them. "Here is your reward!" the Horned God bellowed as the serpents' jaws closed on Therion's penis and testicles and on Amaranth's pudenda. Twin screams of agony rent the air, sounding above even the background bedlam of Hell.

"But You *promised!*" Therion cried as blood dribbled from his crotch. "I served You faithfully—"

His plea was interrupted as Satan bit off his head, chewed up his quivering torso, and swallowed him in a single, noisy gulp. Immediately after that, Satan chomped down on Amaranth so that her severed legs fell into the flame on one side and her head and arms and part of one breast fell on the other. Satan smacked His lips. "Those who seek Evil and those who acquiesce to Evil—delicious."

Now the talons came for Brother Paul and Carolyn.

"No!" Brother Paul cried, and the child screamed. They clung to each other—but the terrible claws clasped each body, sliding on the mucus and diarrhea that coated Satan's nails, and wedged between Brother Paul and Carolyn. They were wrenched apart and lifted high in the steaming air. The two snakes slid down Satan's forearms, their venom-dripping jaws opening wide.

"Take me! Spare her!" Brother Paul screamed.

Satan hesitated. Both snakes halted, obedient to the whim of their Master. The hideous, huge face loomed close. "The price of her is two orbs," Satan said. And the python on Brother Paul's side lifted its tusk-like eyeteeth toward his eyes. Its skin was mottled, its other teeth irregular, and its breath stank of ammonia.

"These—" The snake's head dropped toward Brother Paul's groin. "Or these. Choose."

His sight—or his manhood. To save his daughter. The choice was worse than Satan's decision might have been! How could he give up either one?

Yet—if either of his organs had sinned, it was surely not the eyes. Let him be more like Jesus Christ, innocent of sexual lust. He would have little use for it in Hell, surely.

Even as that decision formed in his mind, the serpent struck down. Its jaws closed about his scrotum, the teeth punching in like the spikes of an iron maiden. There was a flare of unbearable agony, and Brother Paul screamed. Not only with pain, but with loss.

As the blood dripped down from his bitten, empty crotch, Brother Paul saw the other claw return Carolyn to the pentagon. She was sobbing uncontrollably, having been witness to it all.

Lee strode forward, caught her hand, steadied her, and put his arm about her shoulders. The pentagon platform began to move back down the track, away from Satan, away from Hell.

Then Brother Paul was lifted the rest of the way to the Horned God's maw. Headfirst he plunged into the cavernous mouth and slid down the greasy gullet into the guts of the Devil. Now he was one with Satan.

II
Revelation: 21

*According to one humorous legend of the
Creation, God formed Adam and Eve by cutting
them apart from a single original hermaphrodite.
Their bellies were left open as the result of this
separation, so He gave them each a cord of clay or
whang string leather to use to sew their bodies up.
Adam, in the fashion of the male, took great long
stitches with the result that some of his cord was
left over and dangled in front. Eve, in the fashion
of the female, made tiny neat stitches with the
result that she ran out of string and was left with a
slit at the bottom of her belly. She begged Adam
to sever his extra length and give it to her so that
she could finish the job, but he was selfishly unwilling. And so it has been ever since, this con-
tention between men and women over "That
Little Piece of Whang," because the men refuse to
give it to the women and will only lend it to them
briefly.*

Brother Paul landed—in a plush modern office.
"Please be seated," a pretty secretary said. "The Prince
of Darkness will be with you in a moment."

Nonplused, he looked around. Could this be the inside of Satan? What had happened? Every office ar-

29

tifact was in place from the electronic voicescriber to the soft classical music issuing from concealed speakers to the holographic photograph of a pleasant rustic scene mounted on the wall. Something was wrong!

Suddenly his bowels reacted with the letdown. He had not expended the content of his guts during the river crossing. "Please, Miss—is there a—a rest-room here?"

The shapely woman made an indication with one thumb. There was the sign: MEN. Had he looked about more carefully, he would have been able to spare himself the embarrassment of asking—though he could have sworn the sign had not been there a moment ago. With grudging gratefulness he pushed open the door and went through.

All was in order. Brother Paul positioned himself, took down his trousers (he was now informally garbed in civilian Earth-style clothing)—and discovered what he lacked. His penis was intact, but he had no scrotum and no testicles. The skin of that region was smooth and unscarred; it was as if he had never had anything there. There was no pain, no discomfort. He might as well have been an immature boy—with no prospect of ever maturing. He was a eunuch.

He sat on the aseptic sonic-flush toilet and relieved himself of the material portion of his concern. He reached for the toilet paper—and saw words printed on it. He held it up to read. It said: BROTHER PAUL CENJI.

Every piece of paper was printed with his name.

He smiled. Hell had surprises yet! He reached behind—and paused. Was he to wipe his ass with his own name?

Well, why not! It was only a joke like the toilet paper that said "Never put off till tomorrow what you can do today" or "Get a load off your mind" or "Film for your Brownie." A fiendishly minor joke. His pride had better things to feed on than this. He took the paper and completed his mission.

"The Horned God will see you now," the secretary announced as he emerged. She *had* to be Amaranth, this time in a minor part—but what about his seeing her body crunched into pieces and dropping down . . . ? He squelched that thought; she was indicating another door, and obviously all her appurtenances were intact. Rather than stare at them a second time with more than sexual curiosity, he walked on through.

Satan came forward to shake Brother Paul's hand heartily. The Horned God was human-sized, had human hands and feet, and wore a conservative, circa 1995 plastic business suit complete with Gordian-Knot tie. Only His small, neat horns betrayed His nature. "So good to meet a good man!" He said.

Brother Paul gave up trying to make sense of things. He was here, and this was surely another aspect of Hell. The Devil would have His way, regardless. "It has been an interesting experience, so far," Brother Paul said.

"It has not yet begun," Satan said pleasantly. Who played this part, Brother Paul wondered. There seemed to be only one reasonable prospect, yet that—well, who could make sense of Hell anyway! "Please make yourself comfortable. This may take some time."

"Eternity?"

Satan laughed with mellow empathy. "Not that long, I trust."

The question burst out before Brother Paul knew it was coming. "You just swallowed me! How is it that I'm here, in this office—and that You're here, in human size?

"I am everywhere," the Devil said easily. "I am in you, and you are in Me. Evil is ubiquitous; it has no limits."

"But—"

"If you feel more comfortable knowing the specific geography, I shall provide it. I swallowed you; you are now in My belly. You are being digested. My Stomach acids will dissolve away, layer by layer, all the protective mechanisms you have clothed yourself with, until the fundamental truth of your being is achieved. Then, and only then, may you be fairly judged."

"But you—"

"I am in Myself too. I am everywhere. At this moment, a myriad of other souls are being similarly interviewed in separate offices. I am with each—within My own belly. Only when a given soul is properly processed is it ejected for conveyance to its permanent station.''

''Defecated out?''

Satan made a little gesture of unconcern. '''Most souls are shit; they must be treated as shit. This is, after all, the region of just deserts.''

''I think my soul is shit too,'' Brother Paul said. ''I saw it once when I was in meditation. However, it was pointed out to me that shit is ideal compost, a necessary stage in the renewal of life—''

''Well, we shall find out for sure, now. Shall we proceed?''

Brother Paul smiled wanly. ''Have I any choice?''

''Oh, yes! Choice is the worst torture of all. Indecision can be far worse than wrong decision. Would you rather postpone this interview?''

Where would he stay, during the postponement? In one of the several sub-Hells he had toured? ''No. Let's get it over with.''

''You are intelligent. Were there more like you, My own Redemption would arrive more quickly.''

''*Your* Redemption?'' Brother Paul asked, astonished.

Satan shrugged. ''I am supposedly anti-life. It is my ironic torture to be associated with procreation, for with every act of procreation there is another soul, new life. I am the Lord of Evil, and as Evil triumphs in the world, a greater percentage of souls must come to Me. Thus My punishment is governed by yours and outweighs that of all human souls combined. I wish there would be fewer people born and that more of them would go to Heaven. When *no* souls come to Hell, I will at last be free—and I fear that will be a long, long time yet.''

''I never thought of that,'' Brother Paul said musingly. ''God assigned to you all the dirty work—''

''Precisely. Now if you will lie on that couch, please—''

''This is a psychoanalysis?''

''The ultimate. Not for nothing does that term contain the word *anal*. Sigmund Freud originated the couch posture so that his patients would not see the look of shock on his face as he heard the horrors in their case histories. I really do not suffer from that particular problem, but the couch does seem to work adequately for contemporary occidentals."

Brother Paul spread himself on the comfortable couch. "What now?" he asked. "Do I just talk, or—?"

There was a rustle of papers. "According to your dossier, there was a certain matter of—a clothespin."

The clothespin. Instantly Paul was a boy again back on Earth. It was his first time out in a new neighborhood, and he knew no one. He saw a group of children seated in a circle behind a building. They were little girls no older than he, playing some kind of game with many exclamations and titters.

"Can I play too?" Paul inquired.

They looked at him, the stranger, with merry incredulity. "You're a *boy*!"

Paul's lip pushed out in mild belligerence. "S'not s'pose to be sexcrimination. A boy can do anything a girl can do."

They responded with a spontaneous burst of laughter.

"Well I *can*!" he insisted.

"That's what *yoooou* think," one girl said, greatly elevating and extending the *you* so that it sounded almost like a train whistle.

"I can play your ol' game as well as you can!" It wasn't that he cared about their game; his fledgling pride was at stake.

"Pride," Satan said in the background. "One of the Seven Basics. Relates to the Suit of Pentacles. Misapplied Pride brings more souls to Me than any other thing except perhaps Greed—which ties in to the same Suit."

The girl studied Paul. She was elfin with curly reddish hair, quite cute. She reminded him of someone—but of course all little girls were played by the same actress. "Wanna bet?"

"Sure I'll bet!" But he was uneasy. These girls were too certain of themselves, too full of some secret. They knew something he didn't. Yet he had no way to retreat.

"Okay, let him play," the redhead decided. This was

answered by another outbreak of mirth. Strangely, some of it seemed embarrassed; one child was blushing. "But you must promise never to tell."

"Okay, I promise," Paul said. "What's the game?"

"Clothespin," she said, and there was yet another general titter. *What was so funny?*

"Okay," he repeated. "How do you play it?"

"It's a contest," she said. She held up a clothespin—the old fashioned kind without a spring, just a cylinder of wood bifurcated at one end. The prongs normally slid over the clothes, pinning them to the clothesline so that the wind would not blow them away before the sun dried them out. This was a big clothespin, about fifteen centimeters long. There was a blob of grease on the solid end. "You push it in."

"In?" This made no sense to him.

"Like this," she said. She bent her knees and hiked up her dress, showing that she wore no panties. The space between her legs was cleft by a hairless crease quite unlike his own apparatus; he was both fascinated and alarmed. She was incomplete! She fitted the clothespin into the crevice and slowly slid it into her body, one centimeter, two, three, four. "Whoever gets it in deepest wins."

Paul was not entirely naive about sex. He had heard stories and seen suggestive things on TV and had been able to piece together a fair picture of the mechanics of human copulation. After his initial surprise at his first direct view of the secret region, he was able to integrate the mental picture with the physical geometry. He recognized this game of "Clothespin" as preliminary, surrogate fornication. But more immediate, and far more important, he realized that he had lost his bet. This was not a game a boy could play, for he had no *place* to insert the pin.

She withdrew the clothespin and held it up, glistening with the spread grease. "Now you try it. My mark is there." And she scratched the wood with her fingernail, indicating the level of deepest penetration.

All eyes turned to him expectantly, the laughter barely suppressed. Oh, they had shown him all right! He was stuck in an impossible position. Outwitted by a bunch of dumb girls!

Then he had an inspiration. Girls had more apertures than boys had—but he still did have a place. He took the clothespin, took down his pants while the girls went into a fury of guilty tittering, and jammed it in to the shocked amazement of his audience.

Paul won his bet—and the contest. But at a price. No one told on him, for the girls were well aware that they could not do so without incriminating themselves, and adults tended to take very dim views of children's private pleasures and explorations. So the matter never came to the attention of the parental authorities. But these girls attended the same school Paul did, as it turned out, and some of them were in his own class, and every time he met one of them she would giggle secretively and pass on without speaking to him. He lived in fear that an adult would catch on to the secret. He should have accepted defeat, rather than the victory.

For when the clothespin came out, there had adhered to it a blob of shit.

"So that was the root source of your vision of the Turd back in Triumph Seven, Cup Seven!" Satan exclaimed gleefully. "Oh, beautiful; this one will go into my special file!"

Brother Paul knew he was blushing furiously with the shame of that memory. Naturally Satan was delighted; this was Hell. No physical pitchfork could have given him equivalent agony. Yet it was a relief to know this consciously now.

"You chose to seal off the original episode," Satan continued. "The memory drug withdrawal must have also helped to bury it. But it remained in your subconscious, prejudicing both your self-respect and your relations with women. Shit was your nemisis—and now we know the truth."

But that was hardly the whole story.

"Hmm," Satan mused. "There remains opacity. We have peeled off only one layer of the onion." He leafed through His papers. "Was it that episode with Therion? No, that was entrapment and too recent. It is necessary for you to realize that your control of these Animations is not complete. When you enter the area of special expertise of another person, his knowledge and thrust preempt the scene. This was especially true in the early stages before your discipline asserted itself. Thus you were only partially responsible for the act in the Castle of the Seven Cups and cannot be damned to Hell solely on that account. The detail—"

"I don't want to review the detail!" Brother Paul cried.

"You forget where you are," Satan reminded him. "It is necessary to appraise your total record; we do not do shoddy anal-ysis here. Therion has had an anal fixation since his childhood, much stronger than yours; yours was merely a reflection of each boy's normal progression through this stage on the way to maturity. But the resolution of that belongs to his analysis, not yours. In this case he indulged in passive sodomy, then attempted to eject the result onto the face of the girl: symbolic defiling of all women in the exact manner of his namesake. The final effort he placed in the Seventh Cup for you to find. Thus he sent you into an extraordinary sequence—"

"Therion—did all that?"

"He dictated the scene. You merely played the role he specified for you—as others played the roles you specified for them in other scenes. Your will normally dominates; this was an exception owing partly to your private feeling of guilt. You were not properly aware of the nature of the role and would have balked it had you known. So you are guilty of laxity, not intent. We shall have to look deeper to judge you properly."

"But I participated!" Brother Paul cried in anguish.

"So you believe that even in the absence of knowledge or intent, you were culpable because of the act?"

"Yes," Brother Paul said without full conviction. "I *should* have guessed or stayed off those drugs. I should have kept control so as to prevent it happening."

"Then you must answer for it," Satan said. "You

must do penance, and the penance is this: provide a species-survival rationale for sodomy.''

"You want *me* to justify human homosexuality?'' Brother Paul demanded, shocked.

"I don't *want*; I *require*,'' Satan said. "You seem to be having the damndest trouble remembering your situation. Kindly confine yourself to the issue: sodomy is not identical to homosexuality. The former is an act; the latter is a preference.''

"My situation,'' Brother Paul repeated. He could not at the moment imagine anything more hellish than this penance.

"No stalling,'' Satan said. Flames danced about Brother Paul's feet: hot-foot galore. The pain was intense.

"I'm answering!'' he screamed, and the flames subsided. Rationale? What rationale could there possibly be? Sodomy was an abomination!

The flames began to rise again. And under that savage prodding, Brother Paul vomited out his answer, the connection between feet and mouth virtually bypassing brain. "Reproduction is essential to the species. Therefore, it is compulsory behavior, rather than voluntary. Animals have in-heat cycles, with the smell of the female coercing the male to copulation. But human beings are more intelligent; they take longer to mature and have much more to learn. So they need a family situation with a male staying close to help protect, feed, and educate the offspring—''

"I question the relevance of this line of exploration,'' Satan said. "It sounds like an argument for heterosexuality.'' The flames reappeared, flicking playfully at Brother Paul's toes. His feet now seemed to be bare.

"It's relevant!'' Brother Paul cried. "I am not talking about homosexuality, as you pointed out. I'm talking about the rationale for an act that may occur in a normally heterosexual situation.''

"Well, I'll allow it this time,'' Satan said. The flames subsided again.

"So in primates the heat cycle is abandoned,''

Brother Paul continued hurriedly. "Sexuality is peren-
nial. The female can be receptive any time of the day or
year, and in this way she holds her man. But sometimes
the family is interrupted by circumstance, such as war or
natural catastrophe. A function that goes too long
unused is apt to be lost, such as man's former ability to
manufacture ascorbic acid in his body. Vitamin C. So
the sexual drive in men is continuous and insistent.
When there are no women, it expresses itself in various
alternate ways—and one of these is sodomy. If it were
not so, the drive to indulge in the sexual act with
another individual might atrophy at the peril of the
species."

"Yes, that will do nicely," Satan said. "Is sodomy
therefore a sin?"

"Well, considered that way, in special cir-
cumstances—"

"You see," Satan said decisively, "there is no such
thing as objective sin. A person only sins when he does
what he believes to be wrong. Your definition of sin
does not, upon reflection, include involuntary sodomy.
Case dismissed."

Maybe so. Brother Paul would have to sort it all out
more carefully at another time. "Therion—he served
you well, if selfishly. Why did you kill him?"

"I did not kill him. There is no death in Hell. That's
the Hell of it! Death would represent escape from
retribution. I merely tortured him a little. A well-
deserved humiliation, preparing him for the penance he
must do."

Again Brother Paul wondered who was playing the
part of Satan. It had to be Therion—yet how could he
talk about himself this way? Unless this whole
Animation really was guided by some Godly power,
and this role was part of Therion's penance. Was there
any way to be sure? "But if he made a bargain with You
to bring us all here—"

"The Horned God makes no bargains! All souls that
are My due will come to Me in due course. Why should I
bargain for what is already Mine?"

"But you accepted *my* bargain—to spare Carolyn."

"Not really. She is innocent—not even a clothespin mars her record. She is as yet unborn. I cannot take her. And you—were already in My power."

"Then why did You torture me by threatening her?"

"This is Hell," Satan said simply. And of course that was true. Brother Paul realized that he had taken too narrow a view of Hell. Torture came in many forms —and the worst of these were internal.

More rustling of papers. "Why don't you computerize your damned records?" Brother Paul inquired irritably. Satan merely chuckled, and Brother Paul realized: this, too, was Hell.

"Sexual and/or scatological repression is not after all the root," Satan said. "Let's try the racial motif. You are of mixed ancestry—"

"Let's leave my ancestors out of it," Brother Paul said, fearing what would come out. "*They* are not on trial—" But the review was upon him. One did not get to argue much in Hell.

It was 1925. She was a young black woman too intelligent to remain in the ghetto. She had come to the high-rise district seeking quality employment. She had not been successful. This was not entirely racism; the fact that she was female had a lot to do with it. Now she was walking back to the apartment which she shared with another aspiring woman, because her money was running low and she still had to eat. It was early evening.

"Well, now!" A white man stepped out in front of her.

Instantly she reversed, fleeing him—but another man was behind her. He caught hold of her. There was the gleam of a knife. "You jus' be quiet, Brown Sugar," he said. "We ain't goin' to hurt you none—if you know your place."

She knew her situation, if not her place. She did not struggle or cry out. And they were true to their word. They did not beat her; after both had raped her, they let her go with only a perfunctory admonition about keeping her mouth shut if she didn't want them to come back and squeeze the chocolate milk out of her tits.

They were pleased; they had saved two dollars apiece for a cleaner lay than the local house would have provided.

She kept it quiet. There was nothing she could do about it, for she didn't know either man. And if she *had*, it was the word of one nigger gal against two white men: forget it. She was a realist. She bought herself a good knife as insurance against future episodes, continued on her quest, and got her job. It was a good one as maid to a wealthy white family; they treated her well.

Then she learned that she was pregnant.

Her livelihood was destroyed, but not her life. She went home to her family and birthed her bastard son, and his skin was much lighter than hers. She raised him well with pride, for that light color was a mark of distinction. He was handsome and smart, and he married an open-minded white girl. Their daughter was lighter still, and race was less of a barrier than it had been. She married a white man who claimed to have some Indian blood somewhere in his ancestry; he was a career diplomat. Their son was Paul. He was no darker than a pure Caucasian with a summer tan—but he was one-eighth black. They went to Africa, partly because it was a prestigious, well-paid position. There was a political flare-up, minor on the world scene but quite serious for Americans in that region. Paul was hastily shipped out at the age of four; his parents wanted to assure his safety, if not their own.

Paul's paternal uncle took him in. Man and wife were conservative with an image to maintain; that little bit of Indian blood in their ancestry was a secret blot. They never told Paul he was black though this was the age when black was beautiful. Paul went to a white private school and associated only with whites. There was, of course, token integration at that school, but the occasional presence of blacks made no difference to Paul. He was not of their number. He had "passed."

He started school—with the snickering girls—but before the year was out his foster parents moved out to the country in the north. Paul had trouble in school, not so much with the teachers but with other children who teased him with the special cruelty only children understood. When he came home with a black eye, his foster father acted: "That boy is going to learn self-defense. We'll put him in a karate class."

There was such a class at a community center in a neighboring town; Paul and his foster father walked in and saw the people practicing in their white pajama-like outfits, landing on mattresses. "How much?" the father asked the instructor who was a young man in his mid twenties, mild-mannered and not large—hardly the type one would fear in the street. The rates were cheap. The man paid the money, completed the necessary form, obtained a pajama uniform called a *gi* for Paul, and left him there. Paul was about to learn self-defense.

Paul was nine years old and small for his age. The *gi* hung on him hugely. But there were other children there his size, and the instructor gave him personal attention for the first classes. The instructor's name was Steve—he demanded a no more formal address—and after Paul saw what he could do, he understood why there was no disrespect.

This was a judo class, not karate; they had walked into the wrong room. But as it turned out, judo was far better suited to Paul's needs than karate would have been, for it enabled a person to defend himself without hurting his opponent, and Paul did not like to hurt people. Judo was the science of throws and holds and, after those had been mastered, strikes and strangles and assorted leverages of pain. With this science a charging giant could be hurled violently to the ground and held there until he yielded. Two or more attackers could be tumbled into each other. A man with a knife or club could be rapidly disarmed. Yet the salient features of judo were courtesy and self-improvement. Students gave to their instructor and each other the respect due to people capable of dealing death—and of refraining from it.

It started slowly. First Paul had to learn to take falls so that he could be thrown to the mat without being hurt. Then he worked on basic throws. To his surprise, his first partner was a black girl slightly smaller than he was. But she wore a yellow belt, one grade higher than his white one, and he quickly discovered that she could beat him in physical combat and hold him down so that he could not get up. He developed an instant respect for this martial art; for if a girl who weighed less than he could do that to him, what might he do to a larger boy—once he learned judo?

At the end of the first class Steve took him aside. "How did you get that black eye, Paul?" he asked as if it were not obvious. He had the girl, whose name was Karolyn, follow Paul's instructions and reenact the way the school bully had stepped forward and punched with his right fist into Paul's left eye. Steve nodded. "Here is what you do for that. First, try to get away from him; step aside and run if you have to. Don't let him get close to you."

"But then the other kids—"

Steve nodded. "When, for one reason or another, you can't escape, you must defend yourself. There are many ways, but for you I think this is best." He summoned another boy, larger than Paul. "*Nage no kata*, second throw, Uki," Steve told the boy. The boy closed his fist and shot a punch at the girl's head. She blocked it up with her left forearm, whirled, caught his arm with her right arm, and heaved. The boy flew over her back and landed with a resounding slap on the mat. "That throw is called *ippon seoi nage*, the one-armed shoulder throw," Steve told Paul. "You are going to learn it—now."

Paul was hurt many times after that—but seldom did he suffer at the hands of his schoolmates, and never again did anyone land a punch on his face. Judo, to a certain extent, became a way of life for him. He progressed from white belt to yellow belt to orange and green and finally brown. He entered judo tournaments, winning some matches and losing others, but he always put up a good fight and was as courteous in defeat as in victory. Never did he seek a quarrel outside of class—and seldom did anyone seek one with him.

But he always remembered that first class, and how a little girl had overcome him and held him down—and never teased him about it. Paul was somewhat wary of girls in general, but in his secret fashion he loved Karolyn. She left the class a few months after he started, and he never saw her again, but she had left her mark on him in the form of a fond memory.

When Paul was eighteen, his foster parents were divorced. But by that time he was scheduled for college, and an education trust fund that had been arranged long ago by his parents carried him through. After college he sought his family roots—and for the first time learned of his black heritage.

"No, no!" Satan said. "That's not it! That's way too late! You have no guilty race secret; you were not even aware that you were passing—and if you had been, you would have been culpable only for the lie, not the fact. The culpability of your society that discriminated covertly on the basis of race was in any event worse than your own."

"This is Satan talking?" Brother Paul marveled aloud. "The Father of Lies?"

"Satan never lies. It is the minions of God who lie, cheat, steal and deceive—until the fruits of these iniquities come at last to Me. I am Truth—and because the truth is often ugly, I am called evil." The papers rustled again, annoyingly. "I'm going to try a somewhat random shot based on intuition. I suspect the blocked-out secret of your life occurs in childhood somewhere in the foster-parent era. I think it involves a female, but perhaps not in the sexual or racist way. So I want—one day of your life, at age eight."

Paul had to urinate. He wanted to continue sleeping as it was cold out there in the outhouse and scary at night, for there might be a porcupine. One thing a dog never did twice was nose after a porky; that first hellish noseful of barbed quills invariably sufficed. Paul did not care to walk into a porcupine by accident. Better simply to piss in the snow just outside the back door. But—he had to go, and that was the place.

He got up groggily, finding the air oddly comfortable, not cold at all though it was winter. He walked down the hall—and it opened out on a pleasant,

modern, tiled bathroom with a flush toilet—how could
he have forgotten about this? He stood at the toilet and
let go. The sensation was immensely gratifying; the
liquid flowed and flowed, seeming to have no end, but
rather gaining in force and conviction.

Then he felt something strange. A wetness about his
middle, as if he were standing waist deep in a hot bath.
Yet there was nothing visible. He fought off the sensation—but it would not be denied. With slow horror,
the realization forced itself upon him: he *was* standing
in brine. Lying in it. For he was still in bed; everything
had been a dream. Except the urination.

As usual, he had wet his bed. He opened his eyes. It
was dark. It was still night. Too early to get up. Well, he
was comfortable where he was; the rubber sheet sealed
the depression of the sagging bed so that his hot bath
stayed with him. So long as he kept the blankets on top
and dry, he was all right.

He remembered when it had started two years ago.
They had put him in a hospital for observation, and in
five days there he had been so tense he never wet the
bed, though they "forgot" to bring him the bedpan for
as long as 24 hours at a time. One morning there, he had
awoken to spy half a dozen nurses clustered just outside
his door, whispering with animation. Were they talking
about him? "Don't tell him . . ." but the words trailed
into unintelligibility. There was hushed laughter like
that of the clothespin girls, only these were big girls.
"The way *I* do it. . . ." Do *what*? "Just shove it *in*."
Surely not a clothespin! Suddenly he caught on: this was
a hospital. They were planning surgery in secret. Don't
tell the patient because he might climb out the window
and escape. Just take the knife and shove it *in*.

Paul lay in the bed bathed in cold sweat that resembled the urine. They were going to cut him open. He had
been assured that they were only going to *look* at him
(which was bad enough) in the hospital—but that was
what they had said the first time he went to the dentist
too. Grownups thought it was all right to lie to children
"for their own good," which usually meant something

painful or extremely unpleasant. It meant that no adult could be trusted, ever.

But the nurses dispersed, leaving him alone with his thoughts. If not now, *when*? All day he cowered in his prison bed, waiting for them to come, for it to start. His appetite decreased. He lost interest in the games provided, in his reading book, in his drawings. What was the use of them in the face of this terrible threat?

At last he was released. The hospital's verdict: there was nothing physically wrong with him. Presumption: he could stop wetting his bed if he wanted to. So he was encouraged to want to. He had to wash his own sheets each day. The word "punishment" was never used, but the message was plain: *You do this awful thing, you clean it up yourself.* Somehow that treatment was not effective. Paul needed no extra motivation; he *wanted* to have a dry bed—and could not. Something always happened in the night, no matter how hard he tried to resist.

He was drifting back to sleep this morning, fortunately. Nightmares seldom came after his bladder was empty. The hospital memory was fading; it no longer really bothered him. So long as he never had to go back for that lurking surgery. Mornings were not so bad. His feet were cold, but he was used to that. He heard the faint, eerie hoot of some wild animal ranging the forest; he was glad he was not out there. He remembered the prior year at the boarding school, he being the smallest of the small, beaten up as a matter of course in the initiation, fleeing, terrified. Yet even this nightmare was not total. One morning one of the bullies, a boy a year or two older than Paul, came in before Paul was up. "Hey, I hear you piddle in bed!" the bully exclaimed. "Lessee." And he ripped off Paul's blanket.

Paul had wet the bed. He had kicked off his soaking pajamas, and they lay in a damp wad at his feet; he was naked from the waist down, steaming in urine. The bully looked for a long moment while Paul lay still, not afraid to move but simply having no option. He had long since lost his pride of person as far as his body went. Then the bully replaced the blanket and went away without comment. Later that day, the bully talked to Paul privately "When I piss last thing at night, sometimes I just stand there at the pisser a while, and then a little more will come. Then some more. Maybe if you waited long enough, you could get it all out, and—" He shrugged. He was trying to be helpful.

That bully never bothered Paul again; his sympathy had been aroused. A few days later, in the presence of a group of boys, another bully came to Paul. "I won't hit you any more," he said, and they shook hands. "And if he *does*, we'll hit *him*," one of the larger boys said. And after that no one picked on Paul. Yet, for him, the school remained a horror; he just wanted to get home.

Now he was home and satisfied. He knew when he was well off. Sometimes he imagined this was all a long, bad dream, and that he would wake up and be four years old again in Africa in his happy real life, but for two years the conviction had been growing that this would never happen. *This*, now, was his real life; the other was the dream.

His feet had stopped hurting with cold; instead they were flaming as though a fire blazed about them. That was nice. Paul fancied he could see the leaping flames, gold and yellow, sending sparks up toward the ceiling. He could lie here forever enjoying that bonfire. If Hell were the place of heat and flames, he had no fear of it; better to go there than out into the snow on a windy morning.

The clangor of the alarm jolted him awake. He hadn't realized he had made it back to sleep. No question about it; the thin cold light of dawn was seeping in. Mornings in winter were so *bleak!* He lingered for a moment more, than took a breath, held it, gritted his teeth, and threw off the blanket. Oh, it was cold! The floor was wood, but it was so cold his flame-tender feet could not tolerate it; he danced from toe to toe with the acute discomfort of it. He dashed naked downstairs to the bathroom; it had no toilet since there was no running water in this room, but there was a pitcher by the table. Once all houses had had oil heat and citypiped water everywhere, but the crises of energy and water and pollution had driven many families out into the wilderness where the air was still clean and it was possible to be largely self-sufficient. Water that was carried by hand was seldom wasted; that helped the declining water table.

He sloshed some water into the basin, soaked the washcloth in it, then gritted his teeth, closed his eyes, and stabbed the wadded cloth at his chest. The shock was like ice, for winter in an unheated house brought ice very close. Sometimes the kitchen pipes froze, so that water could not be pumped inside, and they had to break the ice and dip it out in a wooden bucket. But soon his chest warmed the cloth somewhat, and he rubbed it in a zig-zag pattern down and around, getting his stomach and thighs. Then another clothful for his backside. He moved rapidly, for his teeth were chattering, his skin blue. Still, this was no worse than swimming in the mountain pool in summer; the water rushed through a narrow channel from its origin somewhere high in the mountains and was so chill he dared not dive in, but had to walk in slowly, letting his feet grow numb, then his shins, and slowly up until at last his whole body was numb and he could swim. Some people *could* dive in, venting a scream of reaction as the chill struck them all at once—but they were better padded than he with subcutaneous fat. That was the secret of the walrus. Paul was skinny; the cold went right through to his bones, and when he got out those bones radiated it back into his flesh. It took him half an hour to get warm again. But he liked swimming. It lifted him free of the visible ground, making it seem as though he were flying. Flight represented a kind of escape, however transitory.

In less than a minute he was through washing. He dumped the basin into the tub, whose drainpipe poked through a hole in the wall to empty into the weeds outside, and he charged back upstairs. Theoretically this expenditure of energy should warm his body, but the magnitude of cold was simply too great to be dented by such measures. He used no towel; the water dried as he

moved. Now at last he could dress, and that was a comfort. The worst of the morning was done. Pants and
shirt and sweater and socks. He knocked his boots
together at the heels before trusting his feet to them;
once he had donned them without doing that, and he
felt something funny, and found a big black multilegged
roach inside. That had been enough to condition him
for some years yet. He was not bug shy, but he didn't
like such things in his shoes. Some bugs liked to bite.

Down to the warm kitchen heated by the wood stove.
These same power crises had made wood fashionable
again, especially in the country where wood was free for
the picking up and cutting. That stove was lit in the
morning and kept going all day; sometimes when it was
zero outside, it was a hundred in the kitchen in the old F
degrees the backwoods people still used. In real degrees
C, it was minus 18 out, plus 38 in.

Paul liked the stove; there was just room behind it
next to the back wall where he could sit, enjoying a
steady temperature around 40° C. He could never get
too much heat; it reminded him of the old happy years
in Africa when it had always been warm physically and
emotionally. The two were strongly linked for him. But
no time for that now; his cracked-wheat porridge was
ready, and he had to hurry. He poured some white
goat's milk on top to cool it enough for the first spoon-
ful and started in. It was good, filling stuff, and there
was always plenty of it; he never went hungry.

"I wonder if we're getting anywhere?" Satan murmured. "Well, we have plenty of time. On with it."

Then the rush to cram into galoshes, overcoat, mit-
tens, and hood, tying it close about his face to protect
his ears. It was a long walk to school, but not bad once
the path had been beaten down. It was cold out, but the
wind was down; an inch of snow (a scant two centimeters in real measure) had fallen in the night, but this
hardly obscured the deep track that had been broken
through the crust last week. Snow crusts were
something; they formed when the sun melted the top
layer of snow, and then the night froze it back tight like
ice on a lake. Once he had slipped on a hard crust at the

top of the hill, and been unable to regain his footing because only an axe could cut through it when it was strong, and had to slide helplessly a quarter kilometer to the bottom. No harm done; it had been fun in fact. Another time he had stamped his foot to break through a thin crust to find the solid ground some centimeters below. Suddenly he had sunk down another ten centimeters: that was not ground, but a second crust! The ground was deeper than he had remembered. Then that, too, had broken, and he came at last to the *real* ground, hidden beneath three crusts, a full meter down. Once a crust was covered by new snowfall, it never melted until spring. Like life in a way; once he settled into a new level, he could not go back to the old one. Sometimes he tunneled under a crust, hollowing out a snow cave, using the crust as a roof. Snow was cold, but it had its points.

He crested the ridge and started down through the forest on the other side. Here there was wind; it whistled through the bare trees. Beeches, sugar maples, scattered clumps of white birches, scattered patches of white pine—which, of course, was not white but green, even in winter. It was four kilometers to the school, but he was used to the walk and liked it. The animals were harmless; he saw their tracks crisscrossing in the fresh snow. Sometimes he would spy a deer bounding away. He had never seen a bear though they were present. But at times the snow itself was more interesting. One night there had been a freezing rain; it formed icicles on every twig of every tree, weighting them down. The forest had become a fairyland of glassy pendants, tinkling as his passage disturbed them. He had never before witnessed such absolute beauty! Maybe part of his attraction was its fragility, its crystalline evanescence. In one day the ice had been dirtied and broken, and in three days it was largely gone. Trees were beautiful too—but you could always see a tree. The ice forest had been a once-in-a-lifetime experience, treasured less for its nature than for its rarity.

He passed a large old oak tree leaning over the trail. "Far and wide as the eye can wander, heath and bog are

everywhere," he sang aloud, picturing the snow as
heath and bog. "Not a bird sings out to cheer us, oaks
are standing gaunt and bare. We are the peat-bog
soldiers, marching with our spades, to the bog." He
liked folk songs and enjoyed singing and humming
them, but he couldn't do it at home. His foster father
objected, calling it noisemaking. "But for us there is no
complaining, winter will in time be past. One day we
shall cry rejoicing: homeland, dear, you're mine at
last!" He felt the tears coming to his eyes and got
choked up so he couldn't sing any more. Would winter
ever pass for him?

Down the mountain two kilometers, then up the next
slope. This was a wilderness route though there was a
plowed-out road he could have used. The problem with
the road was that it went by the house of Mrs. Kurry.
That story went way back to last year. One day at
school, Paul had washed his hands and noted how dis-
tinctive the surface of the bar of soap was: firm yet im-
pressionable. His artistic sense was awakened. He put
the bar against the tap and twisted. Sure enough, there
was a neat circular indentation as if a spaceship had
landed in this miniature planet, melting the very stone
by the heat of its jet, then departed, leaving only this
melt mark on the airless surface. But later that day there
was an outcry: "This water tastes like soap!" Oh oh—it
had not occurred to Paul that soap would attach to the
tap; he had been contemplating the other end of it, the
art. He confessed what he had done, accepted his
ridicule, and cleaned it off the tap, and forgotten the
matter. But others had not forgotten. To them, this was
an injury due to be avenged.

Another day Paul had enjoyed himself in new, light,
fluffy snow beside the road to school by lying on his
back and waving his arms to make "Angels" and
running around saplings, one hand on the trunks to
guide him in a perfect circle, to leave donut-shaped
paths. How easy it was to form geometric shapes in
nature if you only knew how! It was merely idle play on
the way to school, not taking long enough to make him
late. It happened to be near Mrs. Kurry's house. She

stormed out and delivered the worst verbal abuse of his life. She accused him of ruining her trees, cutting a hole in one of her tires, and being sassy—when he tried to explain that he had not harmed the trees, knew nothing of her tire, and did not possess a knife. "You did it!" she screamed. "Just like you broke that tap at school!" And she chased him off.

The matter had not ended there; there was a letter to the teacher, complaints to Paul's family, and a charge from her house whenever he passed by. But he had to go to school, and this was the only road. Finally this alternate trail through the forest was set up so that Paul would not have to pass her house. His life had been made harder, and he had been terrorized—because this neighbor had borne false witness against him.

"Ah, yes," Satan observed. "We have her here in Hell now. Beelzebub's dominion; I must make sure the Lord of The Flies has her doing penance for false witness." The papers rustled as He made a note.

At school it was okay. The kids hardly teased him anymore about his hand twitches or compulsive counting of things, and he had a lively interest in many fields, so it wasn't so bad. He had a couple of stomach aches in the course of the day, but he was used to these. Only when a bad one struck, the kind that hung him up writhing in agony for half a day straight, did he really mind—and fortunately those powerful ones did not come often. Today was just a minor-pain day, no problem at all.

He finished his written work early and doodled on his paper, trying to draw a realistic dormer window—the kind that poked out of a slanting roof. A straight window was easy because it was all straight lines, but a dormer had all sorts of angles that were hard to visualize. It was difficult to draw it on a flat paper so that it looked real, and he wasn't quite sure it could be done at all. After all, *it* was three dimensional. But it was a challenge. Maybe if he angled a line *here*—

Uh-oh. The teacher had called on him, and he hadn't heard her at all. His classmates were laughing at him. They thought he was stupid, and he suspected they were

right. Why couldn't he pay proper attention? Others
were smart; *they* paid attention. And he had lost his inspiration for the dormer.

On the way home he heard the distant barking of a
dog. The hair on his skin reacted, and he looked about
nervously, hoping the animal didn't come this way.
Once he had petted a strange dog, and it had jumped up
and bared its teeth in his face with such a growl he had
fled in tears. Other children had thought that very
funny. Last year some lumbercamp dogs had charged
him in a pack, barking, nosing up, scaring him. One had
nipped him in the rear, but no one paid attention. They
always said that a barking dog didn't bite though that
was manifestly untrue. The thing was, a twenty
kilogram dog seemed a lot bigger to a twenty-seven
kilogram boy than it did to a seventy kilogram man. But
today Paul was lucky; the distant dog went elsewhere.

Actually, the dogs were not nearly so bad as the Monster. At least he could *see* them. The Monster was quite
another matter. It followed him home from school each
day, huge and malignant, like a centipede the size of a
dragon with deadly pincers in front and a ten meter long
sting tail behind and little glowing eyes on the ends of its
eye stalks that could twist about to see anything. Its
myriad side legs stretched out to comb the brush: that
was to prevent Paul from hiding in a bush in order to let
it pass and get ahead of him. If that ever happened,
Paul would have power over the Monster because then
he would be following *it* and he would have *seen* it. But
he dared not ambush it because of the extreme care it
took with bushes. He had to see it from *behind*. That
was the law of their encounter.

He looked back, feeling that prickle of apprehension
up his back. Nothing was visible. That was also the way
of it; the Monster could retreat in an instant. If Paul
only had eyes in the back of his head . . . the thing was,
it could only approach him from behind, from the direction he wasn't looking. When he turned around, the
direct force of his vision made it back off, giving him
more leeway. But if he should run without turning back
to look, too long, it would overtake him and—

No! Paul stopped, nerved himself, turned, and strode
back down the snow trail. He would show it he was not
afraid of it though he trembled in his knees. He would
spot its tracks, *proving* it had been following him. That
would be a point for him. Once he got an advantage,
however trivial, he would be able to use that leverage to
drive the Monster back and back until finally it was
gone. Then it would seek some other prey instead of
him.

There were no tracks, of course; he should have anticipated this. Its hundred padded feet made little im-
pression in the snow; each carried very little weight, and
the Monster was very cunning about brushing away any
telltale marks. Almost too clever for him. . . .

Paul turned about again. With a soundless gloat the
Monster resumed the pursuit. Paul looked back, but it
had dodged out of sight already. He could not defeat it
this way. Now he had to re-retrace his path, enduring
the hazard again. He had only complicated his journey.

Strange that the Monster never pursued him in the
morning. Maybe that was because then he was fresh and
vigorous—or because he was going toward the long
chore that was school. Why should the Monster interfere when he was heading *in* to trouble? It preferred
to go after him when he was on the verge of safety. But
mostly, he thought, it was because the shadows were
lengthening in the afternoon. The Monster was a
devotee of shadows, a beast of darkness, whose strength
increased as light decreased.

"You were a bit too smart for the Monster," Satan
remarked appreciatively. "I remember with what
gnashing of tooth it complained about the way you kept
backing it off, just when it thought it had you. We
finally had to reassign it." Infernal humor!

Now, as Paul came near the crest, he saw the late sun
shifting through the trees, making the forest brighter,
prettier, as though there were a clearing. In the summer
this effect was enhanced, shaping seeming glades where
ferns and flowers grew lovely. In winter the entire forest
was lighter, so the effect diminished. Still, in places it
remained strong, and this was such a place. But Paul

gave no glad start of discovery; instead he averted his eyes from the effect, breathing hard, and ran until he could no longer see it.

He made it home. Junie was nibbling the bark of a tree near the house; she made a little bleat of pleasure and plowed through the snow toward him. He liked Junie as he liked all goats; not only did she provide good milk, she was affectionate. He stroked her white-striped nose. She was a Toggenburg, the handsomest of goats. Too bad she couldn't come to school with him; if the Monster came, she would just butt it with her sawed-off horns. No one won a head-to-head collision with a goat!

But he had chores to do. First he had to split tomorrow's kindling for the stove, then wash out last night's sheets. The splitting was fun; he liked wood, and he liked the feel of its splitting. The first split was hard, halving the log; but doing the halves was easier, and rendering each quarter into fine kindling was easiest with such a rapid feeling of accomplishment. If only the problems of life could be divided and conquered similarly!

Laundering the big sheet was not fun. The water was cold, making his hands get pink and hurty, and it was hard to wring out. He twisted it, on and on, until it resembled a giant rope, a hawser like that used to anchor a ship, but there was always more water in it, waiting to drip, no matter how hard he squeezed. But it had to be done.

He looked at the drips descending from the sheet. He was suddenly thirsty—and he had forgotten to tank up on water. He was under a proscription. They had taken him to a doctor one day about the bed-witting, and the doctor had said: "'No water after four in the afternoon.'' And that had been the word. It had had no effect on the bedwetting, but it made his evening life a torment of thirst. Now he put a corner of the wet sheet between his teeth, tasting the faint remainder of urine, helping to hold it while he wrung it out with both hands (he told himself), and sucked a few precious drops surreptitiously. It wasn't enough, but it helped some; even a single drop became gratifying.

In the evening his foster father read to him: stories of adventure, fantasy, history—all fascinating. Paul was in love with the past, the future, and the imaginary. Those other realms were always so interesting, partly because of their exotic nature and partly because they were not *here*.

But at last it was full night and time to sleep. Paul had a lamp, a dim night light, but it wasn't enough. For now the ultimate dread of his existence loomed, and the name of it was Fear. Yet it was admixed with wonder, too, that lured him back again and again to—

America! Perhaps only the foreign born could appreciate the full meaning of that word. He had come to find the glories of the new land spelled out by a single beautiful song. He did not know its title or all its words and could not fathom its allusions, but he did not need to. This song—it was not so much a reflection of the new world, it was the new world itself.

He could see the vast terrain, covered with fruited plains and waving with amber grain and studded with jewel-like alabaster cities that gleamed under the spacious skies. Magnificent purple mountains extended from the ordinary sea in the east, that he had crossed, to the wonderful shining sea in the far far west, almost beyond imagination. It all blended into a vague yet brilliant image somewhat resembling a single field where the great trees became smaller, dwindling to saplings and finally to brush and green fern and pretty flowers. A field of rapture whose brief image brought warmth to his being. America! America! He loved her through that song.

Yet America was the city too—a great metropolis whose architecture scraped the sky, the smoke of industry rising up toward God. Cars, trains, ships, aircraft, spacecraft, printing presses, atomic power plants, huge solar reflectors in orbit—the wonderful technology of civilization. Nature and Science: two images, each alluring.

The two fragmented into four, and these became framed and frozen. Four pictures seemingly innocent—yet taken together, they were nightmare.

1. A woman walking along a city street, a small boy at her side.

2. The woman in a vidphone booth, the child looking in through the glass.

3. A man standing in a clearing, a lion at his side. Nearby, a lightly but richly clad woman, lying on a pallet.

4. The man holding the lion in the air, chest high.

What was the secret of these still images that made them horrible? His mind proceeded inexorably to the interpretation though he dreaded it.

America! Yet somehow the rousing cadences echoed hollowly, for the city through which he walked with his foster mother was not exactly alabaster. Nevertheless, it had some of the luster and excitement characteristic of the new world. It was not lonely like the farm; there were people, and stores, and television, and things happening. A happy picture.

One of his earliest memories of Africa was not Africa at all, but the vision of Tomorrow. Tomorrow was a row of houses down the street, and he knew he was going down that street and that someday he would be there at those strange houses instead of here in the familiar. Suddenly Tomorrow came, and it was called America, and he was unprepared for it. He had thought his parents would be there with him. There were nice people in the new world, but all he really wanted was to go back home.

He realized that the city could be a trap. His foster mother went into the glassy doorway to play with the marvelous contraption called the vidphone: some mysterious adult business of the machine age. Then she put her hand to the door to come out again, but the door was stuck. She could not leave. Sudden alarm; the machines could not be trusted, the city would not let go. The promise of America had become a threat even to its own people.

Paul's foster father preferred the farm, while his foster mother preferred the city. The two seemed destined never quite to meet. Paul did not understand the laws of the conflict; he saw only the opposing forces: the city and the country. The woman was the creature of the city, the man of the country. They were married, yet could not unite. He could call neither one good or evil, right or wrong; both were good, both right—yet they warred.

The man stood in the country amid the trees, the symbol of strength, dominating the lion. The woman was now in his power, spirited from the vid-trap to the pallet, sedated. Surely the man would prevent the lion from doing her harm!

Paul wandered one day through the open fields so like the glorious spaces of the song. He had not chosen, *could* not choose between the rival forces; both city and country were parts of America, the promised land, Tomorrow. At the foot of a grassy hillside he saw a skull. It was the vast white hollow-eyed bone of a cow. He realized that this dead thing had once been part of a living animal similar to the animals he knew like Junie. Now it was defunct, its warm flesh gone, its hooves nevermore to walk the green field. Had it mooed high, or had it mooed low? He could not know; it was gone. He looked upon the fact of death, the face of death, and began to realize the utter finality of it. *Nevermore!* How had it died? Maybe an African lion had killed it.

Now the man was holding the lion in the air, happy with the beast, smiling. Yet death was in that picture: not the specific act of killing, but the morbid knowledge that death had come and swept its scythe and left its mark, and nothing would ever take that mark away, for it was final. The lion had fed. The pallet was empty. The country had devoured the city. The man was holding up the lion to see how much weight it had gained.

Now the field that was America was intertwined with the stigmata of horror, terror, and death. The fear was real, the fear was ultimate; by day it could be largely avoided or blunted, but by night it became overwhelming. He was gifted, cursed, with a graphic imagination; when darkness cut off normal sight, his mind's eye filled the world with spectral images so real that he could see every detail. Light was the only defense; so long as his eyes remained open and seeing, the nightmare was held at bay, like the Monster of the forest.

It was the body that haunted him. The body that had not quite been in the four pictures, but that he knew was there, perhaps in the hidden fifth picture. The body with the flesh torn off where the lion had fed; the hollow, sightless eyes, the bleached white bones protruding from that which had once been—

Screams, screams in the night! It was a sight too mind shattering to face, yet too persistent to ignore. It impinged upon his consciousness, inescapable no matter how he fled. It loomed in fair fields, it cruised by like the engine of a locomotive, always lurking, a mass of horror driving him relentlessly toward insanity. It impinged upon his very soul, and almost, now, it had *become* his soul.

"Now I lay me down to sleep, I pray the Lord my soul to keep," he whispered. "If I should die before I wake, I pray the Lord my soul to take." He repeated it in singsong, in the tune he had learned for it, trying to blot out the horror, to shove it away so he could sleep at last. But it would not be denied, and every flicker of the lamp brought it closer until he fancied he could feel it touching his cold toes, nudging them, where he could not quite see, and he dared not look. How could he look at a feeling? How he wished day would come to release him from his torture. But the somber mass of the night loomed between him and day, forcing its torture on him. Tomorrow—yet this *was* Tomorrow, and so there was no escape. This night's Tomorrow would only start the cycle again; he was bound to it with no relief possible. For the horror was what was past, not what was to happen. With sudden inspiration, he modified his prayer: "May I sleep—and never wake," he said, and then he slept.

"And so you sealed it over," Satan said as Brother Paul lay bathed in sweat steaming like urine, eyes staring, hands twitching. "You had adapted to everything in your youth, except for that. You could neither explain it nor accept it. You chose to block out that entire segment of your life; that was the only course available to you, given your then existing needs and capabilities. But of course it did not leave you. It remained as subconscious motivation. The five great forces of your life—Fire, Water, Air, Earth and Spirit—evoked piecemeal by the cards of the Tarot. The Fire of the burning wood, granting temporary relief from the encompassing cold; the Water of your wet bed, while yet you suffered from thirst; the Air of the violence about you in the form of Mrs. Kurry, the dogs and the invisible Monster, not to mention the gas in your tummy that caused you small and great pains; the Earth of your ruptured self-esteem, your neurotic twitchings, lack of social status; and the Spirit that ruled over all of you supreme: Fear."

"Fear," Brother Paul repeated weakly.

"Yet you had a lot of frustrated talent, for art is a thing of the Spirit," Satan continued. "You might have been a sculptor, but your soap carving on the tap scotched that. You could have gone into music, but your parents stopped your singing in company at the outset. You had fair artistic talent and could have been a painter—but your teacher thought your drawings mere distractions. So your potential achievement of self-esteem and escape from nothingness via the route of creative expression was denied, and in the end you had to write it all off as a loss."

Brother Paul did not argue.

Satan shook his head. "This is a tough one! I had figured you for hidden sexual or racial sin, considering your background, but fear is not a sin by conventional definitions. Cowardice is another matter—but there is little to suggest you were ever a coward. You tried to fight back, but were overwhelmed by events."

"But the sealing off—I finally gave up on the problem," Brother Paul said, not caring that he was arguing against his own interest. "I couldn't face the fear, so I fled it. I—"

"You are honest; that's the most awkward thing about you," Satan said. "You were uprooted, removed from your home and family in Africa, and planted in new soil. But your foster parents had problems of their own. It was in part the city-country schism. Their lifestyles differed, and they could not agree, so they engaged in a decade-long tug-of-war that terminated in separation and divorce. Your fragile new roots were broken again as you shuttled from city to country, needing both, needing a unified family. You finally got the country—at the price of the family. You were too small to understand that it was not your fault; when your foster mother returned to the city, you thought *you* had driven her away: figuratively killed her. You were unable to stand on one foot, on half a family—not in your root-pruned condition. So it is scarcely surprising that you fell. Your bedwetting, twitching, and nightmare were merely symptoms; it was no longer possible for you to survive whole and sane in that situation. So—you stepped out of it when you had the opportunity—by orienting your life around the lifestyle of judo and sealing off your memories of home. I really hesitate to condemn you to eternal damnation for that.''

"You have already done it," Brother Paul said. "You have opened out my secret. Now Hell is with me—in my memory where it once was shut out."

"But you are stronger now than you were then," Satan pointed out. "You have regrown your roots in the Holy Order of Vision. Your life in that capacity has been exemplary ever since you suffered your Vision of Conversion. And in fact you have not been dragged before Me kicking and screaming; you descended voluntarily to Hell itself. Your last free act before being consumed by Me was to plead for your innocent daughter, who does not even exist yet, named in honor of a girl you admired twenty years ago, and for her safety you sacrificed your manhood."

Satan paused thoughtfully, rustling His papers again. "Of course, that was governed by your fear of losing your sight, so that you would not be limited to the nightmares of perpetual darkness, the Monster and the Corpse. But overall, the nobility of the sacrifice outweighs the specific motive of choice of punishments. No, I'm very much afraid your case remains in doubt. You *do* have evil on your conscience, and you are humanly fallible, but there is no clear shifting of the scales."

Brother Paul was coming out of his lingering shock of memory. This might be an Animation, but those memories were real. Yet Satan was correct: he *was* stronger now than he had been as a child: he had a much broader perspective. He could appreciate how much beauty and good there had been in his sealed-over life; it had been a shame to obliterate that along with the unfaceable. Satan had made an accurate assessment. "Do with me what you will," Brother Paul said. He was discovering a genuine, fundamental, disconcerting respect for Satan.

"I shall put you to the torture of the Three Wishes," Satan decided. "Three because it took me three attempts to evoke your guiltiest secret. I am always fair."

"Three wishes?"

"That is correct. I will grant you three wishes—and upon the use you make of them, shall you be judged."

"But I could simply wish for Salvation!" Brother Paul protested.

Satan shook His horned head again. "So hard to deceive an honest man! Now I must confess the trap: you could wish for Salvation—and you would lose it because your wish was selfish. I would honor it by shipping you to Heaven—you alone, not your friends or your daughter—and the Pearly Gates would not open for your selfish soul. You cannot knowingly seek purely personal gain by demonic means."

"That rules out a lot of things," Brother Paul said. "But I don't see that it should be a torture even so. There are innocuous wishes I could make."

Satan smiled, and now the tusks showed. "You will surely find out."

"Do I have any time to think about it?"

"You have eternity. Right here."

"Oh. Very well. I wish for knowledge of the true origin and meaning of Tarot."

Satan nodded slowly. "You are a clever man. I perceive the likely nature of your following wishes."

No doubt. Brother Paul hoped that the responses to the first two wishes would enable him to phrase the third one in such a way as to obtain the answer to his quest here. If he finally discovered the way to learn whether there was a separate, objective God of Tarot—

"But knowledge itself is neither good nor evil," Satan continued. "It is how you acquire it and what you do with it that counts—as you shall discover. There-fore—on your way, Uncle!"

Suddenly Brother Paul dropped through a hole in the floor. He slid down a chute that twisted and looped like an intestine. *Oh, no!* he thought. *I'm to be shit out, colored brown, like the insult of the Dozens game!*

But as he reached the nadir, the passage closed in about him, squeezing him through a nether loop, then upward. Fluid surrounded him, moving him hydraulically on. The pressure became almost in-tolerable as the tube constricted yet more. Then there was an abrupt release as he was geysered up and out with climactic force. He had a vision of the Tarot Tower exploding. He sailed through the air, looking back, and realized: this was indeed the meaning of that card, the House of God or the House of the Devil. This was Revelation! *He had been ejaculated from Satan's mon-strous erect phallus.* He was the Seed, proceeding to what fate he could not guess.

III

Hope/Fear: 22

When the High Patriarch of the Christians in Constantinople made a motion, the priests would diligently collect it in squares of silk and dry it in the sun. Then they would mix it with musk, amber and benzoin, and, when it was quite dry, powder it and put it up in little gold boxes. These boxes were sent to all Christian kings and churches, and the powder was used as the holiest incense for the sanctification of Christians on all solemn occasions, to bless the bride, to fumigate the newly born, and to purify a priest on ordination. As the genuine excrements of the High Patriarch could hardly suffice for ten provinces, much less for all Christian lands, the priests used to forge the powder by mixing less holy matters with it, that is to say, the excrements of lesser patriarchs and even of the priests themselves. This imposture was not easy to detect. These Greek swine valued the powder for other virtues; they used it as a salve for sore eyes and as a medicine for the stomach and bowels. But only kings and queens and the very rich could obtain these cures, since, owing to the limited quantity of raw material, a dirham-weight of the powder used to be sold for a thousand dinars in gold.

—*The Book of the Thousand Nights and One Night:* translated from Arabic to French by Dr. J.C. Mardrus, and from French to English by Powys Mathers: Volume I, London, The Casanova Society, 1923.

The first thing Brother Paul saw was the star. It hovered just above the horizon, bright and beautiful and marvelously pure: the Star of Hope.

But immediately he felt fear: where was he? Was this another aspect of Hell? What menace lurked in this unknown region? He hardly dared move until he knew whether he stood on a plain—or the brink of a precipice.

Fortunately he had not long to wait. Light grew; it was breaking dawn, brighter in one portion of the firmament, giving him convenient orientation. He knew which way North was. Now if only he knew where in the universe *he* was. Not Planet Tarot, it seemed; the vegetation, air and gravity were too Earth-like to occur anywhere but on Planet Earth. But he needed to narrow it down more than that! It had to be the temperate zone, for now he saw that the trees were deciduous.

Perhaps he had seen the Morning Star, actually the Planet Venus, symbol of love. He hoped that was a good sign. But other stars could shine in the morning too, depending on the season, cloud cover, and mood of the viewer.

He stood on a pleasant hillside. It was evidently spring. Though the morning was cool, it was not unpleasant, and the odors of nature were wonderful. Flowers were opening, and they seemed to be of familiar types though he could not identify them precisely. If he had his life to do over again, he would pay more attention to flowers! Carolyn would have enjoyed this scene.

Carolyn—where was she now? Not until the recent review of his past had he realized consciously the rationale of her naming. Carolyn, one-sixteenth black, in honor of the all-black Karolyn who had shown him what judo could do and never snickered. Satan had said

Carolyn did not yet exist—yet she *did* exist, for he knew her and loved her and she was his daughter. The colonist child was merely the actress, standing in lieu of the real Carolyn, who was—where? He could not believe she was a creature solely of his imagination; he was emotionally unable to accept that. Well, at least she had avoided Hell; probably Lee had taken her back out of the Vision. Thank God!

Or was it Satan that deserved the thanks?

Music interrupted his thoughts. Beautiful, flute-like—was the melody the "Song of the Morning"? Edvard Grieg, who composed it as part of the famous *Peer Gynt* suites, had lived in the late 19th century, and he was Swedish—no, Norwegian. Could that be where and when Brother Paul found himself—in historical Europe? Given the capacities of Animation, this was well within the range of possibility. How he would love to meet that marvelous musician, one of his favorites! But no, this melody was not that; one passage had merely seemed similar. So—forget Grieg, unfortunately. Satan would hardly have granted him that incidental pleasure.

But why guess at all? The tune issued from the vale to the west. Brother Paul walked toward it. He realized he was wearing a belted tunic and crude leather shoes made comfortable by use. But something itched him—ouch! He suspected it was lice. That put him back somewhere in the Middle Ages, probably Europe. Sanitation was not well regarded then. Not by the Christians. In fact it had been said that Christianity was the only great religion where dirtiness was next to Godliness. The Moslems in particular had ridiculed that attitude, perhaps angered by the impertinence of the Crusades. Only in relatively recent times had the Christian attitude changed.

The musician came into view. He was a young man, tall and slim and strong, garbed in garishly colored pantaloons and jacket and hat. One slipper was blue, the other red. His stockings were the reverse. There were small bells on his knees, and he wore a bright blue cape. The brim of the hat spread so widely it flopped down over his eyes. Yet this comic personage seemed in no way embarrassed. He rested on the ground under a densely leaved tree, and he was playing on a strange double flute, his right hand fingering the holes on one side, his left the other.

"Pan pipes!" Brother Paul exclaimed.

The man stopped. He looked up questioningly. "Ja?" he inquired.

Brother Paul did some quick readjusting. That sounded like German! He was not proficient in that language, but he might get by. "I—was admiring your music," he said haltingly in German.

"The shepherd's flute," the man agreed in the same language. His accent was strange, but not unintelligible. "It sets the mood for the day. Will you join me?"

"I would like to," Brother Paul said.

"Have some bread," the man said, tearing off the end of a long loaf and proffering it. This was hard black stuff, but it smelled good.

"Thank you," Brother Paul said. "I fear I have no favor to return. I am a stranger here, without substance."

The man smiled. "There are no strangers under the eye of God."

"None indeed!" Brother Paul agreed, encouraged. "I am Brother Paul of the Holy Order of Vision." He broke off, uncertain whether that would make any sense in this context.

"Would that have anything to do with the Apostle Paul's vision on the road to Damascus?"

"Yes," Brother Paul agreed, gratified. Here was a kindred soul! The actor was obviously Lee, but now the role itself was harmonious. "For both my Order and myself. We believe that the foundation of present-day Christianity was when the Pharisee Jew of Tarsus was converted to Christ. To a considerable extent, he made Christianity what it is. More correctly, he laid down the principles this great religion should follow although many bearing the title of Christians have strayed from those precepts. We of the Order of Vision try to restore, to the extent we are able, the Christianity of Saint Paul's vision. A faith open to all people, regardless of the name they choose to put upon their belief." He knew he was not speaking with the eloquence he wished, handicapped by the language, but it was getting easier as he progressed. Lee, of course, knew all this—but it was necessary to get it on record for this Animation, as it were anchoring the philosophical basis.

"Very well spoken, Brother! You are then a traveling friar?"

"No, not at all. I am here—well, by accident. I don't even know where this is. Or *when* this is. I am from America, circa 2000 A.D." How would *that* go over?

The man smiled again, shaking his head. "I regret I know of neither your Order nor your country, and I surely misunderstand your calendar. But I am ignorant of the fine points of religion; my folk always believed religion originated with fear. I have no knowledge whether this is true. But on geography I am more conversant: this is the land west of the Rhine, north of the Alps, and this is the year of Our Lord 1392, and I am a simple itinerant minstrel, entertainer, and magician. I go by many names, none of them significant; you may call me simply *Le Bateleur*, or the Juggler."

"The Juggler!" Brother Paul repeated, astonished. "Thirteen ninety-two!"

"You seem surprised, friend. Have I given offense?"

"No, no offense! It's just that—in my framework—which seems to be some six centuries after yours—your name is the title of a—what some call a fortune-telling card!"

The man waved a flute in a careless gesture. "This, too, I do, if there be an obolus in it." He flipped the flute in the air and caught it expertly. "Do you wish your fortune told?"

"I, uh—no thank you. If an obolus is a unit of money, I have none." Brother Paul seemed to remember a medieval coin worth a cent or so; this could be it. "In fact, I seem to be without resources and cannot repay you for your bread unless there is some service I can do."

The Juggler looked at him appraisingly. "I will accept payment with a mere song."

"A song?" Brother Paul found himself liking this unpretentious yet talented character, but this was confusing. "I do not claim to be an accomplished singer, though I do enjoy the form."

"I will give you the tune so that you may hum as I play." And the Juggler put his shepherd's flute to his lips and played an oddly sad melody.

"I like it," Brother Paul said. He began to hum, picking up the tune readily. He remembered how, as a child, he had been rebuked for humming. But now he was freed of that geas and could enjoy it.

As he mastered the song and hummed more forcefully, the Juggler changed his playing. Now it was the descant, complementing and counterpointing Brother Paul's voice. The pipes with their linked yet separate themes were lovely in themselves; but now, augmenting Brother Paul's voice, they lifted the song into a creation of such simple beauty that he found himself in a minor transport of rapture. Music soothed the savage breast indeed.

When it finished, the Juggler smiled. "Brother Paul, man of Vision, you were unduly modest. You have a voice second only to that of a castrato."

Brother Paul suffered a feeling of horror quite removed from the intended compliment. In medieval times young boys with good voices were castrated before puberty so that they could retain their sweet high ranges and continue singing in church choirs. The Bible forbade any man "injured in the stones" to enter a congregation of the Lord, but the Church ignored that when its convenience suited. What about himself: had he recovered his masculinity, or was Satan's excision permanent? The Juggler had spoken figuratively; Brother Paul's voice remained tenor since castration after the age of puberty had no immediate effect on range. Yet—

He could check readily enough. But not right now! "I thank you for the bread—and for the song. I must be on my way. Could you direct me to the nearest town or city?"

"Merely follow the river, friend! There are hamlets

throughout, and eventually to the north you will come
to the great city of Worms, the first Imperial Free City
of the Empire.''

"Worms! I remember the Diet of Worms, where
Martin Luther—'' He broke off. The Diet of Worms occurred in 1521—a hundred and thirty years after the
year this was supposed to be. He remembered that date
with special clarity because there had been a joke among
his schoolmates about the "diet of worms" they would
have to eat if they misremembered that date. One
thousand, five hundred, and twenty one worms to be
exact.

"You have friends in Worms then?'' Of course the
pronunciation was different with the *W* sounding more
like a *V*, so the joke was no good for adults.

Brother Paul cut off his continuing, worm-like
thought and answered. ''Uh, not exactly. But perhaps I
shall find what I seek there.''

"May I inquire what you seek? It is not my business,
but I have made many contacts in the course of my
travels and perhaps can help direct you.''

"I am looking for a deck of cards called the Tarot.''

The Juggler's brow furrowed. ''Ta-row? I think I
have heard of some such pastime indulged in by the
wealthy.''

"They are special cards with pictured trumps and
numerical suits. We use them as an aid to meditation,
but they have a long and checkered history.'' But the
Juggler's obvious perplexity made him pause. Apparently in this role he had no direct knowledge of
Tarot. ''This is the deck I mentioned where one card has
your name: the Juggler or Magician.''

The Juggler spread his hands. ''I would be flattered,
but this is surely a coincidence. There are many of my
ilk, begging our bread and a night's lodging from village
to village. Are there also cards for merchants and
plowmen and friars?''

"Not specifically. The cards favor kings, queens, em-
perors, and popes,'' Brother Paul said with a smile.
"As you suggested: an entertainment of the wealthy.''

"Worms would be the place to seek then,'' the

Juggler said. "It is the capital of the Bishop-Princes and a center of Empire intrigue. I wish you well."

"Thank you." Brother Paul rose and oriented northward.

"Move east until you spy the river," the Juggler advised. "The roads are better along its bank, and the villagers are accustomed to travelers."

Brother Paul nodded appreciatively and walked east.

By mid-afternoon he was hungry and footsore. He had found the river and a suitable trail north, but the villagers were not particularly hospitable to one who had no money. This idyllic historic land had its drawbacks. But he plodded on.

A party of ill-kempt soldiers rounded the turn, going south. Brother Paul knew that excellent armor and mail were available to those who could afford it in the fourteenth century, but these men were more like rabble. Instead of chain and gauntlets and swords they wore doublets with patches of leather sewn on for protection, their hands were bare and calloused, and they carried assorted knives and staffs evidently scrounged from what was most readily available.

They were upon Brother Paul before he realized their nature; because he was hot, grimy, and tired he had not been paying proper attention to his surroundings. "Out of the way, ruffian!" the leader said, striking forward with his staff.

Brother Paul reacted automatically. Adrenaline flooded his system, abolishing his fatigue. He stepped aside, reaching out with his left hand to catch hold of the moving staff. He turned to the left, his right hand coming down on the soldier's right hand, pinning it to the staff. Now he was beside the soldier, his two hands on the staff along with those of the other man. Brother Paul bent his knees, pushing the staff up and forward, causing the soldier to overbalance. He heaved—and the man flew over Brother Paul's right shoulder to land resoundingly in the dirt. The staff, by no coincidence, remained in Brother Paul's hands.

"Sorry," he said in his imperfect German. "I thought you meant to attack me." Better to put the most positive face on it!

But now the other soldiers ringed him, knives drawn. They looked ugly, in feature and attitude. "Who are you, churl?" one demanded.

"Just a traveler to Worms," Brother Paul said innocently.

"Who's your Lord?"

They thought him a servant. "I have no Lord. I'm just looking for the Tarot deck—"

The soldiers exchanged glances. "Sounds like a heretic to me," one said, and the others nodded agreement. "No protector, interfering with honest troops—let's teach him his place."

Uh oh. Brother Paul looked around, but there was no retreat. They had him, and they meant trouble. They had delayed their revenge only long enough to ascertain that there would be no likely retribution from some powerful noble who might have sent this stranger on some mission. If Brother Paul tried to escape, he would get stabbed by a dirty knife. If he fought—the same. Better to accept their chastisement—and be more careful next time.

"We'll flog him," the leader decided, dusting himself off. Brother Paul had not thrown him with damaging force, and the turf had broken the man's fall, so he had taken no injury worse than bruises. "Strip him!"

Rough hands ripped away Brother Paul's clothing while one of the men unwound a brutal-looking whip. This was not going to be pleasant at all!

They hauled off the last cloth—and paused. "He's gelded!" one exclaimed.

"Must be a slave, escaped from a galley—or a convict. We'd better kill him and cut off his ears; might be a reward."

"Cut off his ears *first*," one suggested. "I want to hear how a gelding screams."

Now Brother Paul knew he would have to fight. He had no choice. These were brute men to whom life was cheap, and they had no mercy. By beating and killing others, they sought to redeem their own sorry lot. The leader looked like Therion. Brother Paul braced, noting the position of each. If he caught one and threw him into two others—

"What's this?" a new voice demanded.

All turned, startled. It was a priest in black robe with a silver cross glinting at his throat. Even without this uniform, his demeanor would have cowed strangers. It was as if light glinted from his steely eyes.

"It's nothing, Father," the chief soldier said. "We caught this felon, and—"

"A heretic," another put in.

"Allow me to be judge of what is or is not significant, and who is or is not a heretic," the priest said sternly. His pale eyes glared down on Brother Paul as from a great height. He rubbed his nose with two fingers, squinting appraisingly. "Are you not the eunuch of the Apostle?" he demanded.

Startled, Brother Paul could not answer.

The priest gestured imperiously. "The Holy Office wants this miscreant. Garb him and bind him; I will convey him to Worms myself."

"Yes, Father," the soldier agreed, cowed. "But can you handle him alone? We could hamstring him for you. He's a rough—"

The priest peered down at the man. Something very like a sneer curled his aristocratic lip. "Your tongue wags rather freely, minion. Is it too long?"

"Father, I—"

"The Holy Office might arrange to have it cut shorter so that it will no longer interfere with your work."

With a visible gulp and tightly closed mouth, the soldier turned to get to work on Brother Paul, and the others jumped to help. They could easily have over-powered the priest, but this thought apparently was not in their repertoire. Quickly they replaced Brother Paul's tatters and tied his hands behind him with a length of cloth. It was evident that the mere mention of the Holy Office put a chill into the stoutest military heart.

"Good men," the priest said gruffly. He lifted two fingers in a careless benediction. "God be with you. Be about your business."

The soldiers bowed their heads. "Thank you, Father," one said and hastily retreated. In moments they were away and out of sight.

From the frying pan into the fire?

The priest considered Brother Paul again. He lifted the crucifix in one hand. "Miscreant, kiss the divine symbol of your Savior," he snapped imperiously.

The memory of a friend suffering and bleeding on that cross was too fresh. "Kiss my ass," Brother Paul muttered in English. He had read of the corrupt, venial medieval priests, and this one seemed typical of the breed. He spoke of tortures more readily than he spoke of the love of Jesus. Better the untender mercies of the soldiers; at least they were not such hypocrites. When Jesus Christ had gone out for his second crucifixion, men of this ilk had been awaiting him.

"I could have your ears sent to join your privates," the priest said warningly. Then he smiled. "Do you not know me, Brother Paul?"

Amazed, Brother Paul recognized him. "Juggler!"

"Stumble onward, friend; the ruffians may be suspicious. When it is safe, I will release you." And Juggler gave him a cuff on the neck that landed without force. What an actor he was!

Brother Paul stumbled forward, hunching his back as if cowed. "How—how did you—?"

"I followed you because my mind was in doubt about you. When it seemed you were authentic, I donned one of the disguises in which I am versed."

"Just in time, too! They were going to kill me! But why should you—?"

The Juggler shook his head ruefully. "My friend, I apologize. I took you for a spy of the Inquisition, but such a person would never have sung the heretical melody or have suffered himself to be humiliated as you were by those soldiers, and a eunuch could not have been admitted to the Holy Office. I realized I had misjudged you."

"The Inquisition? I?" Brother Paul laughed. "I abhor the repression for which the Inquisition stood!"

"So do I. If I were to fall into the power of the Holy Office—" The Juggler shook his head gravely.

"But why should they bother you? A mere minstrel and juggler, however talented—"

"Friend, I must confess that I juggle more than batons," Juggler said, untying Brother Paul's hands. "I am a *barba*. An Uncle."

"Uncle?" Brother Paul repeated blankly. He seemed to remember Satan using the term.

"A missionary of the Waldenses."

"The Waldenses!" Brother Paul had heard that name before. A historical sect, persecuted for their heretical beliefs.

"My partner fell victim to the Black Death. I would have saved him if I could—but it was in God's hands, not mine. Now I continue alone, for the believers must be served. But I fear lest my mission be incomplete."

Now the Juggler quickly removed and reversed his priestly robe. On the inside was his peasant-magician garb. The silver cross was shoved into a deep pocket with a contemptuous twitch of his lip. Now Brother Paul understood the necessity for the Juggler's dramatic abilities. The life expectancy of a suspected heretic was brief indeed. How much worse for a heretic missionary!

"Juggler—it may be presumptuous to ask—but do you think I might accompany you? I don't know my way around and have no money, but there might be some way I could help if you tell me what to do, and perhaps your route will take me where I am going. I bear no malice to your sect; in my framework there are many Christian and non-Christian religions, and tolerance is part of our custom and our law." Thanks to John Murray and others.

The Juggler turned to him seriously. "Brother Paul, I was hoping you would make the offer. I think I followed you in the hope that you would turn out to be a compatriot. You see, there are certain aids I need when performing my tricks—and I must perform or the Holy Office will be suspicious, and suspicion is nine-tenths of

the law. I do not cheat anyone—my faith forbids
that!—but I must put on a realistic show. Only in that
manner can I justify my presence so that I can meet with
those to whom I bring my message.''

"And what is your message? I am a man of some
religious scruple myself, and while I would not seek to
interfere with your belief, I—''

"The Waldenses follow precepts similar to those of
the Albigensians. The Albigensians were suppressed by
the sword and cross two generations ago, so we profit
by their misfortune and tread carefully. A number of
their survivors have joined us. We rely on the authority
of the Bible, rather than that of the Church. We em-
phasize the virtues of poverty, and so we cater chiefly to
the poor. We insist on the direct relationship between
man and God so that priests become irrelevant. We do
not believe in confessions or prayers for the dead or the
intercession of Saints. Men and women are equal. We
do not venerate the cross, which is the torture implement on which Christ died. We missionaries are
known as the *barbe* or Uncles to those we encounter of
our faith and to those we convert. Because we spread a
message that runs counter to that of the Church—indeed, we feel Christianity could dispense with the formal Church entirely and be the better for it!—we are
deemed heretics and suffer the opprobrium thereof. Yet
we see the temptations of Satan on every side while God
remains aloof. We feel that if God recruited as actively
as Satan does, this would be a better world. Therefore,
we proselytize.''

"There is little in your philosophy to which I take exception,'' Brother Paul said. "My sect honors the Bible,
but also respects the texts of other religions, such as the
Buddhists and the Moslems and the Confucians. We
would not abolish any sect, but rather seek to coexist in
peace with all faiths. Yet I can see that much of your
philosophy of religion has come down to my own time
and has been incorporated into the faiths of my world
including my own Order of Vision. The Quakers honor
the direct relation between man and God, calling it the
'Inner Light,' and the Jehovah's Witnesses attempt to

combat Satan by active recruiting, and we take what amount to vows of poverty at the Holy Order of Vision—'' He spread his hands. ''There is too much to cover at the moment.''

''I had hoped this would be the case. Your Order sounds like a sister school.''

''It may be,'' Brother Paul agreed. ''We do not seek converts, but we do lend support to those in need of faith.'' He paused. ''You remind me of someone I knew—in my own time. He—'' He broke off. He was getting so carried away with this play that he was forgetting who was playing what part! This *was* his friend Lee in a new guise. No need to disrupt the scene by remarking on it. ''But of course that is irrelevant. I believe your message should be spread, for this age has need of it, and I will help you in what ever way I can.''

''Then let me show you the lesson plan,'' the Juggler said. ''Our devotees are mainly illiterate peasants. They are good people, but they could not read the Bible even if they were permitted to possess it. Even if it were translated to their language from the Latin. What point is there in an unreadable, unavailable Word of God! Yet we dare not carry the Bible with us or anything else that might betray our nature to the Holy Office. So—we use these little pictures whose real nature we carefully conceal from the minions of the Church.''

And the Juggler produced a pack of thirty drawings. Brother Paul looked at them as he walked beside his friend, amazed—for these were very like the Major Arcana of the Tarot. Suddenly he realized that Satan was honoring his first wish: knowledge of the true origin and purpose of the Tarot. ''This—this is what I seek!'' he exclaimed.

''When you named the Tarot, I was sure you were attempting to trap me,'' the Juggler admitted. ''Yet not *quite* sure—and I could not condemn you on the basis of mere suspicion because that is the way of the Holy Office we abhor.'' He shook his head sadly. ''What a fine world it would be if one man trusted another and had that trust returned! Is this the case in your world?''

''No,'' Brother Paul said. ''Not yet.''

"We conceal our card lessons in the one place the Holy Office will never suspect: the pack of playing cards used by gamblers and wealthy degenerates," the Juggler said, passing the rest of the deck to Brother Paul. "These become the minor cards of the greater deck, the whole of which we call the Tarot, or Tzarot, the ruler of cards. We have not changed the minor cards, for that would betray our secret, but we have adapted them symbolically to our purpose. Each of the five suits represents—"

"*Five* suits?" Brother Paul asked, astonished.

"Some common decks have six, others four—in fact there seem to be many variations in number and symbols as each local printer or copyist innovates to suit himself. But we feel the appropriate number is five to represent the five fundamental elements as taught by the ancients."

"The Ancients!" Brother Paul repeated, thinking of something the alien Antares had said. A Galactic civilization that had existed three million years ago and disappeared.

"The Sumerians, the Egyptians, the Minoans, the Eblans, the Hittites, the Greeks, the Megalithic society—all the ancient peoples who knew so much more than history has credited them with," the Juggler said, and in that moment it was indeed Antares that looked out of his eyes, smiling sadly.

"Oh. Yes. Certainly." Animation though this might be, it seemed important not to introduce anachronism. But there was another matter. "*Five* elements? Fire, Water, Air, Earth, and—?"

"And Spirit," the Juggler said gently. "That which distinguishes man from animal. Man has conscience; man knows right from wrong. Man ate from the fruit of the Tree of Knowledge of Good and Evil and thereby separated himself from the ignorant beasts. Some call that a curse; we call it man's most important attribute."

"Spirit," Brother Paul repeated, appreciating it. It seemed that he had always known it. "What separates man from beast."

"The other suits may be interpreted on many levels,"

the Juggler continued. "As virtues or as classes of
society or qualities of character. There is the Stave of
Fortitude—or of the peasant. The Cup of Faith—or of
the Church." He made a wry face. "Much good the
peasant gets from the corrupt established Church! Then
there is the Sword of Justice—or of the military." He
smiled at Brother Paul's expression; there had not been
any direct association of justice and military in his own
recent experience! "The Coin of Charity—and of the
merchant. And of course the Lamp of the Spirit—and
of our wandering souls, seeking to bring that light to
those ready to receive it."

"The Waldenses," Brother Paul said, nodding.

"Or *any* good people of whatever faith who follow
their conscience and seek love and truth," the Juggler
amended. "As the early Christians did before they were
corrupted by power. We Waldenses claim no special
privilege or right; we merely do what we can, hoping our
seeds will find fertile soil."

And the most fertile soil came from compost, fed by
fecal matter. Satan had made Brother Paul into a seed
and planted him here. What meaning did that have?

"This picture, The Juggler, represents—me," the
Juggler said with a smile. It was, indeed, the Tarot
Juggler or Magician—a gaudily dressed man standing at
a table upon which various items of parlor magic rested.
"The Juggler is of course the master of disguises—as we
Waldenses have to be. At times he may appear very
much the fool. But the sight of this image alerts the
faithful, and when I see the countersign, thus—" He
made a gesture with his forefinger like a figure eight
turned sidewise. "That is the double symbol of the sun
and moon, two circles touching, the eternal progress of
day and night reflected in my hat." And he took down
his floppy hat to show how the rim formed a similar
lemniscate. "I know then to whom to address myself
after the show is over. Circumspectly. Usually the believer will find some pretext to bring me to his home,
and I will conduct the lesson there. Thus is another
segment of my mission accomplished under the danger-
ously sensitive nose of the Holy Office."

"Beautiful," Brother Paul murmured. "In my day, these cards have lost much of this meaning. You hide them under superficial interpretations so that the Inquisition will not suspect, and those superficial aspects have carried through so that most people do not even suspect the primary purpose."

"That is exactly as it should be," the Juggler agreed, pleased. "It means the Holy Office will not prevail in your land either." He indicated the next card. "This is the Lady Pope. Do you know the legend of the Popess?"

Brother Paul nodded affirmatively. "However, our researches show that no such person existed historically."

"Perhaps not on that level. But symbolically she certainly exists! This is the way we see the Church, the Whore of Babylon who has taken upon herself the attributes of secular power and become as one with the kings of the flesh. This picture follows naturally on the first, as a false Pope follows a false Magician. A harlot disguised as a priest, treading in the footsteps of a priest, disguised as a juggler. Those of true faith will perceive the reality behind these facades."

"Yes, I should hope so," Brother Paul agreed.

"Now here is a very special representation," the Juggler continued, showing another card. "Kindly admire the art."

"But it is blank!" Brother Paul protested.

"It is and it isn't," Juggler said. "Some say this is the Holy Ghost, the invisible Spirit of God. But we prefer to call it the Unknown—that ineffable force that governs the life of man."

"Fate!" Brother Paul said. He remembered this card now from his rapid tour of the gallery under the Pyramid.

"Perhaps. It is really up to each person to interpret it for himself. If he draws a card randomly from the deck and this one appears, it is a signal that he is proceeding on erroneous assumptions and should re-examine his situation."

"Interesting," Brother Paul said, more than interested. "Is there a particular reason it appears here in the deck, right after the Lady Pope, rather than at the beginning or end? I note it has no number."

"It is numberless and also infinite," the Juggler agreed. "Therefore, it has no assigned place in the deck. When the cards are arranged in order by number and suit, the Ghost is inserted randomly. We do try to keep it with the Triumphs because often we separate them from the suits in order to avoid suspicion, but if it falls among the suits and turns up in the course of a card trick—well, it is merely a blank card of no significance." He contemplated the empty card a moment. "Seldom does it manifest this early in the deck. There must be a reason for that but I confess I do not fathom it. Perhaps it relates to you." And Antares looked out at him again.

Brother Paul shrugged. "I do seem to be an unknown quantity in this world." The Ghost concept was growing on him. He had never, before he entered the Animations, suspected that a thing like this could be in the Tarot—but it seemed it was. Or once had been.

"Next come the Empress and Emperor, of equal rank according to our precepts, lawfully wedded. We believe in the married state and find the celibacy now fashionable in the Church to be hypocritical. God did not create man and woman that they should not know one another and not have the fulfillment of families! There are so many innocent bastards sired by priests! They breathe on young women during Confession and get them unknowingly excited, easy prey for lechery, and such women dare not expose their seducers lest the seducers charge them with heresy and destroy them without trial. Better those priests should marry and be openly fruitful as the Holy Book decrees."

"Yes . . . " Brother Paul murmured. But he, without testicles—what of him?

"And the Pope himself," the Juggler continued, showing the next. "So like the Emperor that one can hardly tell the difference, adorned with costly robes, coronets, scepter, on a throne yet! What would you take the meaning of this image to be?"

"That the Church has become overly materialistic," Brother Paul said promptly. Never before had it occurred to him that the close similarity between Emperor and Hierophant (Pope) was not coincidental!

"Very good, Brother Paul; you have a very quick perception! We feel that when the Church consented to be endowed by the Roman state, she became morally corrupt and lost the mandate of Christ. She has been led astray by worldly power, dominion, and wealth—as any religion *would* be, however pure its original tenets. We protest against all religious endowments and *any* temporal powers of clergy."

Brother Paul had to interrupt. "In fairness, I must say that this situation is much improved in my day, perhaps again because of your efforts. The Catholic Church stands as a bulwark against oppression, and its priests are persecuted by totalitarian regimes. In broad parts of Asia it has been almost entirely suppressed, and in Europe during recent political upheavals priests were tortured. In Latin America—" But he had to stop, prompted by the Juggler's look of perplexity. There *was* no "Latin" America at this period of history.

"Perhaps in your day the Church has recovered some basic humility and purpose," the Juggler said. "But right now the Pope is weighted down with those odious instruments of torture called crosses and other ornaments never authorized by the Scriptures. Call it heresy if you will, but we insist on separation of State and Church, not this ludicrous and oppressive amalgam. Why, the Cardinals are so greedy for power they contest with each other for the papal throne."

"Ah," Brother Paul said, remembering. "The Great Schism! Three Popes—"

The Juggler smiled. "Not quite that bad, yet. Fourteen years ago, when Pope Gregory XI died—is he in your records? The one who ended the 'Babylonian Captivity' of the papacy by returning to Rome from Avignon, France—"

"Babylonian captivity for the Whore of Babylon!" Brother Paul interjected, laughing.

"Just so. When Gregory died, the Roman mob

pressured the Cardinals to install a local boy. Rome is
an unruly city, and non-Italian popes don't feel quite
safe there, perhaps for good reason. The Cardinals
responded by electing Urban VI. I do not claim Urban
was a bad man as these things go; he was an uncompromising reformer who yielded to no man on
matters of principle."

"Trouble, surely!" Brother Paul murmured.

"Correct. His harsh mode soon alienated the Car-
dinals, especially the French ones. They declared his
election null and elected Robert of Geneva, who became
Pope Clement VII and took up residence in Avignon.
He had to; his life would have been hazardous in
Rome! Three years ago Urban died, but that did not re-
solve the problem. The Italians replaced him with Pope
Boniface IX."

The Juggler pinched a louse out of his hair with obvious satisfaction. "So now we have two popes," he
continued. "Which is the real one and which is the
Antipope no one can say for sure. In Italy it is best to
say Boniface; in France say Clement." He made a
gesture of good-natured helplessness. "How glad I am
that we Waldenses do not recognize either of these
clown priests! But make no mistake, either one would
string me up by one foot if he caught me or any other
barba. The *men* may be ludicrous, but the *office*
remains powerful."

Brother Paul thought of some of the politics of his
own period and had to agree. "If it is any comfort to
you, this eventually got straightened out. In my time
there is only one pope. But of course there are many
Christian religions who do not follow the Catholic
pope, so in that sense it is more confused than ever."

The Juggler continued on through the deck, picture
by picture, while Brother Paul listened so raptly that he
felt no further fatigue despite the distance they were
walking. Here at last was True Tarot!

They followed the Rhine downstream, coming to a
village in the Holy Roman Empire—a region that would
be known in Brother Paul's day as Germany. The

Juggler was exceedingly cautious in populated areas, fearing overt persecution; the Empire was not the safest place for Waldenses this year.

Much of the region was forested and beautifully unspoiled, but the fascination of the Tarot was such that Brother Paul hardly noticed where they were going or what was around them. The individual trees could have been twentieth century skyscrapers or completely alien life forms, and he would have passed them blithely by.

At the village the Juggler set up his table and performed his cardboard miracles, and he was a most proficient stage magician who obviously enjoyed amazing the credulous and making children laugh. The peasants threw small coins in appreciation: not many, for they were poor, but even an obolus went a long way here.

However, no secret signal was given, so there was no ministering to the Waldenses faithful. "I did not expect a contact here," Juggler confided. "Up nearer Worms there are more believers. I'll make arrangements to spend the night in a stable."

"The stable was good enough for our Savior's birth," Brother Paul murmured. He already had a load of lice in his clothing, so could not take on many more bugs from the environment. His feet were sore, his muscles stiffening, and his unfamiliar clothing was chafing the skin raw in places; *any*where was fine for a rest. When he slept, he would dream of Tarot—assuming he remained in this situation now that his wish had been fulfilled.

Next morning he remained in the fourteenth century, his body stiffer and rawer than ever with assorted welts from the bites of unseen insects. But fresh water and some more black bread made him feel better, and the resumed walk gradually worked out the kinks. He was not comfortable, but he could get by. But he wondered: why was he still here?

As they trekked north toward the great free city of Worms, the Juggler abruptly staggered. "Ah, the thirst!" he cried.

Thirst? Brother Paul caught his arm, steadying him.

The man was hot! "Friend, you have a fever!" Brother
Paul said. "You must rest; I will fetch water to cool
you."

The Juggler slumped down against a tree. "I fear it
will do no good," he gasped. "I felt it coming, but tried
to persuade myself it was not." He vomited weakly,
soiling his uniform.

Alarmed, Brother Paul hurried to fetch water from
the river anyway. But when he reached the bank, he
found he had no container for it. He had not thought, in
his worried haste, to bring one of the Juggler's trick
cups, and in any event that would have been too small.
Maybe he could find something by the bank—

He ran along the riverside, searching desperately.
There was nothing. But his friend was gravely ill!

He burst through a copse of trees. There was a girl
dipping water from the river. She had an earthen
pitcher in each hand and was evidently rinsing them out,
swishing water in them and pouring it out again. Over
her shoulder near the eastern horizon he saw the first
star of dusk. Uncommonly bright, almost blindingly
brilliant. He suffered the feeling of *déjà vu*.

But he had no time to figure it out. "Miss, oh Miss!"
he called. "Fraülein—may I borrow a pitcher?"

The girl looked up, startled. She resembled—but of
course Amaranth played this part; why did he keep
being surprised by the new ways in which the basic cast
appeared?

"I have a friend, sick," Brother Paul explained
breathlessly. "He needs water."

She hesitated. "Sick?"

"A fever, vomiting, thirst—"

"The Black Death!" She got up so hastily she
dropped a pitcher in the water and fled.

He had no time or reason to pursue her. What could
he do with a woman anyway, had he the time and in-
clination? He was a eunuch. He sloshed into the water
to recover the bobbing pitcher before it sank. At least he
had that!

The Juggler was worse when he returned. Brother
Paul splashed water on his friend's face and on his hot,

dry skin. He offered a cup, and the Juggler gulped avidly.

Now Brother Paul saw it: black spots forming on the man's skin. "Uh oh."

"It is the Black Death," the Juggler said. "I buried my companion, may God accept his soul, and I hoped I had escaped—" He looked up, alarmed. "My friend, get away from me! You cannot save me; you can only infect yourself."

"No danger of that," Brother Paul assured him. "The plague was spread from rats to men by infected fleas."

"Fleas! But fleas are everywhere!"

He was right. Lice, nits, fleas—there was no escaping them here. Probably fleas had left the dying *barba* companion and hidden in the Juggler's clothes. Now, after the incubation period of several days, Juggler had come down with it. Rat fleas might spread it, but they didn't need rats once they infested human clothing.

"You saved my life from the soldiers," Brother Paul said. Actually, he might have fought off the soldiers successfully—but it had been no certain thing. "I will do what I can for you."

The Juggler retched again. "There is only one thing needing doing for me, friend—and that is more than any man can ask of another, were it even possible."

The man was extremely sick, and Brother Paul did not know how to care for him. Even with hospital care, the outlook would be doubtful, for the bubonic plague had killed about a third of the population of Europe in the latter part of the fourteenth century. Even had Brother Paul known where to get help, he would not dare to take the Juggler there. A heretic missionary in a time of persecution—no, he could not seek help! "What is this impossible thing?"

"My mission," the Juggler said. "There are good people who depend on the Uncles to uplift their faith. They should be told—that they must wait a few more months, until the persecution dies down, until the next *barba* comes. They must not give up hope!"

"I can tell them that," Brother Paul said.

"But they are hidden—and to seek them out is to risk discovery by the Holy Office—for you *and* them. You dare not—" the Juggler lapsed into silence for a time. He was fading rapidly. When a killer disease took hold of the body of a medieval man, already weakened by fatigue and malnutrition, its ravages were swift!

The Juggler summoned strength. "Take the sacred pictures, friend. Guard them well. They must not fall into the hands of—" He had to stop, gasping.

"I will guard the Sacred Tarot with my life," Brother Paul said soberly. "The Inquisition shall not have it."

The Juggler could no longer speak. His fevered hand touched Brother Paul's in mute thanks. He shuddered, trying to vomit again, but nothing came. Then with what seemed a superhuman effort he managed a few more words. "Abra-Melim, the Mage of Egypt— Abraham the Jew in Worms—tell—" He choked—and before Brother Paul could help him, he collapsed.

Brother Paul tried to revive him with more water, to make him comfortable—but in a moment he realized that his friend was dead.

"Let him only change parts . . ." Brother Paul prayed, feeling an intensity of loss that threatened to overwhelm him. "Let the role die, not the player—" But he could not be sure that prayer would be answered, for this was an aspect of Hell.

IV

Deception: 23

There is no more immoral work than the "Old Testament." Its deity is an ancient Hebrew of the worst type, who condones, permits or commands every sin in the Decalogue to a Jewish patriarch, qua *patriarch*. He orders Abraham to murder his son and allows Jacob to swindle his brother; Moses to slaughter an Egyptian and the Jews to plunder and spoil a whole people, after inflicting upon them a series of plagues which would be the height of atrocity if the tale were true. The nations of Canaan are then extirpated. Ehud, for treacherously disembowelling King Eglon, is made judge over Israel. Jael is blessed above women (Joshua v. 24) for vilely murdering a sleeping guest; the horrid deeds of Judith and Esther are made examples to mankind; and David, after an adultery and a homicide which deserved ignominious death, is suffered to massacre a host of his enemies, cutting some in two with saws and axes and putting others into brick-kilns. For obscenity and impurity we have the tales of Onan and Tamar, Lot and his daughters, Amnon and his fair sister (2 Sam. xiii.), Absalom and his father's concubines, the "wife of whoredoms" of Hosea and, capping all, the Song of Solomon. For

the horrors forbidden to the Jews, who, therefore,
must have practiced them, see Levit. viii. 24; xi. 5;
xvii. 7, xviii. 7, 9, 10, 12, 15, 17, 21, 23, and xx. 3.
For mere filth what can be fouler than 1st Kings
xviii. 27; Tobias ii. 11; Esther xiv. 2; Eccl. xxii. 2;
Isaiah xxxvi. 12; Jeremiah iv. 5, and (Ezekiel iv.
12–15), where the Lord changes human ordure
into "Cow-chips!" Ce qui excuse Dieu, said Henri
Beyle, c'est qu'il n'existe pas,—I add, as man has
made him.

——*The Book of the Thousand Nights and a*
Night: Translated and annotated by Richard F.
Burton: Volume Ten, n.p., The Burton Club, n.d.

Brother Paul collected the Juggler's things into a little
pile, then set about burying him. The actor, in this role,
was not mutilated: that was a minor relief. That cir-
cumcision of Jesus had been uncomfortably convincing!

Brother Paul did not want to bury the man just
anywhere, but lacked the strength and will in his grief to
be choosy. So he cut a stick with the Juggler's magic-
tricks knife and used it to excavate a shallow grave. He
was afraid this would be scant protection against the
ravages of scavenging animals, but it was the best he
could do.

He did not know what manner of ceremony the
Waldenses used at a burial, so he said a few words of his
own choosing. "May the mission on which this good
man went be somehow fulfilled." Yet he knew from
history that, in the narrow sense, it had not been.
Juggler had died in vain. The Waldenses had never
gained many converts although their ideas had had
broad influence.

Now he sorted through the Juggler's belongings.
They were routine: the reversible cloak, jacket and
pants; the infinity-rimmed floppy hat; the vials of
powder for coloring fire and other special effects; the
trick wand that sagged limply when held one way, yet
was stiff when held another way (oh, the phallic symbolism there!); the cup and knife and coin. The twin-
bodied flute. That hurt most of all, for it was the in-

strument that had summoned Brother Paul and brought
the beauty of song into his fourteenth century life. Such
a pitiful remembrance! But these items were overwhelmed by the significance of the Tarot deck, the true
original of an idea that had branched into many forms.
This, perhaps, was the true mission of the man—giving
to the world the truth in Tarot. In that sense, maybe the
Juggler's mission had not been futile.

The crescent moon had risen. Brother Paul went to
the river to wash and drink, then looked back toward
the grave site. He was horrified to see two wild curs approaching it, sniffing. "Hey! Get away from there!" he
cried. The dogs paused, hearing his voice, poised for
flight. But then they spied the moon and lifted their
muzzles to bay at it. Brother Paul knew that canines,
being nose-oriented, had difficulty dealing with a thing
they could see but not smell; one sense told them it was
there, but another denied it. A man who heard a voice
but found no person there was similarly perplexed,
calling it a ghost. A dog merely howled.

Something attracted his attention almost at his feet. It
seemed to be a crayfish trying to climb out, as though
attracted also by the moon. Or attracted by the grave,
Brother Paul amended his thought with a shudder. He
looked again toward that grave and saw the silhouettes
of the dogs sitting there with two giant trees rising to
frame the moon like dark castles. A pretty nocturnal
scene, in its way—but also as horrible as his own vision
of the field with the lion. Death lurked beneath each:
not the brief shock of violent destruction, but the
lifelong grief of the loss of a loved one.

He strode toward the dogs, and they skulked away.
The grave was undisturbed—but how long would it
remain so? Yet he could not remain here indefinitely to
guard it. The Juggler would simply have to take his
chances in death as in life.

The night was warm. This must be the season of the
"Dog Days"—hot. When the "Dog Star" Sirius was
prominent . . . that must be the star he had seen in the
morning or evening. He could survive the night's temperature without trouble.

Brother Paul found a suitable tree and climbed to its crotch, bracing himself and squirming around until reasonably comfortable. Before he knew it, he slept.

He woke hungry and with additional stiffness. There might be fruit trees in the forest—but he did not know where to look and did not want to steal. Obviously this Animation was not yet through with him, and he did not wish to become one of the failure statistics, i.e., dead. Satan had promised him information on the True Tarot; Satan had not promised he could take it with him from the fourteenth century. He would have to shift for himself until he could demonstrate his ability to survive here indefinitely.

Yet what legitimate way was there to obtain food? He did not want to get too close to villagers because he had to hide and preserve the invaluable Tarot deck. He was an obvious stranger, speaking awkwardly, not to be trusted by the clannish locals, and liable to suspicion by soldiers. If he even showed his face in a village, he might be mobbed. Unless—

He almost fell out of the tree. Well, why not? It had worked for the Juggler!

With nervous confidence, Brother Paul descended, stretched his cramped limbs, urinated against the roots of the tree, and donned the magical robe. He was about to do tricks for his dinner. His strangeness should only enhance the effect.

First he rehearsed the tricks. His own youthful experience stood him in good stead; he could do sleight of hand as well as was needed. He hated to have to use the Sacred Cards for parlor tricks, but they were his best tool—and indeed, he had used Tarot in this capacity before. He riffled through the crude cards, making sure he could handle them with sufficient dexterity. They were printed cards, but not uniform; probably some kind of wooden block print, itself hand carved, for it would be over half a century before the printing press was developed.

Then he put them away and turned over some rocks

and was lucky enough to spot a small harmless snake. "Easy, fellow," he murmured, catching it and putting it in a tied handkerchief. "I will let you go in due course." Yes—he was ready.

He set out again, following the trail to the north, working the kinks from his body. He did not feel good, but he felt halfway confident. There had to be a village along this trail somewhere, and now he had no intention of avoiding it.

It turned out to be surprisingly easy. His bright Juggler costume identified him instantly, and within moments of his appearance at the next village there was a crowd around him. Without further fanfare he set up the table a villager brought and began his act. He made a small silver coin appear between his fingers, vanish, and reappear from the ear of the nearest urchin. He poured water from one cup into another, then showed the second cup to be empty. He waved his wand—and the little snake appeared on the table and slithered away. Finally he did tricks with the cards, making the Ace of Wands come up repeatedly, no matter how carefully it was shuffled into the deck.

Suddenly, in the midst of his act, he remembered what had somehow faded from his consciousness for the past day. *This deck had five suits.*

He continued almost mechanically, going through his limited repertoire while his mind and eye reviewed the suits. Wands—Cups—Swords—Coins—and Lamps, just as the Juggler had told him. Ace through ten in each, plus Page, Knight, Queen, and King. Fifty numbered cards in all, plus twenty Court Cards and thirty Waldenses Triumphs—a deck of one hundred cards in all. A magical number in this age and his own!

How had the scholars of later centuries missed this obvious clue that their decks were incomplete? 100 was a number to conjure with while 78 was a nothing. They must have looked at individual cards, instead of at the deck as a whole. Almost literally missing the forest for the trees.

Maybe this was another aspect of the Tarot he had yet

to discover. He could not leave this framework until his *whole* wish had been granted—including the ramifications of it he had not known about.

He wrapped up his show and made his bow. A few small coins were set on his table. Success! Now he could buy some food, and no one would question his presence here. He could survive.

As the crowd dispersed, a young woman approached hesitantly. "Sir—your cards—is there a picture of the Juggler among them?"

The Juggler. He had not employed that card or any of the Triumphs in his act, both because they were too valuable to risk and because he feared they might arouse suspicion. He had promised to keep them out of the hands of the Inquisition, and this was best accomplished by keeping them out of sight. But how could he deny the card that stood for his dead benefactor? Slowly, he nodded.

She made a sidewise figure eight in the air with her forefinger. "*Barba*," she whispered. "We have awaited your coming! Please, visit our hut tonight."

Brother Paul paused in chagrin. Here was Amaranth in a new part, delivering the signal of identification for the Waldenses. Of course these believers were on the lookout for traveling entertainers! Why hadn't he thought of that when he set out to imitate his friend? He should have answered no about that card so as not to arouse false hopes.

Yet he had promised to inform the believers of the delay before the next Uncle came so they would not lose hope. This was his opportunity. He had almost forgotten that commitment, but had no alternative now. "Miss, I regret to inform you that—"

"Oh, don't speak about it here!" she protested, glancing nervously over her shoulder. Sure enough, another villager was approaching, and Brother Paul had to break off.

"Then you will perform for us tonight," Amaranth said brightly. "We will give you supper and straw for the night."

"Uh, yes, that will be fine," Brother Paul agreed

lamely. He smiled at the other villager. "I trust you enjoyed the show?"

"That snake—it was alive!"

"Of course," Brother Paul said with a smile. "I would not want to conjure a *dead* snake."

The man's eyes widened. "Then you are in league with Satan!"

Uh oh. These primitives believed in magic. He had made his show too good. He was, perhaps literally, in league with Satan, but that was not relevant to this issue. "No, it is merely a trick. I caught the snake in the forest this morning and hid it in my sleeve. Don't tell anyone!"

Disappointed, the man departed. There went a close call! He could not afford to be too convincing!

There was nothing resembling a supermarket here, but there was a local baker from whom Brother Paul obtained a loaf of black bread. His stomach did not like the stuff very well; it was too much like his childhood bread. But at least it was familiar.

In the afternoon he ranged the area and managed to catch several beetles and caterpillars: ammunition for the evening show. He spotted one rather pretty little stone and pocketed that too, although he wasn't sure he could use it in a magic trick. He chatted with people who were curious about news of the world—and fortunately the world was limited to a few square leagues in their awareness.

In the evening the young woman fetched him to her hut, which actually turned out to be a good sized cottage some ten meters by five with a thatched roof, and constructed of fairly sturdy hand-hewn beams. Inside, however, he discovered it did double duty as a shed for animals; straw was on the floor, and the ambient odor was strong. But what had he expected among peasants? The lowest classes of the medieval societies had never had a good life and always had to live pretty much from hand to mouth.

This house was crowded with people of all ages. "*Barba!*" an old woman cried. "I feared I would die before I had your blessing!"

And he had to tell them he was not the Waldenses missionary. This was going to hurt. Yet they deserved to know the brutal truth: that the true Juggler had died of the plague not half a day's walk from here, trying to reach them. "I regret to explain that I am not—"

"Oh, it's all right, Uncle," she said. "We are all of the faith here. From all the villages around, we have come. Some will be punished for failing to work for their Lords today, but they had far to travel to get here on time. A young couple have delayed marrying lo these many months so that you could do it, and we have a child sick near to death, and we all stand in such desperate need of your counsel, for our life is hard and some of us have suffered in the persecution and we know not even how to pray properly to God for relief. We have had no one in a year to preach the True Faith to us, and now at last you have come, and what a blessing it is! If I die tomorrow, I die happy, for I die with my faith uplifted by your touch!" And she held out her withered hand to be touched.

And what was he to say now? At such sacrifice had they gathered to meet him, risking their very lives to have the blessing and encouragement of the *barba*. How great was their simple faith in the terrible shadow of the Inquisition! How could he tell them now that the true missionary was dead?

Suddenly he appreciated with much greater clarity the situation of the Universalist John Murray who was prevented by a lack of wind from sailing away and going about his business until he agreed to preach at the local church. Murray had not felt qualified, yet—

Yet if he, Brother Paul, did not tell these good people the truth, he would have to impersonate the Uncle they thought he was, the representative of a religion to which he did not belong. Even if that could be called ethical, he wasn't sure it was possible. And how could he participate in such a terrible lie?

The old woman was waiting. He had to do something now! Should he kill her with the truth or provide salvation with a lie? Was this a test of his own mettle? If he lied, he was surely doomed to Hell. Yet how many other people would the truth doom?

Brother Paul touched her hand. "It is your own great faith that uplifts you, good woman," he said gently, knowing she would misinterpret his words. *If this be the road to Hell, so let it be.* "I am only a man."

"Yes, yes!" she breathed raptly.

"No man can stand between you and God. You have no need of priest or *barba*, so long as your heart is open to Our Lord."

"Ah, but you make it so clear!" she exclaimed. "Oh, Uncle, my faith has wavered so often, but your words restore it stronger than before! Give me your blessing!"

"My blessing means no more than that of any other person," Brother Paul said, troubled. No matter how he tried to defuse the lie, it became stronger like her faith. "There is no special power in me; I am as nothing, unworthy. I have no avenue to God that is not as readily available to you. I could say the words, but that would not—"

"Say the words!" she cried raptly.

There was no way out. "May the blessing of Our Holy Father be upon you," he murmured.

It was as though she had been reprieved from Hell. Her wrinkled face was transformed by rapture.

Now the others crowded in, nudging the old woman aside, and she suffered herself to be moved, oblivious in her joy. "The *barba* blesses us all by his presence," a man said. "Come, Uncle—we must tend first to the child, lest she die unclean." He hustled Brother Paul to the corner where the child lay on a straw pallet amid flies.

Brother Paul looked at her again on the verge of protesting the confusion of identities. But as he looked, he recognized—Carolyn. This girl was about twelve years old, but so wasted and thin she could have been eight. Yet the face—obviously it was the same actress, and so, in the terms he dealt with, the same girl. She had not escaped Hell's aftermath after all. Satan had betrayed him. He should have guessed when Lee showed up in this sequence! Now—he had to save Carolyn again. If he could.

What was her illness? Should he ask? No, he could get no useful answer. Had it been anything routine, she would have recovered on her own. Malnutrition? Then why hadn't it affected other members of her family? It must be some individual, slow debilitation, not susceptible to the treatment available. Something like— cancer.

In which case, nobody could save her. The medical technology for abolishing cancer had not been developed until the 20th century. The *barba* had a hopeless task. Even the genuine Waldens Juggler could not have done what these people hoped.

But if she died, here in Animation, would she also die in real life? He was uncertain. Some people did die in Animation—and the odds seemed against his own survival. But some survived. If a person *thought* he died in Animation, would his life expire in his mundane existence? The witch-doctor power of Voodoo suggested this was a solid possibility. Suppose a person only played the part of a character who died and knew that—could he then survive?

What was the present state of Lee, his Good Companion? Infused by the aura of Antares, he had played the role of Jesus Christ and had not died. But historically, Jesus had risen again. Now Lee, as the Juggler, had died again, more convincingly, for he was no longer the Son of God but a mere mortal man. A played part or reality?

If the player died, surely his part died too, for a dead person could not animate a living one—not in this manner. Antares was a special case. If a part died, the player might live or die, depending. If a part lived, the player *had* to live. Therefore, the only way to be certain was to keep this part alive; then he would know that Carolyn lived in all forms. Even though the form he loved had not yet been born in his own time framework.

The logic might be suspect, but his feeling was not. He *had* to save her. Though Satan Himself dictated otherwise. To Hell with Satan!

"I will try," Brother Paul said, realizing that these words committed him with finality to this part within the play. He was impersonating the Juggler, the part that belonged to his friend. He was deceiving these good people. *The Moon*, he thought, experiencing the awful poignancy of it. *Planet of deceit*. He had thought his honor was his most important asset; now Satan had shown him it was not. For the sake of an unborn child, the mere part in a play, his honor was forfeit.

If this manifest failure in his character damned him to Hell, he thought again, so be it. These people might be illusory, and this play might be scripted by Satan, but Brother Paul was what he was in reality or imagination. He had to try to save this child.

He knelt beside her and put the fingers of his right hand to her forehead. The flies buzzed up angrily. Her body was not feverish. Was this a good sign? Maybe not; cancer would not necessarily cause a fever. His left hand took her thin right hand. How bony her fingers were!

"My dear," he said.

There was no perceptible response. Her breathing continued with labored regularity. She was asleep, but not blithely so; he feared she was locked in some internal nightmare as bad as his own.

He concentrated, willing her to wake, to recover. Antares had told him he had an aura and that this might be used to heal; Jesus Christ had implied the same. If this were true, he might be able to help this child. "Wake, little one," he said, praying for it to happen.

But it did not happen. His prayer met a blank wall. Brother Paul was not Jesus Christ; he could not heal by mere touch and will. Not even when the subject was his daughter.

At last, defeated, he rose. "We cannot know the ways of God, except when He wills it," he said sadly. *What had he done wrong?* "I will see this child again." And he would. Again and again, for this was the one defeat he could not accept as final.

The old woman nodded soberly. Had she expected more from him?

Brother Paul returned to the center of the room. All eyes followed him expectantly. He had come prepared to put on a magic show, but this was obviously not what they had come for. They wanted a message from the Waldenses, an affirmation of faith.

He had in effect perjured himself when he ministered to the child. Should he aggravate it now? He looked at the faces of old and young, shining with hope, and knew that he had to complete his own damnation. He could not destroy their belief when he knew there was no alternative for them. Both true *barbe* for this route were dead, and it might be another year before another set came this way. Better a makeshift message than none at all. Even the actors of a play written in Hell deserved some consideration.

What of the Juggler? What would *he* have done in this situation? Brother Paul knew: he would have given a ringing presentation of his faith. Now Brother Paul had assumed the missionary's place; was there any more fitting way to repay the favors the Juggler had done him? What better epitaph than a declaration of the message the Juggler had sought to bring!

"Brothers and Sisters of the faith," Brother Paul began, experiencing sudden stage fright. "I—am a novice. The true *barba* who was instructing me, guiding me, to whom I was apprentice—that good man perished before he could reach you. I beg your indulgence, for I have not before presented the message of the Waldenses alone."

No one responded. They took his words as mere apology, the ritual modesty, missing the literal import. He was the uncle, the religious guide; experience made little difference. So his partial confession of his deceit was no confession at all. Satan made it very easy to sin!

Well, he would simply have to do it. He would give them the message of the Waldenses as well as he was able. It was not a bad message—not at all.

"The Waldenses follow precepts similar to those of the Albigensians," Brother Paul began. But immediately he saw that it wasn't going over. These people had no knowledge of foreign religious philosophies or the history of heretic sects; they simply believed in the word of the *barba*.

He tried again. "The Waldenses believe that people should return to the principles that Jesus Christ and the Apostle Paul established. Simplicity, humility, and disinterested love for all mankind." But this wasn't working either. It was a lecture. The Juggler had spoken clearly and rationally to Brother Paul, but that was one literate, educated scholar communicating with another. Peasants and serfs needed something more tangible. The Juggler, when doing his magic show, had appealed to the least sophisticated element of society with the same finesse he had shown Brother Paul. He had been a man for all levels.

It was not enough for the people to desire enlightenment; it had to come in palatable form. These people were what they were: uneducated. Philosophically they were like children: ready to learn, but with limited intellectual experience.

What he really needed was a programmed lesson, preferably illustrated. Pictures were great for illiterates.

Pictures—programmed text. Suddenly it burst upon him. *Of course!*

Brother Paul brought out the thirty Tarot Triumphs. He extracted the Fool and showed it before him. "Look at this buffoon!" he exclaimed. "He walks with his eyes to the sky while the town cur rips the pants off his bum!"

Now they responded with appreciative surprise. Now he had their attention. Now he could score!

"It is hard indeed for a rich man to approach God," Brother Paul said. "'Or for the powerful noble, or the proud priest. What is wealth or power or pride to God? Better to leave all that behind, and seek God with a heart unfettered by worldly things. To be like the Fool, stepping boldly toward his goal, eyes fixed on the splendor of the rainbow, seeking God with pure, selfless love."

There was a murmur of agreement; the poor people were receptive to news that the poor could achieve salvation more readily than the rich. That the buffoon might be nearer to God than the Lord.

"Even if at times it hurts," he concluded, rubbing his own posterior as if it were sore. "For the dogs of Manor and Church have sharp teeth."

The peasants' faces burst into appreciative smiles. The arrogance of the civil and religious authorities was a chronic sore point with them, and they liked hearing them likened to dogs. No doubt about it: Brother Paul was uttering heresy by the definitions of this medieval society—and he was enjoying it.

"This picture is Everyman," he continued. "Every person who seeks truth and enlightenment. He does not have to wander the countryside; the way is prickly enough though he never depart his village. His companions may laugh—yet he presses on, his eyes fixed on that glory that awaits those who persevere despite ridicule and even torture. Call him a fool—but those who laugh are the real fools."

Some peasants started to laugh—then caught themselves. Others began to laugh at *them*—and suffered similar second thoughts. Most nodded knowingly. They were all fools in this room, suffering persecution for their particular faith in God. Brother Paul had scored again—thanks to the card. It was a good feeling.

"Yet is it better to have some direction," he continued with more confidence. "And so we have the Juggler—" he held up the appropriate card— "who comes in many forms, but always with the same message. It is the message of Jesus Christ, the first great Magician, who sought to lead erring human souls to the majesty of God. Even with that divine example to follow, many of us can hardly find the way. It is as though the message is magic, appearing and disappearing, eluding us just as we seek to grasp it." And the wand appeared in his hand, waved, and vanished.

He paused. They were with him now, raptly studying the little picture. It spoke better than his words ever could—but it needed interpretation. Perhaps the picture messages could have been made more obvious—but then the Inquisition would have deciphered them too. They had to be clear—only when properly explained. Like locks, they had to open to the proper keys—and resist all other efforts. Indeed they did this; imposter philosophers had missed the point of Tarot for centuries! Alas, even the deck of the Holy Order of Vision was sadly flawed, distorted by a chain of errors of interpretation—yet he had never realized this until he came here to the late fourteenth century. Satan had granted him his wish in full, providing not only the authentic original deck, but also its proper meaning. Yet he had to work out much of that meaning for himself; there was no instant comprehension of a philosophy as complex as Tarot.

Brother Paul held up the Lady Pope. "Yet who tries to give us that divine message? The Whore of Babylon!" He was interrupted by a shout of savage laughter. Oh, yes, they were familiar with that story! "The Church has become a giant succubus, tempting us with the promise of Salvation but leading us into damnation."

He showed the Ghost card. "It is hard to know right from wrong. 'Tell us what to do!' we cry, yet the answer is a blank space. We are all creatures of ignorance. Only God knows all, the Infinite, the Holy Spirit, the Ghost! Our past, present and future are all clouded by the unknown. Who knows which of us will die tomorrow—" He paused, thinking of the sick girl.

Then he thought of himself. His whole participation here was another unknown. In fact, his mission to Planet Tarot in that distant, almost forgotten other reality—

He cut off that line of thought and followed through with the same presentation the Juggler had given him, through Empress, Emperor, and Pope. Already he felt like a true Waldens missionary.

Now he came to Love. Except that this was not Love, primarily, but Choice. Through the centuries, he now realized, this card had been interpreted according to its purposely misleading illustration, rather than its more fundamental meaning. Iconographical transformation. Interpreting from the superficial image, rather than comprehending the intent of the symbol. Similar confusion must have phased the Ghost entirely out of existence! It was blank, therefore it stood for nothing, therefore it did not exist. Lord, how many fools had tinkered with Tarot!

But back to Choice: "A person cannot serve both God and Mammon. Riches and worldliness may be very tempting, but their benefit is superficial. Evil often puts on a fair face—yet it remains evil." He himself had been deceived by that fair face in the form of a sparkling intellect when he selected Therion to be his guide in the First Animation. What a price he had paid for that error! Yet it had forced on him a profound humility without which he could not have progressed this far through the rest. After compost, everything smelled better. "Do not choose Love of Possessions over Love of God! Give your heart and soul to Jesus Christ. Dedicate yourselves to doing good—"

A small sigh interrupted him. It should not have been audible over the general rustle of the people in the crowded room, but it sounded like a clarion in his ear. The sick child!

He broke off the presentation and went to the child and took her limp little hand again. "Do not choose the wrong path," he murmured only for her. He became oblivious to the rest of the room. "Come to the light, for we love you."

A tremor passed through her body. Her eyelids flickered. But she did not wake.

Brother Paul felt a horrible premonition: if he did not rouse her now, he would never succeed because she would fade out of part and life together. Whether the strain of three Animations was bearing her down, or whether her physical condition was causing her part to fade with her, or a combination—she was going.

He could not *let* her go. He had never known her before the Animations, and what he did know was only a young colonist playing a part. But somehow he was sure that there was—or would be—a Carolyn, his daughter. Who would die—or might never exist—if he let her go now. Ludicrous as it might seem to take this premonition seriously, he believed it.

"Pretty child," he murmured, speaking to that most

precious spirit he sought, oblivious to all else. "You can only exist if someone believes in you. *I* believe in you. Someone must love you. *I* love you. Someone must need you. *I* need you. If you pass on, I shall have to go with you wherever your spirit leads. You are my future. Without you, my love is wasted. My life is empty. You must wake for me." And he put both hands on the sides of her face, cupping it tenderly, smoothing down the straggly hair, and leaned over and kissed her forehead. There were tears in his eyes, and as he came near her they spilled out and fell on her pale cheek.

He felt a power stirring like the flux of a magnetic field as it might feel to the magnet. It was the aura. *Oh, God*, he prayed silently. *If there is healing power in me, let it heal her now.*

"So much care," the old woman murmured, "for a child he doesn't even know." She was speaking with awe, not with cynicism.

"The *barba* reflects the love he speaks of—the love of God," another said.

If only that were true! Brother Paul's affinities seemed to be much closer to Satan than to God. He had bargained with Satan to save Carolyn from Hell—but had not thought to save her from death. That was the fallacy in dealing with the Devil; no man could outwit that horrendous evil intelligence. Had Satan granted his wish for Tarot knowledge—at the expense of his friend Lee and his child Carolyn?

Somehow he didn't believe that. *Couldn't* believe that. He had to have faith that Satan, like God, kept His word. Satan could not accurately judge souls if He were corrupt Himself. So this had to be another trial, not a punishment. Maybe Brother Paul was being offered another chance to promote his own private welfare at the expense of hers. To renege on his deal with Satan. All he had to do was let her die and return with his knowledge of Tarot.

"Wake," he murmured desperately. "There is so much for you to live for! Remember the field of flowers, the pine trees, the pretty stones." He almost said "airplane" but caught himself in time.

Her eyelids flickered again. "Stones . . . " she breathed.

All little girls liked pretty stones! This was fair game. "At the edge of the river," he said urgently. "All colors, rounded, some with streaks of brown or red. Each one separate, each one precious—because it is yours, because you value it. Nothing else can take its place." With inspiration, he reached into a pocket, his fingers sifting through what was there. He found what he wanted, brought it out, pressed it into her hand, and closed her fingers about it. "A stone!" he said. "The most wonderful thing there is! A little chunk of God."

Her hand tightened, feeling the contours of the stone. "Yes. . . . "

"Most wonderful—except for a little girl," he amended. "The stone is nothing without you. It needs you! Take care of it."

A shock of realization went through her. Her eyes popped open. She looked at him, her eyes suddenly great and blue, too large for her face, strikingly beautiful. Her lips trembled, then parted. "Uncle," she whispered.

"Glory!" the old woman exclaimed. "She wakes!" Tears of joy streamed down her face.

Brother Paul felt tears on his own face again. He squeezed the child's hand gently. "Rest, Precious, rest. God is with you." And this was no line in any play; he had never been more sincere.

"God . . . " she repeated weakly.

"Only have faith in Him; you are His child. No one stands between you and Him. Put your soul in His care; He will not betray you." He squeezed her hand again. "God loves you. This you must believe." Yet there was an underlying current, for when he said God he also meant "I". This was his child too, and he loved her. And had it really been God who had restored her—or Satan?

"I believe . . . " she said dutifully.

"I believe . . . " the old woman echoed.

"It is a miracle of healing," the man said.

The child's eyes closed. She was sleeping now, a small

smile on her face, the stone tightly held. Brother Paul released her hand and stood up. "It shall be as God wills," he said. "I do not know whether God will take her today—or in twenty years. But she is a creature of God—as are we all."

"Yes, Uncle!" the woman agreed. "How wonderful is the faith you bring!"

"It is the love that Jesus Christ showed to man," Brother Paul said. And silently: *Thank you, Jesus!*

He thought of returning to his Tarot presentation—but decided against it. The recovery of the child was a better message than any other. If it were really recovery, and not some temporary remission. . . .

Next morning Brother Paul resumed his journey toward Worms. He already knew as much about the Tarot as he had ever hoped to learn—but it seemed this "wish" had not yet run its full course.

He hoped the sick child recovered fully. It was uncertain at this stage. He had wanted to make provision for news of her progress, but knew there was no safe way to handle this. Even a cryptic message: THE LAMP IS LIT or THE LAMP IS OUT could be hazardous to the health of the messenger—and perhaps the child too. What would the Inquisition do to the living evidence of heretic healing? And peasants could not travel far freely; they were fairly well bound to their lots by the ties of the feudal system. Any man who did not pay his required rents on time, or serve on his Lord's estate, or appear at the regular church services—that man was in trouble.

Brother Paul did not like impersonating the *barba*, but now there seemed to be no way to avoid it. Only soldiers, minstrels, and the aristocracy could travel freely without being challenged. Soldiers went in groups, and the Lords and priests had horses and retainers. Had the soldiers he had encountered before been quicker witted, they would have been suspicious of a priest afoot and alone; fortunately the Juggler's bold ruse had worked. Brother Paul did not care even to attempt impersonating a bishop!

He approached another hamlet. But before he could set up his show, a child hurried up. Children seemed to be ubiquitous messengers, perhaps because they were not yet locked into the labor system. "Juggler—the Lord of the Manor suspects—you must go!"

Brother Paul did not question the message. There could have been an informer at last night's meeting. A horseman could have ridden at night, carrying the news: a heretic missionary! He packed up his equipment immediately and departed the village. He was weary—but this was no place to stay.

He cleared the village, but now was not sure what to do. He had not eaten in several hours, though the pangs of hunger had not yet touched him. He was more tired than he really should be, and the thought of sleeping in another tree crotch did not appeal. Yet if the villages were not safe—

The path led up a hill—and there at the height, gruesome in the gloom of husk, was a gibbet. A man was working at it, taking down the rope. He spied Brother Paul. "Too late!" he called down cheerily. "You missed it. He's already been hanged, taken down, drawn and quartered."

Brother Paul paused. He was not feeling good, and this did not improve his outlook. Since he might be under suspicion himself, he could not openly express his revulsion. "Well, I had a long way to come."

"You should have hurried." The man's tongue ran around his mouth, tasting the memory. "It was something to see! He must've kicked his feet a full minute! Still, it was too good for him. I'd have had him quartered live! Stealing the Lord's best horse, running it half to death—we're well rid of him!"

So a poor peasant had been executed publicly for stealing a horse. Well, that was justice in the medieval age; horses were valuable.

"But stay around," the man said. "Almost every week we have a new show. Mostly foot hangings, but some of them aren't bad. They—"

"Foot hangings?" Something piqued Brother Paul's curiosity, morbidly.

"Right. For minor stuff like killing a peasant or fucking a witch." The gibbetsman laughed coursely, but Brother Paul was not certain this was humor. "String him up by one foot, let him swing a day. Some are tough; they don't seem to notice it. But some scream like all hell, and some die without a mark on them."

Hanging by one foot. Now Brother Paul recognized what had jogged his curiosity. One of the Triumphs of the Tarot was titled the Hanged Man, and that man was suspended by one foot. He had put another interpretation on that card before, but naturally it related to this crude medieval torture. The Tarot reflected the life of its times. How much misinterpretation there had been in subsequent centuries of *that* card!

Brother Paul shook his head and moved on, feeling worse. But he had hardly put the gibbet out of sight when he heard something. A horse!

He hurried off the path. Maybe what he heard was innocent—but he could not take the risk. Even though he had merely impersonated the *barba*, he had spoken heresy, which was against what this medieval culture called the word of God, and that was a serious matter. The Inquisition—

The horseman passed. Brother Paul heaved a sigh of relief and returned to the path. He would go as far as he could while light remained, watching for a good place to spend the night.

His groin hurt. He paused to explore it, for a moment harboring the wild hope that his genitals were somehow growing back. This was not the case; there was merely some sort of swelling there, perhaps of the lymph nodes. It made walking awkward. As if he didn't have problems enough, without food or lodging or water—

Water! Suddenly he was ravenously thirsty. Was there a spring near here? The path had strayed away from the great river, rising into the hills; he needed water *here*, not a league away.

He staggered, feeling dizzy. He was hot, burning up; he knew it though he had no objective way to check his temperature. His skin itched.

Slowly the realization dawned. He had observed these

symptoms before. In the Juggler—just before he died.

He had the dread plague.

Brother Paul fell headlong in the path, striking heavily and rolling part way over. He saw the moon hanging in the gloomy dusk sky. Isis, Goddess of Luna, the principle of female deception, stared obscurely down at him from her filling crescent: the face of the womb. Somewhere a sad hound bayed.

It was no time at all—but also an eternity of fading in and out, retching, burning thirst, pain. Discovery; exclamations. "Get it off the road!" But he remained because no one would touch him for fear of contamination. Then one came who was willing, and Brother Paul was dumped unceremoniously into a wagon. He bumped along, being taken—where? Obviously to the burial dump for plague victims.

He tried to say something, but his mouth would not work properly, and the noise of the wheels was loud. And what difference did it make? He would soon be dead anyway. Satan had granted his wish. He had not wished for life. Not his *own* life.

Lights shone: lamps in the night. Buildings loomed. He was coming into metropolitan Hell. The demon driving the wagon stopped to converse with a devil guarding the gate to some torture station. Money changed hands. Money—the love of which was the root of all evil. How fitting that it dominate the rituals of Hell! Then the two of them came back to Brother Paul and hauled him out of the wagon and walked him through the narrow portal of the building. They dragged him stumbling upstairs and finally laid him out on a pallet. Maybe some vivisection to lead off the festivities. . . .

Troubled unconsciousness. Something at his face: he felt wetness. The water torture! But he was so parched he had to gulp it down. Then other tortures; bitter herbs to eat, cold washing of body, sleep.

Now he woke in a clean bed. A man about his own age stood over him. He had a full black beard, above which dark, seemingly hooded eyes looked out. "I think you have passed the nadir, stranger." The voice was familiar.

"I have the Black Death," Brother Paul said. "My companion died of it."

"Many do. You came close. But I have a certain finesse with herbs, and your constitution is strong." He drew up a wooden chair and seated himself beside the bed. "The question is, why did a castrate Waldens *barba* stricken by plague call my name?"

Brother Paul focused on him, confused. "Your name?"

"I am Abraham the Jew."

Oh. "My companion gave me two names before he died. One was yours. I did not realize I spoke it aloud."

"Fortunate for you that you did. I am interested in strange things—in magic and sorcery and odd faiths. So when the burial detail heard you name me, they brought you here. I saw at once that you were of a heretical sect—but what is Christian heresy to a Jew? I neither gave away your secret nor let them dump you to die. Intrigued by curiosity, I paid their fee and gave you drink and medication. Now I seek my reward: complete information on you and your magic."

Could he trust this man? Did it matter? Evidently this was not formal Hell, after all, but a continuation of the medieval vision. Brother Paul decided to tell the truth or as much of it as made sense. "I am no *barba*. I am a stranger to this realm, who was befriended by a Waldens missionary who had lost his companion. Then he died, and I took his place."

"A risky impersonation. Are you not aware what they do to heretics?"

"I was fleeing the Holy Office when I fell ill," Brother Paul admitted.

"You say the *barba* named me. Where did he get my name? I have not before had dealings with the Waldenses. In fact, I had not realized they were into sorcery."

"Only the magic of God's great love," Brother Paul said. "The rest is stage trickery to entertain the masses and allay suspicion. I suppose the Waldenses keep track of those who might help them in emergency, and you were the one for the city of Worms."

"That seems reasonable," Abraham agreed. "For as it developed, I *have* helped you. Yet surely they were aware that all Jews are grasping usurers and that I would not help one of their number unless they made it amply worth my while." He smiled briefly. "I am sorry you are not the real Uncle; I am most curious what payment they proposed to proffer. What was the other name the dead man uttered?"

Brother Paul concentrated, and it came back. "Abra-Melim, the Mage of Egypt."

The Jew shook his head. "That name means nothing to me. And Egypt is far away from Worms."

"True." Brother Paul felt tired already. He dropped off to sleep, and Abraham let him be.

He woke later—perhaps it was another day—feeling stronger. The Jew's herbs must have been potent! Some sound had disturbed him. Maybe it had been the Jew delivering food; at any rate, there was a sweet roll and an ewer of milk beside his bed, though he was alone.

Brother Paul began to eat and drink, glad for his hunger; he was definitely on the mend. He had thought he was finished when he came down with the bubonic plague, but of course it was not a hundred per cent fatal. Good care had been all that he needed. How fortunate that he had cried out Abraham's name in his delirium!

Abraham the Jew—there was a nagging familiarity about him. Shave off that beard and—of course! He was Therion in this new role.

What did that mean? The Good Companion had died; now he was again in the power of the Evil Companion. Lee had been the Wand of Fire; Therion was the Sword of Air. What did this devious servant of Satan have in mind for him this time?

Now he heard voices and realized that this was what had awakened him. One was Abraham; the other—no, it could not be the Juggler, for he was dead in this sequence. A stranger, then.

What stranger would seek him out? Had the Jew, angry because he could not repay his board, betrayed him for a price to the Inquisition? If so, how could he escape? He was feeling better, but not that much better. This was the first food he had eaten in perhaps two days: good, but hardly enough.

". . . minstrel, ill with the Black Death," Abraham's voice came more clearly. "No harm in him."

"I shall be the judge of that," the other responded firmly. "There is news of a shameless heretic in this region."

"Heresy!" Abraham snorted derisively. "Your entire Church is a heresy by our definition!"

"Jew, you have had an easy life in this fair city," the other retorted grimly. "It could become more difficult." There was cold menace in the too-familiar voice. It sounded so very much like the Juggler in his guise as a priest.

"I merely expressed a viewpoint." Abraham's voice had turned conciliatory; the threat had had its effect. "To us, there is not a great difference between Christians and the Moors. Both of their founders were prophets subscribing to our principles; both cults are comparatively young."

They had evidently halted on the landing near Brother Paul's door, engrossed in their unamiable dialogue. "Jew, you do not draw on an inexhaustible supply of tolerance," the other said warningly. "I will interview this man."

"I do not know whether he is in fit condition to be interviewed," Abraham protested. He spoke loudly and clearly—obviously intending Brother Paul to overhear. That did not seem like betrayal—yet the ways of the Evil Companion were invariably devious. "He is merely a stage magician who fooled me into supposing he might possess real magic; a charlatan. Of no interest to your Order."

"Jew—" The freighting of that single word was eloquent.

"Well, we shall see." Abraham opened the door.

Brother Paul refused to play a game of deception by

feigning sleep. He had had enough of deception!
"Greetings," he said as they entered. He continued
munching his bread.

The visitor wore a white habit with a black mantle:
the classical garb of a Dominican monk. His beard was
neat, his eyes piercing, and he had an air of grim concentration. "I am Brother Thomas, a Black Friar," he
said.

It was! It was Lee in a new part! He *had* survived the
death of his prior part! "How glad I am to see you,
friend!" Brother Paul exclaimed.

The Friar looked at him sternly. "Have we met
before?"

Of course Lee would play the part properly, inflexibly; that was his way. And what a part he had now!
He had become his former enemy, the Inquisition.

Lee had also, in life, been something of a racist. Now
he was a "Black" Friar. It was only a name, of
course—but in these Animations names were often a
vital part of the symbolism. Lee was really making up
for past indiscretions! Of course, since this was an
aspect of Hell, Satan might have required—

"Perhaps he performed a show at your house, one
time," Abraham said. And what of Therion: he had
ridiculed the Bible, and now was a Jew. Satan had given
him a hellish assignment too!

"Let him speak for himself." The Friar's penetrating
gaze swung to bear on Brother Paul again. "Juggler,
why did you address me as 'friend'?"

Brother Paul had allowed his racing thoughts to
distract him from his present situation. Now he had to
play his own part. "I thought I recognized you, but I
may have been mistaken."

Brother Thomas's glance was too keen. This man
would make a devastating enemy! "Surely we have not
encountered each other before; I have no connection
with stage magicians or others of that ilk. Yet there is no
doubting the flash of recognition that illuminated your
features just now."

This was awkward. Surely Lee-the-player recognized
and remembered Brother-Paul-the-player. But this part

of "Brother Thomas" had not met him. So the Dominican would have to verify by some legitimate means what the player Lee already knew to be the case: that Brother Paul was playing the part of a heretic missionary. Probably, by the standards of historical Dominicans, Brother Paul's own Holy Order of Vision was heretical. So he was in trouble, regardless.

Or *was* he? Lee would play the part of Brother Thomas straight, inflexibly accurate—but the player was limited in his interpretation of the part by his own background. Brother Paul would not be able to best a true Dominican in theological debate; after all, Saint Thomas Aquinas, from whose name this part had probably been drawn, had been a Dominican—perhaps the most redoubtable Catholic theologian of all time. But Lee was no Dominican, in life, and no Catholic. He was at a disadvantage. So was Therion, whose Horned God was the antithesis of the Jewish Jehovah. Brother Paul found he rather enjoyed the irony.

"You do not answer?" the Friar demanded. "This is suspicious."

And suspicion was tantamount to conviction with the Inquisition! He had to get talking! "I am not a common juggler," Brother Paul said. What was the best line to take, knowing that part of this man knew the truth, and so could not be deceived? How close to that truth could he come without, by the rules of this grim game, giving away the Waldenses and thus betraying his promise to this same player in another guise? Yet Brother Paul's own religious and ethical scruples prevented him from lying. The *barba* impersonation was a very special case. Never, since he joined the Holy Order of Vision, had Brother Paul failed to honor the truth as he understood it. He had once concealed his childhood fears even from himself, and his one-time addiction to the memory drug had caused other obscurities in his life. That was over; he did not intend to practice concealment again, no matter what pressure Satan applied.

"And what would be behind that innocent facade?" Brother Thomas inquired. He was intent, expectant, closing in on the heresy his memory from his previous

role knew was there, if only he could prove it *here*. Yet
Brother Paul perceived a misgiving in him, the suppressed regret of a man who did what we required
though it was personally painful. Lee wanted to lose this
fish—but as the Black Friar he was bound to do his utmost to reel it in. And his chances of failure were
diminishingly small.

*Oh, Satan, you have crafted the most artistic fiend-
ishness yet! You have forced us to destroy ourselves,
knowingly.* For even Therion, in the role of a man who
had harbored a heretic, would be doomed.

Well, why *not* the truth? Extraordinary measures
would be required to extricate themselves from this
maelstrom. Brother Paul had told it before. The other
players had assigned parts, but Brother Paul played
himself, even when he assumed another role as now. He
was himself pretending to be the Juggler, not himself
cast in the role of the Juggler. A difficult but key
distinction. He was under no obligation that he knew of
to make pretenses. "I am a visitor from another—"

But his own self-protective censor cut him off. There
were different levels of truth here in Animation. He had
experienced how directly these visions could affect the
people within them. If he said something here that convinced the Friar that he was a lunatic or a heretic, he
could lose his part. And for him, unlike the others, his
part *was* his life. This was not worth the risk. "Land,"
he finished lamely. Then, before the Friar could follow
that up, he added: "I am a Brother of a Christian Order
there."

"Would that land be Italy?" Brother Thomas asked.

Italy—the home of the Pope (one of them, anyway)
and of the Waldens heresy. Loaded question! "No. It is
across the ocean, perhaps unknown to you. But we have
Dominican monks, and I thought you were one I knew
until I saw that you were merely another of that excellent Order." Which disposed of the recognition
problem—he hoped. "We believe in the original
message of Jesus Christ and the Apostle Paul." Brother
Paul was not about to be caught up in any great

ignorance concerning Jesus or him namesake Paul; he was on secure footing here.

"Those are apt beliefs," the Dominican observed wryly.

"The Holy Bible is an apt tutor."

"Now that I can agree with," Abraham put in. "Certainly the Hebrew Text which you refer to as the Old Testament. To us, Jesus was merely a man—a good man, perhaps, and a prophet, but nevertheless a man. Jesus was a Jew; he followed the Scriptures we originated and codified." In this role, Therion could not challenge the origin of the Old Testament, whatever private doubts he had.

"Yet you slew Him!" Brother Thomas snapped. "For that you are forever accursed!"

Abraham spread his hands disingenuously. "An unfortunate complication. Your Saint Paul was also a Christian killer, you know. Remember how he had Stephen stoned?"

Oh, Therion was enjoying this now!

"Saint Paul repented!" the Friar said hotly. "He himself suffered stoning for his Christian faith!"

"And now you Christians are eager to stone your own kind, calling them heretics when they protest the manifest corruption in your ranks."

"The Holy Office does not stone Christians," Brother Thomas said stiffly.

"No. The Holy Office merely strings dissenters up by the thumbs like so many carcasses of venison with a scribe meticulously recording every scream. How your Jesus must appreciate those screams!"

This was getting dirty. The Dominican blanched. Brother Paul knew Lee was remembering his role of Jesus in the other Animation and his own objection to the very evil Therion now pointed out. Oh, telling thrust!

This also suggested why a Jew might help a Christian heretic. The Jews had known centuries of persecution at the hands of righteous Christians, many of whom were hypocrites with little inkling of the original precepts of

their religion. Now the Waldenses, like other sects
before them, were advocating a return to those original
precepts—and were suffering similar persecution.
Therion, as a member of another persecuted sect, could
play this role with gusto. For who had been more
vilified by Christianity than the Horned God?

Brother Thomas had recovered somewhat. Lee, as a
Mormon, also knew the meaning of persecution. The
Mormons had had to migrate more than once from
hostile country to preserve their freedom of worship
only to have that country, in the form of the expanding
United States of America, annex their new territory and
outlaw their style of marriage. Yet he had a role to play
here, and he would play it well. "The Holy Office takes
no joy in suffering. But it is not always easy to salvage
the immortal soul of a hardened heretic. Surely the
momentary discomfort he may feel during interrogation
is an infinitesimal price to pay for his release from the
eternal fires of Hell. The boil must be lanced, though it
hurt for an instant, lest it poison the whole."

That was a good statement, Brother Paul thought.
Lee was coming through well in this very difficult role.

But the Jew was pressing for the kill. It was The
Dozens, again. "I think Hell might well be a better place
to spend eternity than among hypocrites."

"No, the hypocrites are relegated to the infernal
regions," Brother Thomas said evenly. "There they suffer the eternal torment they so richly deserve."

Abraham affected surprise. "With no reprieve?"

"With no reprieve. They had their chance in life."

"No rehabilitation?"

"No rehabilitation after death."

"Not even if the hypocrite sincerely repents his
hypocrisy?"

"No, once he is damned, he is damned forever."

"Is this what your Jesus Christ said? That there be no
forgiveness when the prodigal son returned?"

"Forgiveness in *life*," the Dominican said grimly.
"There must be a point of no return," and that point is
at the terminus of life. At death the decision is final.
This is the reason we labor so diligently to save a per-

son's soul in time by whatever means we possess. We do not wish *any* immortal soul to suffer indefinitely." He glanced piercingly at Abraham. "There may still be time even for you, Jew."

Abraham laughed. "I do not fear Satan! I'd prefer to live as Jacob did, money-grubbing and lusty, cheating and being cheated—and human throughout. When the time comes, I will wrestle with God as he did, and we shall see what we shall see. Yahveh will understand."

This was Therion's interpretation, Brother Paul thought. He doubted a genuine Jew would have put it that way. Therion, like Lee, was limited by his own religious background. Thus God was cast in a Satanic mold.

But strait-laced Lee could not accept such a statement and neither could the Dominican Friar. "God accepts no money-grubbers, no cheaters, no lust! You blaspheme!"

"God seems to accept the Holy Office," Abraham remarked.

But Brother Thomas was too worked up to grasp the full nature of that insult. "*No* culture could justify such things. They are abominations before God!" This too matched what Brother Paul knew of Mormon tenets; the forbidden fruit of the Garden of Eden was sexual intercourse. But because God had commanded man to be fruitful and multiply, Adam and Eve had chosen the lesser of evils and indulged in the fruit of sex. This really was not too different from medieval Church doctrine to Brother Paul's mind.

The problem was that Lee was far better versed in *The Book of Mormon* than in the Bible. A number of names overlapped, but they stood for different people. The Jacob of the Mormons was not the Jacob of the Jews.

"Your God accepted a man who sent his own firstborn son out into the wilderness with his mother!" Abraham said. "Abraham's firstborn was Ishmael—and he cast him out in favor of his second son Isaac. From Isaac and his cheating second-born son Jacob are the Jews descended, and from them came the Jew called Jesus, whom you—"

He broke off, for Brother Thomas was staring at him.
Oops—the Baal-worshiper Therion had allowed his personal feelings to carry him away, forgetting that in this
part he was the Jew. As Therion, it was natural that he
resent the exclusion of his philosophic ancestor Ishmael—but as the Jew, he had fluffed his part.

That fluff could give the advantage to the
Dominican—and undermine Brother Paul's own
position. His own role was at stake; Abraham knew his
Waldens association and Brother Thomas suspected it.
Discovery or betrayal would probably finish him.
Would Therion sell him out to protect himself? Therion
certainly would! He had to step in.

"There may be misunderstanding," Brother Paul
said carefully. "Abraham was the father, according to
the Bible, of Ishmael by his wife's maid Hagar.
Abraham's wife Sarah was barren, so she gave him her
Egyptian maid for the purpose of siring an heir. This
was standard practice in those days, for to the nomads
children were vitally important. The custom seems to
derive from the Hurrians. Plural marriages were permitted, and no blame attaches to Abraham for this. He
would have been remiss had he not taken steps to
provide offspring, to continue the tribe."

The Friar might have objected—but the player Lee,
sensitive about the furor over the former Mormon practice of polygamy, could not bring himself to do it. The
Jew was happy to have his namesake Abraham de-
fended, and the player Abraham eager to have his fluff
covered. So Brother Paul had the floor—for now.

"The problem came because, though Ishmael was the
first son, Isaac was the legitimate son. God made Sarah
fertile at the age of ninety, and Abraham was a hundred
when Isaac was born. So it was a remarkable circumstance, unanticipated. There was fierce rivalry between the two women, and in the end the only way
Abraham could settle it was by sending away Hagar and
Ishmael. But Yahveh looked after them, and their
descendents became the Arabs—actually more
numerous and prosperous than the descendents of
Isaac, the Jews. So it was a difficult situation, and an

unkind compromise had to be made, but I don't think blame should attach to either the Arabs or the Jews for that."

"Attach the blame to the Hurrians," Abraham said, relieved.

Brother Thomas was not so eager to let it go. "Yet I believe the Jew said something about Jacob, cheating and lusting and fighting with God? This sounds heretical to me."

Meaning that if Brother Paul tried to defend such actions by Jacob, instead of denying them, he might be accused of heresy himself—the very thing he was trying to avoid. Once the Inquisition put him to the torture on this pretext, the torturers would quickly extract from him the rest of his information. Therion, obviously unsympathetic to the children of Isaac despite his present role, was ill-equipped to reverse himself there. So it was Brother Paul's problem again. Had this been engineered by Satan? Regardless, it was hellish.

"Those were hard times," Brother Paul said carefully. He felt as if he were treading a thin sheet of ice covering the rumbling maw of a volcano. One misstep, a single mischance—doom. Satan charged a high price for the wish He granted! "Abraham had many problems and very difficult decisions. His son Isaac had his own problems; it was all he could do to protect his pretty wife Rebekah from the attentions of other tribesmen. Isaac's twin sons Esau and Jacob were rivals for his favor; Isaac tended to favor the strong hunter Esau, while Rebekah liked the more moderate Jacob. So there was a very human dissension in that family too. It might be taken as an analogy to the contrasting pulls of the rugged country life of the nomads, and the more comfortable, settled life of city peoples." And there was his own crisis: country vs. city! "In which direction would this tribe go? Thus the strife was subtle but intense. Jacob, as boys will, made a deal with Esau to obtain his brother's birthright and followed it up by tricking their father Isaac into granting his blessing to Jacob. This was a form of cheating. But the point is, the men of Biblical times were human with human stresses and failings, and they did make errors of judgment and passion. They were a great trial to Yahveh.''

"Yes," Abraham agreed, and Brother Thomas nodded. So far, so good. But he wasn't out of trouble yet.

"Jacob was cheated in his turn, perhaps in retribution," Brother Paul continued. His hands were sweating; surreptitiously he wiped them on the blanket. "When he worked for seven years to marry the fair Rachel, he discovered after the consummation that her father had substituted her older sister Leah. Now he had to work another seven years for Rachel. He was actually allowed to marry Rachel within a week, however, so he did not have to wait; he had two wives while he worked off the debt. And perhaps the hand of God was in this too, for as it turned out, Rachel was barren. So it was Leah who provided him with a number of fine sons. Then Rachel, to preserve her status, gave him her maid for procreative purposes in order to have at least a surrogate son. So Leah gave him *her* pretty maid for another son, and—well, you could call this lust, but I don't think that's quite fair. All of it was for the purpose of increasing the size of the tribe, and since underpopulation was the main problem of that day—''

Brother Thomas the Dominican Friar spread his hands. "Brother, I thought you were practicing deceit, but you evidently have a fine knowledge of the Bible."

"It was Jacob who practiced deceit," Brother Paul agreed, weak with relief. "And his father-in-law. Each had his motives—''

"In fact, your knowledge of the Bible is so specific that I suspect you must have been reading it yourself."

Oh, no! Now Brother Paul remembered: in medieval times the Church frowned on common reading of the Bible. It was deemed too important to be left to the run-of-the-mill believer, and instead had to be read and interpreted by the hierarchy. He had marched into another trap.

"In my country, the study of the Bible reaches further toward the layman than it does here," he said. Un-

derstatement of the mission! "And as a traveling minstrel I am accustomed to remembering stories. It is easy
to remember the greatest story ever told." Would that
pass?

"I must accept your credits as a Christian scholar,"
Brother Thomas continued. "I apologize for ques-
tioning you during your infirmity."

Victory! Brother Paul had so phrased his commentary as to defend the Mormons along with the
Biblical Jews, and this had paid off. Multiple wives, for
a good cause. . . .

"Ah, but this matter of wrestling with God—"
Abraham said, unable to resist the gibe.

Brother Paul saw disaster looming again. If Brother
Thomas resumed the fray—

"We all wrestle with God at times," the Dominican
said. "We call it conscience. The human flesh is weak,
while God is strong; we must listen to God always."

"Yes," Brother Paul agreed, relaxing again. So the
dogs really had been called off!

Brother Thomas faced the door. "I apologize again
for the intrusion. Farewell." He crossed himself.

"Farewell," Brother Paul echoed, making the sign of
the cross with his own hand. A true *barba* would never
have done that.

It was a mistake. His hand knocked the table at his
bedside, and the Tarot deck fell to the floor. It landed
face up with a sound like thunder, the cards splaying
apart.

Brother Thomas whirled and stepped back in and
stooped with dismaying alacrity. "What is this?" he
inquired, picking up the cards.

"A tool of the Juggler's trade," Abraham said
quickly. "He performs magic tricks with them for the
entertainment of peasants."

"Magic is heresy," the Dominican said with an
abrupt return of grimness.

"Stage magic," Brother Paul said. Why had this had
to happen now? The worst possible break! Satan's
work, of course. "Sleight of hand. I can demonstrate."

But the Friar was looking through the cards. "Many

of these seem to be conventional images such as are used by riff-raff for gaming. But some are more complicated representations.'' He held up the card for Deception with its sinister Lunar theme. ''What is the meaning of this?''

''That seems to be an astrological motif,'' Abraham said quickly. ''I have made some considerable study of astrology and other types of magic—'' He smiled at the Dominican's expression. ''Do not look so shocked, Friar! Magic is not forbidden to us Jews! In fact we often have need of it to hold our own in this Christian country.''

Brother Paul knew what he meant. The Jews had some of the most authoritative magic in the form of the Qabala, Cabala, Kabbalah or however it was transcribed. They had guarded that knowledge so well that it was unknown to the Christians of this period. Thus the Qabala had no connection with the Tarot although later ''experts'' had done their best to merge the two.

''This is astrology?'' Brother Thomas inquired dubiously. Astrology, if Brother Paul remembered correctly, was regarded as more of a science than magic in medieval times. Thus it was not heretical by Church definitions; indeed, some Church scholars were astrologers. ''Where is the horoscope?''

''The entire deck would be the horoscope,'' Abraham explained glibly. ''The symbols would not be arranged on charts, but on individual cards, and the fall of the cards must determine the reading. This is obviously the planet of the Moon.''

Again, the Dominican's piercing glance stabbed Brother Paul. ''Brother, do you practice divination for your audience?''

''No,'' Brother Paul answered honestly. ''What these pictures evoke is in the mind of the beholders. If you see an astrological symbol in an ordinary Lunar landscape, and wish to pay me a coin for that encouragement, you are a fool and I am richer by that coin.''

Brother Thomas hesitated, then smiled. ''There are many fools in this world,'' he said. He turned again, setting down the cards. "Methinks you are not above preying on foolishness on occasion, Brother, when you are hungry. And the biggest fool of all is the Jew who believes in magic." He crossed himself again and marched out.

"The hypocrite!" Abraham muttered. "His whole Church is built on magic! The reason they burn heretics is that those people practice magic that is outside Church control. They can't tolerate competition! Jesus Christ was a magician; he made water into wine, and a few crumbs of bread sufficient to feed a multitude. *I* seek magic openly—and someday I shall find it!"

Brother Paul found he agreed with him. "There is a lot of hypocrisy in religion. But why have you helped me, knowing that I practice no genuine magic?"

"Well, I didn't *know* that," Abraham said candidly. "I was sure that most of your tricks were innocuous. But I have heard of the Waldenses and their cards, and I suspected there could be magic in it. So—" He broke off, his face twisting into alarm. "The Friar crossed himself. Twice."

"Friars do," Brother Paul agreed.

"When there is a challenge or a threat, they do. But Brother Thomas was departing. Why should he cross himself before leaving the presence of a Jew?"

Brother Paul was getting tired and wanted to sleep again. "Maybe he was warding off heresy."

Abraham shook his head in grim affirmation. "He crossed himself because he believed he had confirmation of the presence of evil. By his twisted definition, I am a known evil, but you—"

"If he really suspects me, why didn't he just take me in when he had the chance? I am weak from my illness; I could not have offered much resistance."

Abraham paced the floor nervously. "That is what *I* would like to know. I would not have dared to interfere, had he declared you heretic; any little pretext will do for a new pogrom! Soft-heartedness can only go so far! I would have had to renounce you, and he knew it. So why should he practice such deception? He surely has great mischief in mind."

The more Brother Paul considered that, the more concerned he became. Suppose the Dominican had decided he had a live heretic on the line—and thought he might reel in more heretics with a little cunning patience? He might indeed pretend to be satisfied so as to reassure the quarry—then watch that suspect. "I fear I must be on my way," Brother Paul said regretfully. Rest seemed wonderful, but not if a conspiracy was building against him and the Waldenses. He had to lose himself quickly.

"I think our minds are moving in similar channels," Abraham said. "The Dominican is unconvinced—rather, he *is* convinced! He smells heresy! I saw his eyes glint when he saw your Tarot. He has seen such cards before, I'll warrant, or heard them described! I believe he has returned to consult the other demons of his Order, and if they don't arrest you they will spy on you, trying to discover your contacts and methods of identification so that they can burn many heretics instead of one. I believe you should escape this city in haste. I shall have to denounce you as soon as you are gone to save my own skin. Are you able to travel?"

"I'm not sure," Brother Paul said. "Your attentions have helped, but the black plague is nothing to fool with; I remain weak."

"No doubt the Friar is certain you can not move about today, therefore is not casting his net quite yet. But tomorrow—" He paused, grimacing. "It will have to be risked," he decided. "I am a Jew; my situation is precarious. I have money, so they deal with me carefully, but it is not wise to push them too far. I will give you directions how to escape, but I cannot provide any material assistance. It must seem that you fled while I was preparing to turn you in."

Brother Paul agreed. He had to move on today, now—for the Jew's sake, his own, and the Waldenses'.

"What was that other name the missionary gave you?" Abraham asked suddenly.

"Name? Oh—Abra-Melim, the Mage of Egypt."

"Abra-Melim, the Mage of Egypt," the Jew repeated, memorizing it. "They have outstanding lore in Egypt. This may be the magician I am looking for. Surely the Waldenses believe the Mage has what I seek."

Brother Paul shrugged as he dressed. "I wouldn't know. It is only a name to me."

"Maybe I should go to Egypt," Abraham mused. "If you slip their noose, it may not be safe for me in Worms for a time." But then he smiled. "But I shall be glad to take the risk if only to aggravate that sanctimonious cleric. Come, we shall effect your escape."

V

Triumph: 24

The chief value of the Bible lies in its moral principles and spiritual guidance. To regard it as authoritative in any other field is to fly in the face of modern knowledge. The Bible is not a textbook in science. Its world view is that of the childhood of the race, and this primitive cosmology is seen in all its references to the physical world. The earth is conceived as flat and stationary. The sky is a canopy or vault through whose windows the rain falls. The sun, moon, and stars are contained within this vault. Beneath the earth is Sheol, the realm of the dead. This world and the creatures in it, according to the Scripture, were made in six days. The world in which the Bible was written was one in which human destiny was determined by the stars, sickness was caused by demon possession, the dead were raised, angels stirred the waters of a pool for the healing of the sick, and the Red Sea was parted.

Many literalists, like Augustine, insist that "Scripture gives no false information" and that if it conflicts with science, so much the worse for science. But others, confronted with the vast discrepancy between the biblical world view and modern knowledge, can distinguish also between the passing and the permanent, between the abiding values of the Bible and their transient setting. They know that changes in civilization do not touch the vital and basic experiences of man. The outmoding of world views cannot belittle the permanence of the Scripture in its moral and spiritual values, its timeless aspirations and deathless convictions. The discoveries of Copernicus, Galileo, and Newton, of Pasteur, Darwin, and Einstein do not in any way impair the universal validity of faith, hope, and love.

—Fred Gladstone Bratton: *A History of the Bible*, Boston, Beacon Press 1959.

Two days later just as hope was rising, Brother Paul felt renewed fatigue and fever. A deep cough developed. It was not a return of the plague, but something else whose symptoms he recognized: pneumonia. He had driven himself too hard, too soon after his prior illness. Now he *had* to rest—or return to Hell permanently. He had not consciously felt threatened by the plague, awful as it was; it was not a disease to which a twentieth or twenty-first century man was attuned. But pneumonia —*that* he respected.

Where could he go? He had headed west from Worms, disguised as a beggar, avoiding any possible contact with likely Waldenses. He had trekked toward France, hoping the minions of the Holy Office would not pursue him beyond the boundaries of the Holy Roman Empire, assuming they picked up his trail. He could not afford any friends, of course; anyone who helped him might suffer at the hands of the Inquisition.

Abraham, despite his protestations, had given him some money and general advice. He might obtain lodging at some isolated farm for a pittance, and no one would know he was there until days after he was gone.

Odd how the roles had reversed. Therion had helped him (apologizing for it by muttering about possible reward and aggravation of the status quo), while Lee was out to destroy him. Satan certainly knew how to turn the knife in the wound!

Brother Paul heard horses on the path. Should he hide—or try to bluff it out? The odds were they weren't after him. What was one suspected heretic in the whole medieval society? Maybe they had never been after him; the Jew had wanted him out, so had concocted the notion of this plot. . . .

No, he couldn't convince himself. This was not the medieval society; it was an Animation set in it. Historical fiction, and he was the central character. All conspiracies would revolve around him.

"Brother, you're paranoid," he told himself. He hunched his shoulders within the cloak and trod on. The sounds of the horse became distinguishable: two horses and the creak of wheels. A fast-traveling coach or wagon. He moved over so as to give it room to pass; a coach probably meant a noble and they tended to be arrogant. The horses could run him down and trample him if he got in the way. Beggars weren't worth much.

The horses came abreast of him, snorting. He glanced sidelong, without turning his head. It was a two-wheeled wagon, canopied, reminding him of a chariot. The chariot of the Tarot of course—power on the move, symbolic of man's journey along the road to salvation.

He kept on walking, letting it pass, still sneaking looks at the horses. The chariot seemed to have slowed, pacing him rather than passing.

"Juggler!" a too-familiar voice called.

Oh, no! It was Brother Thomas, the Dominican Friar.

"Juggler—no need to walk when you can ride," the enemy said cheerily. "How fortunate I am traveling your way!"

Brother Paul considered running. But he could not outdistance the chariot on the road; he would have to go cross country. He knew he could not get far; he was sick and weak and had to rest, while the Dominican was well and strong.

Dispiritedly, Brother Paul climbed up into the chariot beside the Friar. There was a seat there, and he sank down on it with physical relief. What else could he do?

* * *

The chariot halted. Brother Thomas steadied him with a firm hand. "We have a barber who can help you," he said. Was there menace there? A barber—surely not a mere cutter of hair. A medieval doctor. Letting out the bad blood, so the patient could improve. A treatment that could be fatal. "No . . ." Brother Paul protested weakly.

"Have no fear," the Dominican said reassuringly. "Our barber employs only the very best leeches, culled weekly from the Seine."

Bloodsucking worms from the river. Brother Paul thought about vomiting, but lacked the energy. Then something else nagged him. "The Seine?"

"We are a long way from Worms, friend," Brother Thomas informed him. "You slept like the dead—and indeed, I feared that might not be much exaggeration. This is the heart of France, our chief monastery. Is it not beautiful?"

Brother Paul roused himself enough to look. The gate was barred. The windows were small and high. The walls were thick. This was a veritable fortress. "Beautiful," he echoed dismally.

The gate closed behind him. He was trapped—and he had not been able to dispose of the cards. He must have maintained a death grip on them to protect them from the Friar's curiosity. Or maybe the Animation had skipped over this dull passage so that nothing at all had happened between scenes. Animation was real, but on its own terms.

They came to a central room where a great fire blazed in a fireplace. Brother Paul, shivering with a chill, moved toward it gladly. Several hooded monks appeared, closing in about him. "You must rest," Brother Thomas said. "A room has been prepared. We shall take your soiled clothes and provide you with fresh apparel."

Should he try to resist? It was hopeless; he was sick and weak, and they were many and strong. He could gain nothing—and there was always the chance that they did mean well, that the Jew had deceived him about the motives of the Dominicans.

Except for the Tarot. Brother Thomas had seen that deck, and player Lee would have known its nature from his previous part. So Lee knew what he was looking for, and with that deck in his possession he could investigate legitimately and zero in on the secret. Brother Paul's decision to avoid the Waldenses must have nullified the spying strategy, so the Animation had shunted right across to the next contest of wills. The cards were now the key; if Brother Thomas and the Inquisition gained possession of the cards, exposure of the Waldenses was a virtual certainty. The Dominicans would reproduce the cards, put on jugglers' suits, give sermons based on the cards—and take whole audiences into custody, cleaning out entire cities with single sweeps. It would work because the people would believe in the authenticity of anyone who carried such cards—as they had believed in Brother Paul.

Without those cards, Brother Thomas the Dominican would have no certain evidence that Brother Paul was a heretic and no lever to use against the Waldenses. He would be unable to proceed with the persecution. Not according to the rules of this play, no matter how much he knew privately. And Lee would follow the rules, absolutely.

The monks pressed close. This was an Animation; were they real? Maybe he could walk right through them and on through the cloister walls. Yet this too would be misplaying the part, cheating. Satan had sent him here at his own request, as it were; he should not have been surprised to discover Satanic elements of the sequence. Perhaps he played the part of a genuinely historical character, and significant revelations remained. He had to play the animation game or forfeit all that Animation held for him. Which meant that he had to submit now to the power of the monks.

Except for the Tarot deck. If he believed in the play, he had also to believe in the Waldenses who would be routed by his betrayal of the Juggler's trust. They would be put on trial for heresy, perhaps tortured, perhaps burned at the stake. As Joan of Arc had been burned —*would be* burned—in this area a generation hence.

Brother Paul could not allow himself to be the instrument of these good people's doom.

He could afford neither to invoke the power of his disbelief in the reality of this Animation nor to go along with it completely. He had to do the right thing despite increasing pressure. Yet what *was* right in this hell of indecision?

Brother Paul reached inside his robe into the secret pocket. His fingers closed about the deck. He lifted it out, holding it for a moment, gazing on this most precious object he had ever possessed: the True Tarot. He had suffered a tour of Hell itself and the black plague to obtain this cardboard Grail.

He nerved himself. Then, quickly, he hurled the Tarot into the open fire, spreading the cards with a twist of his wrist so that they would burn rapidly.

Brother Thomas screamed as though his own body were afire. He dived at the hearth, reaching in with his bare hands, trying to recover the blazing cards. The other monks rushed to restrain him, thinking him mad—as indeed he was at that moment!—and Brother Thomas had to allow them to haul him away from the searing heat.

Brother Paul knew the agony the Friar suffered; he was experiencing it himself. He watched the cards curl and writhe in the flame as though struggling to escape. Colored tongues danced above the pigments. The heat of the sun, the flames of Hell, the conflagration of the spirit—in microcosm!

The blaze died down. Dismal ashes settled out. It was done; the treasure had been destroyed. The tainted Gift had been rejected. Brother Paul had played the game by the rules and won. At the cost of his Grail. Now at last the Animation could end, releasing him from the torture of his first wish.

They waited, as it were in tableau. Nothing happened. The issue had been decided—yet the scene continued. Evidently Satan had not finished the sequence.

Back into their roles! "You may have destroyed the demon deck, the physical evidence against you," Brother Thomas said. "But it remains in your mind.

Heresy is an affliction not of matter, but of the spirit. It is this we must cleanse—for the good of your soul, and the souls of the other people led astray by heretic teachings."

So there was after all no way to avoid this thing. The medieval Church was partial to physical means to achieve its spiritual ends. The ultimate deprogramming: torture.

"We must take him to the interrogation center," Brother Thomas decided. "This matter must be competently handled."

Brother Paul coughed. This was no polite objection; he felt his fever peaking, and his lungs were rattling. The pneumonia was taking firm hold. He was not in condition to be tortured; he might expire before they got any information from him.

No such luck. Brother Thomas arranged for the best herbal remedies, wholesome milk and bread, a comfortable bed in a quiet room, and summoned no barber. He took very good care of Brother Paul, doing everything medievally possible to promote his health. Was this merely because the role required it—or because of the friendship that had once existed between them in other roles?

He slept and dreamed of Paris: the city he had never seen either in life or in Animation. He woke in his comfortable chamber. He had had no idea that monks lived so well! This was no dark ascetic cell, but a pleasant residence. Yet of course this was the sort of thing the cards of the Waldenses protested: a priestess living like an empress, a priest like an emperor. While the common people lived like the serfs they were.

However, Brother Paul would be glad to trade this fine accommodation for the poor but kindly hospitality of the peasants. It was torture he faced here; he had no doubt of it. At any moment that door would open and he would be taken to—

The door opened. Brother Paul closed his eyes, steeling himself. He was sure that torture in Animation would be just as terrible as—

The scent of perfume touched him. "Am I then so ugly as all that?" a soft voice inquired.

Brother Paul's eyes popped open. A most comely young woman stood beside his bed. Hastily he drew the covers about him. "Who—?" he asked, amazed.

"I am the Lady Yvette," she said, making a kind of curtsy.

She was a beauty, wearing a long tunic under a sideless surcoat, closely fitted so as to make the femininity of her figure quite evident, though her natural endowments hardly required this service. She had a buttoned hood, but wore it unbuttoned under the chin so that a suggestive amount of bosom was displayed. Amaranth, of course.

Brother Paul was not so weak as to be unmoved by her appearance. Yet he was guarded, knowing Satan had placed her in this scene. "What can I do for you, Yvette?"

"I understand you have knowledge of a beautiful set of playing cards," she said.

As expected. Another ploy for betrayal. "I had such a deck, but it was unfortunately lost in a fire."

"Yes, but you could recreate it," she said hopefully.

He smiled. "I am no painter!" Yet he might have aspired to be, once. . . . "The artwork is well beyond my talents."

She looked at him intently. What was behind that lovely facade this time? He had seen her more or less raped in the Black Mass, then reconstituted as Satan's secretary, then as assorted bit parts in this wish-vision. What did Amaranth really feel for him? Once he had thought he loved her, but recent events had chilled that somewhat. "We could employ a good artist. You could describe the pictures to him, and he would paint at your direction. It might take some time, but—"

"I may not have time," he said. "I am to be interrogated by the Holy Order as a suspected heretic."

She raised a finger knowingly. "This set of cards—it would be for the King who is a great lover—"

"Oho!" His own bitterness burst out, surprising him. "You are his mistress!"

She colored. "A great lover of culture," she continued. "Fine sculpture, fine paintings—these things

Charles takes great pleasure in. More than in the government of the realm. If we suggested to him that the culture of the court would be enhanced by a really fine set of cards with mystical elements, I'm sure he would be most intrigued and would commission the very best artist. Especially for cards with magical properties."

"Magical properties? Why should the King care about such nonsense?"

She shook her head so vigorously her bosom bounced. "No, no—magic is not nonsense! And Charles VI is—" She faltered. "His Majesty has a certain peculiar interest in the occult." She leaned forward to whisper. There was no way she could be unaware of what this did to her cleavage. "Some say he is mad, at least at times. So such a device—cards he could use to summon spirits—"

It was coming clear. A king of dubious sanity, interested in art and magic. Maybe they hoped the cards would distract him, while others ran the kingdom. Well, that was not much of Brother Paul's concern. However, if he recreated the Tarot of the Waldenses—that would be a certain route to betrayal. "I am sorry," he said.

She leaned closer, as though concluding that if a study of her globes from a meter's distance wasn't sufficient argument, half a meter's distance might do better. "You don't understand, sir," she said urgently. "If you do this thing for Charles—if you make him happy—the Holy Office can have no power over you. Charles is the King!"

Oho! Her offer had real substance like her bosom. Play along with the palace politics and avoid torture. The notion had an insidious appeal. Still, how could he imperil all the faithful followers of the *barbe*, the missionary Uncles? The Inquisition would surely use those cards to trap unwary believers into admissions of heresy. "No," he said regretfully.

"I would be most grateful," she murmured, touching her bodice with the delicate fingers of one hand. "The set would take many weeks to paint, and I would be with you always—"

And there was the final facet of the offer. The love of a beautiful woman.

She did not know he was castrate. She had been treated much the same way as he had, by Satan's pythons, but apparently that mutilation had not carried over into this sequence. After all, she had her limbs and head back: she had been crunched into pieces by Satan's jaws and restored. Naturally she assumed he had been rendered whole again too.

Her appearance and manner might excite him, but any attempt on his part to follow through would be futile. "Get out of here!" he said savagely.

Surprised, she withdrew. And now he wondered: would he have been able to resist such an offer had he retained his testicles?

In due course Brother Thomas conducted a friendly little tour of the local facilities. Down in the cellar of the building was a dank, old, but serviceable torture chamber.

"Today we merely show you the instruments," Brother Thomas explained with an enigmatic glance. What were his private Mormon reactions to this role? "I must apologize for the gloom. Since Charles VI came to power in France there has not been as rigorous a campaign against doctrinal error as we of the Church deem proper. Thus our facilities suffer somewhat from disuse."

"Unfortunate," Brother Paul said grimly. Inside his stomach knotted.

"However, the situation will surely improve in due course; the sun can not forever remain behind a cloud," Brother Thomas continued. "And it does mean that you will not be subjected to the annoyance of delay."

"Nice." No question about it: Brother Paul was desperately afraid. He had never been tortured in this fashion and knew the Inquisition was expert at this type of thing. This might be a kind of play, but he knew the torture would feel real and perhaps *be* real. Had any of the prior Animation fatalities occurred by torture? It was all too possible.

Brother Thomas drew open a great oaken door and showed the way into the darkest chamber yet. He picked a torch out of its socket, lighted it with his own, and replaced it. Now the room could be seen in all its awful splendor, the details imperfect but still far too suggestive for Brother Paul's taste. It was filled with metal and wooden structures. The purpose or function of some were obscure, while others evinced their nature all too brutally. There was a large fireplace with assorted kettles placed about, filled with water, oil or other fluid. There were knives and irons and axes. Ropes descended from rafters. Chains and manacles were at the walls. Ladders and large spoked wheels abounded.

"You see, the practice of magic by laymen is witchcraft," Brother Thomas said, as though this were a matter of merely academic interest. "And witchcraft is heresy. France has led the world in the definition and clarification of this threat. Our theologians are well on the way to formulating a comprehensive system of procedure that will rid the world of this evil. Archbishop Guillaume d'Auvergne of Paris showed the way more than a century ago, and Thomas Aquinas did much to develop it further. We Dominicans were assigned by Pope Gregory to perform this holy office, subject only to the Pope. We do our best."

"No doubt," Brother Paul agreed.

"Yet we would not willingly cause distress to any person. It is our desire only to abolish willful religious error and establish the truth as it has been declared by the Church. For the good of the souls of all the people. Therefore, we use every device to encourage voluntary renunciation of heresy."

"Such as torture," Brother Paul agreed.

"We prefer to call it interrogation," Brother Thomas said with a wry expression. His eyes met Brother Paul's momentarily, and now there was no doubt about the agony of conscience behind the discipline of the role. "I sincerely hope you will be persuaded to cooperate voluntarily, making recourse to coercive methods unnecessary."

The Vice Squad at college had entertained similar

hopes back in Brother Paul's youth. But seldom was human dignity and freedom suppressed voluntarily. People always fought back, some in token degree, others completely. Brother Paul knew he was fated to be the latter type.

Yet he knew that Lee did not want to torture him. So though the lines of the play were intended to be hypocritical, in this case they were sincere. "I believe you," Brother Paul said. "Yet, merely as supposition, what would become of the soul of a man who betrayed those who had placed their trust in him? If he saved himself from discomfort by yielding them up to the burning stake?"

"Heretics?" Brother Thomas snorted. Yet, again he showed the stigmata of stress. There was a tremor in the muscle of one cheek, and his eyes were narrow. He abated these symptoms somewhat by proceeding to the first implement of torture.

"These are thumbscrews," Brother Thomas said, lifting small metal contraptions and holding them in the light of the torch. "The vise is applied to the tips of the thumb or finger, no higher than the base of the nail, and tightened until the blood flows or the bone splinters. It is amazing how well this promotes confession; often the very first finger suffices. In recalcitrant cases, however, the screws may become stuck, so that they can not be removed except by cutting off the finger. We hope to develop better instruments so as to avoid this messiness."

Brother Paul forced himself to examine the thumbscrews. They were crude things, not screws at all but merely bands of metal, tightened by twisted wires. This was, after all, early in the Inquisition; in the next three centuries the torture instruments would develop greater sophistication—as Brother Thomas had anticipated. In the early days it was possible for subjects to die before they confessed and recanted; in the later days this seldom happened. Should he consider himself lucky—or unlucky?

"Here are the whips," Brother Thomas continued, showing the next niche. "We generally strip the suspect, bind him tightly, and whip him about the back and buttocks. This is the first degree of interrogation. If this is not effective, we stretch him on the ladder—'' He indicated an ordinary wooden ladder. ''And pour boiling fat over his body. Normally he will confess at this time.''

''How convenient.'' This stuff was crude, yet surely sufficient. Brother Paul was sure that he himself could not withstand such tortures. Yet, knowing that many Waldenses, whose only crime was their belief in the original precepts of Jesus Christ and the sanctity of the Holy Bible, would be routed out and similarly tortured if he yielded—how *could* he yield? He thought of the thankful old woman, racked on the ladder, and of the sick little girl with thumbscrews on her thin little fingers. Something very like Satanic rage clouded his vision.

''Suppose the suspect is innocent?'' Brother Paul inquired, surprised to find no quaver in his voice. ''What would your torture avail when a man has nothing to confess?''

''There *are* no innocent suspects,'' Brother Thomas said with chilling conviction. ''There are only taciturn heretics. Those who resist the preparatory interrogation are then subject to the second degree, called ordinary torture.'' He indicated a rope strung over a beam. ''This is for the strappado. The suspect's arms are tied behind his back. He is then hoisted into the air and weights are attached to his feet in order to wrench his shoulders from their sockets without shedding his blood or marking him.''

Dislocation of limbs. That meant that even if the hapless prisoner were released thereafter, he would probably never regain his former health. But of course he would not be released; his agony would end only in death. The prospect sickened Brother Paul, yet morbid curiosity forced him to inquire further: ''And if his taciturnity persists?''

''Then we must regretfully apply the third degree, called extraordinary torture. This is squassation. This resembles strappado, except that he is hoisted higher, then suddenly dropped to within a few inches of the floor. Because stones weighing as much as a hundred kilograms are attached to his feet, his arms are instantly disjointed and his whole body stretched cruelly. Three applications are deemed sufficient to cause death.''

Had they used the kilogram as a unit of measure of weight in medieval France? Regardless, that was more than the weight of a man. By any measure, the business was grim enough! "And if even this does not bring confession?''

"The surviving subject may then be interrogated by special means.'' The Dominican showed a crude pair of pincers. "These are heated in the fire, and when red-hot are used to tear the flesh. Or he may be seated in a metal chair placed over the fire itself so that his posterior slowly cooks. His hands or feet may be cut off. Or—''

"I think that suffices,'' Brother Paul said. Was there a place he could safely vomit?

"I am glad to hear that.'' The look Brother Thomas turned on him was compounded of victory, relief, and barely suppressed horror. *How can we know the dancer from the dance?* Brother Paul thought, appreciating the deepest meaning of the line from W. B. Yeats' poem with sudden intensity. What nostalgia for that 500-year future he felt! How could the Friar live with the conscience of the Juggler within him? Satan was surely testing him as severely as he was testing Brother Paul. "Come upstairs, where our scribe will record your statement.''

"You misunderstand,'' Brother Paul said. "I have no confession to make—except for my belief in the timeless and measureless beneficence of God.''

Disappointment—and muted hope. "You renounce your heretical belief, and take sanctuary in the bosom of the Holy Mother Church?'' Which would mean capitulating and yielding up the information and producing the complete Waldens' Tarot deck from memory, as well as betraying all the Waldenses he already had encountered. Lee did not want to participate in the torture of his friend as surely as Brother Paul had not wanted to hammer a nail through the wrist of his friend on the cross. But Lee also did not want to see the Waldenses persecuted. But he had to play his part faithfully, seeing no way out. "I warn you, you can not escape from our power; no ruse, no false recantation will avail." For him, it would be best if Brother Paul escaped so that neither torture nor betrayal occurred. Thus, this covert suggestion: *at least TRY to escape our power.* Brother Paul might be able to kill himself in the attempt, and that would be better than the Churchly alternatives.

"I mean that I have more than sufficient understanding of the specific instruments of the Church's beneficence," Brother Paul said, gesturing at the assembled torture devices. "Now I must retire to consider my decision."

"Of course." Brother Thomas guided him out, locking the dread chamber behind them. It wouldn't do to have anyone sneaking in here and playing with the instruments! "You may consider as long as you wish—but I regret you must do so without the benefit of water."

Thirst—a most effective inducement! The longer Brother Paul delayed, the worse it would get. Had Lee known of his sensitivity to thirst, dating from his childhood misery, or had it merely been a lucky guess? His torture had already begun!

Back in his chamber, Brother Paul re-examined the barred window. No hope there; it was completely solid, and it opened to an inner court. He would have to depart by the regular passages and doors—which would surely be guarded. Of course he had special physical skills; he could overcome the monks, rendering them safely unconscious by careful judo strangles during the night—

No. First, he was ill; his pneumonia had abated during this rest, but he could still feel its variable fever and the catch in his breath, signaling the involvement of his lungs. Violence and flight would quickly throw him into a potentially fatal relapse—but not so rapidly as to prevent them from nursing him back to health for the torture. Second, he knew that these monks were merely actors to the extent they had any tangible existence at all; he had no moral right to practice violence on them.

Yet the alternative to escape was torture—or betrayal. If he were tortured, he might confess anyway—but possibly the others would be restrained by the same considerations that restrained him—reason, friendship, and ethics—and ease off after token punishment. Then he might be able to get through. Yet if Lee played his role with complete integrity that torture would *hurt*. So the impasse remained.

There was a delicate knock on his door. "I'm here," he called sourly. As if there were any question!

The door opened. Yvette stood there. She had changed her attire; now she was more Italian in style, her hair braided and bound circularly about her head like a coronet. Her dress was closely contoured about her upper body with sleeves closing in firmly about her wrists and the front molded exactly to the shape of her full bosom. The neckline was almost straight from the curves of her shoulders across the uppermost swell of her breasts. In back it became a cape, whose excess material had to be held out of the way by hand. In all, it was strikingly like the costuming in the earliest Tarot cards and most attractive to the male eye. But of course that was the way of Amaranth; in whatever role she played, she had strong sex appeal. The question was, did she have anything else?

"Come," she murmured conspiratorily. "The King has granted you audience."

"What?" He had been distracted by the costume.

"King Charles VI," she said, winking. "I told him of your magic cards, and he is interested. This is our chance!" She took him by the arm and drew him on.

Well, at best it was a chance to make a break. Brother Paul suffered himself to be guided through the silent halls and out into a chariot whose canopy descended to close off the outside view entirely. The ride was rough, but quite private, jammed in with Yvette.

She turned to him, enjoying it. Apparently his prior rebuff had fazed her only temporarily; like a healthy young animal, she had bounced back for another try. And bounce she did; her breasts threatened to detach themselves entirely from the dress. She might as well have been naked above the waist. Yet what use was this to him? Eunuch that he was, the stimulation was all in his mind.

"I do so admire a man with discipline," she said. "If only you perform this service for the King—"

Brother Paul merely shrugged. He was sorry he could not see the great city of Paris. Even in the fourteenth century, it must be something! Obviously Yvette was working with Brother Thomas, carrot and stick under the Devil's direction, trying to lure him into the betrayal he resisted. So both of them took care that he should not pick up any notion of the local geography that might facilitate his escape.

Of course he could simply jump out of the chariot and run—but he was sure guards on horseback were following. No chance there! He had to bide his time, waiting his opportunity—if it ever came.

The palace was impressive both in scale and primitiveness. They entered a huge central hall from which doors led to the kitchen; he knew this by the constantly trooping servants carrying loaded platters of fish, venison, boiled meat, fritters, and pastries.

Suddenly Brother Paul was hungry. This entrance must have been carefully timed to expose him to the main meal of the day. He had been so concerned with thirst he had not realized he had not yet eaten today. He certainly knew it now!

"The King doesn't seem to have arrived yet," Yvette observed. Brother Paul was uncertain how she could tell since this room was filled with people lustily feasting at the long tables. Many of them were well-dressed in fur-lined robes and capes; since the air was chill, Brother Paul wished for heavier clothing herself.

She noticed. "Oh, are you cold? Come over here by the fire." And indeed, there was a raised hearth in the center of the hall with a great fire blazing. But there was no flue. The smoke rose and spread voluminously until it found egress through an aperture high in the ceiling. Well, at least this bonfire was warm! No wonder they needed a large dining hall; otherwise the smoke would stifle everything.

"Let me fetch you some food and wine," Yvette offered solicitously.

Temptation indeed! "Is that permitted?"

"Of course. You are here for audience with the King; he would not let it be bruited about that you were not treated properly. You will always eat well here."

That was not precisely what he had meant. Well, he would experiment. "If I could just have something to drink—"

"If the King enters, there'll be a fanfare and silence. You must face the royal entourage and bow. Otherwise, just stay here and keep warm." She traipsed off, hips swinging beautifully in the gown as she marched toward the nearest table. Now came the test: did this role allow her to abate his thirst, undermining the Friar's coercion?

Brother Paul glanced about. What would stop him from walking out right now while he was unattended? Apart from hunger and thirst. His eye caught that of a guard standing near the wind baffle at an exit. Unattended? Ha!

He refocused his attention on something more positive: the groaning tables of food. Multiple dishes had been set out simultaneously, and with a little analysis he was able to identify a number of them with fair certainty. Beef marrow fritters, a popular medieval dish; large cuts of roast meat, origin dubious; saltwater and freshwater fish; broth with bacon; blancmange, which was shredded chicken blended with rice, boiled in almond milk, seasoned with sugar, and cooked until thick. Surprising how much he remembered once he put his hunger-sharpened mind to it! He hoped Yvette brought him some of that!

But first he hoped she brought him something to drink. She had not answered his plea directly; until he had that drink, he could not be certain this was not merely a refinement of the torture. Maybe he would be allowed all he wanted of thirst-producing food, without liquid.

Dogs chewed on the bones and scraps under the table. No problem with waste disposal here! The diners tore

fragments of meat from the main roasts with their
hands, openly licking off their fingers before grabbing
again. One noble evidently had a cold; he blew his nose
noisily with his bare finger and thumb, wiped the digits
off on his robe, and fished with them in another stew
for a succulent chunk. There were no napkins or eating
utensils.

There was a sound like that of a horn, followed by a
brief, astonished silence. The fanfare announcing the
King? No, a false alarm; someone had broken wind so
vociferously as to be audible above the tremendous clat-
ter of the meal. People in that vicinity edged this way
and that, making exaggerated faces and snufflings, but
it was impossible to tell who was the culprit. Obviously
a meal like this was bound to produce considerable
flatulence, but the proscription against audible venting
was strong. Brother Paul was reminded of Mark
Twain's commentary on the subject, titled *1601*—supposedly a conversation between Queen Elizabeth of
England and her courtiers, including William
Shakespeare. "The pit itself hath furnished forth the
stink," Brother Paul murmured, quoting the famous
playwright's response when accused of authoring the
stench. "And heaven's artillery hath shook the globe in
admiration of it." A fitting comment for this sequence
spawned by the Devil, the Lord of Air. And how did the
Biblical "Wind of God" relate? Could the Suit of
Swords of the Tarot actually embrace flatulence?

But now Yvette was back. She had assembled a splendid platter for him: brewet—pieces of meat in thin cin-
namon sauce; eels in a thick spicy puree; frumenty,
which was a thick pudding of whole wheat grains and
almond milk enriched with egg yokes and colored with
saffron; venison; and several obscure blobs he hoped
were edible by his modern definitions. And—bless
her!—the spiced wine he had requested. The abatement
of thirst!

What a contrast this plate was to the poor fare of the
peasants! But no eating utensils. He could of course employ his fingers, but didn't want to emulate the slobbish
manners he had observed here.

"Use the trencher," Yvette suggested delicately. That was Amaranth speaking, misinterpreting her part; the true medieval lady would not have realized his problem.

Oh, yes—the trencher. A thick slice of stale bread about fifteen centimeters long: the all-purpose pusher, sop, spoon, and plate. Essential in a situation like this.

Brother Paul scooped up some frumenty and washed it down with a gulp of wine. Hoo! That stuff was strong! They had to spice it to cover its rabid bite! Yet if his memory of conditions in the medieval cities was true, this stuff was a good deal safer than water to drink; the alcohol cleaned out the other contaminants. The water of the upper reaches of the Rhine might be sanitary, but Paris was far from that wilderness.

He was allowed to eat undisturbed, standing by the fire, and to drink several tumblers of wine. His head began to feel light; he would have preferred something nonalcoholic, but his thirst overrode that consideration. Apparently it was true: the Inquisition had no power in the palace of the King. If he wanted to avoid torture. . . .

Yvette peered past the pillars that supported the roof. "King Charles has not come," she remarked. "I shall have to take you to his bedroom."

"Is that proper?" Brother Paul inquired.

"Oh, yes—I have been there often," she said, leading the way. Well, he had asked.

But the bedroom, set on a higher level than the main hall, was more than a sleeping place. There was a fireplace set against the wall, and it had a genuine flue so that the smoke was not intrusive. Courtiers abounded; this was evidently a semi-public receiving hall.

The King reclined on his great square canopied bed. The thing was like a chariot, and he the charioteer. He wore a turban-like headdress instead of a crown, but his ornate embroidered robe showed his rank. Regardless, Brother Paul knew him—for he was Therion. As Lee had progressed from heretic to Dominican, Therion had gone from Jew to Monarch. Was Satan taking care of his own?

King Charles VI of France looked up and spied them. "Hey, my pretty!" he exclaimed. "Come up for a kiss!"

Yvette went to him—and suddenly Brother Paul, remembering the conclusion of the Black Mass, could stand it no more. He turned and stalked out of the room.

And Brother Thomas was there before him, present at a suspiciously opportune occasion. "Now you comprehend the alternative. Would it not be better to return to the bosom of the Church?"

The alternative: reprieve through the intercession of the mistress of the Mad King. And Amaranth would play that part faithfully, as the minionette of the Monarch, to spare Brother Paul from torture. The cards were only a pretext. It was not intellectual gratification Charles most craved.

Brother Paul's real choice was between torture—and betrayal of his relation with Amaranth. Whatever that relation might be.

He suffered an indefinable terror. There seemed to be a heavy weight on his chest, interfering with his breathing, yet nothing was visible. He felt completely helpless in the face of this unknown menace—yet there was an ironically voluptuous element. Was he a masochist—one who derived erotic pleasure from pain?

Then an extremely shapely young woman entered the room, whose very presence seemed to illuminate the air. It was Yvette, nude, glowing. He knew he must avoid her, and as she approached he struck at her with his fist; but he felt nothing, only air. She was an illusion.

Then she touched him, drawing off the covers and removing his night clothes, laying him bare before her. Though he resisted with all his strength he could do nothing, for his hands passed through her while hers handled him with substance. He was invisibly bound, and could not move from the bed or change his supine position. He had to lie there in stasis, except for his uselessly flailing arms.

She leaned down over him, her fine breasts dangling

ponderously, and kissed him on the mouth, and her lips were solid. He could not turn his head away or even close his eyes. He remembered that one of the Saints had bitten off his own tongue to prevent contamination in a similar situation, but his jaws were immobile.

Her deep kiss stirred him immeasurably despite his reluctance. He concentrated on diversionary thoughts, on icy-cold showers, on trigonometric functions, and his body relaxed.

But the nymph had only begun to fight. More correctly, to love. Small difference! She moved down and leaned over his hips, lifting up his member and placing it between her smooth breasts. She pressed them together with her hands, his member sandwiched between their protean fullness. The flesh flowed warmly around it, enclosing it with gentle hydraulic pressure. She kneaded her own breasts, and the motions were transmitted to him muted yet quintessentially potent. Under that firm yet fluid incentive, his member swelled until it seemed ready to burst, becoming simultaneously as rigid as cast iron.

But I'm castrate! he cried in his mind. *This can't be happening! I can't react sexually!*

Obviously he *could* react! She had seen his empty scrotum—empty? It didn't exist at all!—and knew his handicap. What did she know that he didn't?

Satisfied with her priming operation, the nymph let go her breasts and lifted them away with a flex of her upper torso. Now his member angled up stiffly. She climbed upon him, moving carefully to slant her posterior and take him neatly into her hot, moist orifice. Once more he struck at her with his fist—and once more her visible body was no more than smoke. Yet her vulva moved down, melting about him, and he felt himself penetrating her, being enveloped. At last the connection was complete, full depth.

Now she brought her lips to his again, and as she kissed him she slid her body slowly up and down, drawing it slickly along his torso and causing his penetration to diminish, then increase again. Her tongue slid between his lips and played with his own in counterpoint. It was the rhythm of coitus, and he had no defense.

It continued for seconds, then minutes; then it seemed an hour. The weight on his body was the same; before it had been nameless, but now it was female. His terror had been replaced by disgust: a mere transmutation of the same emotion. This was merely torture in a different form.

And he realized: his masculinity was like that of a boy before puberty. He could be stimulated to the point of urgency—but could never climax. This could go on until his penis blistered. . . .

The door crashed open. Brother Thomas stood there, glowering. Yvette evanesced: she faded gently away, leaving Brother Paul lying naked with erection.

"So you have lain with a succubus!" Brother Thomas thundered. "Pollution of Satan! You are an unrecalcitrant heretic!"

Brother Paul could not deny it.

Now he was in the torture chamber. Brother Thomas sprinkled Holy Water on the instruments. "Bless these holy mechanisms, God's tools on Earth," he intoned. "Thy will be done."

He put both Brother Paul's hands together in the vise and screwed it inexorably closed. Brother Paul screamed, but the pressure did not abate. The agony quickly became intolerable. The fingernails cracked; blood spurted forth like a series of ejaculations, one from each digit. Flesh and bone were pulped together. He knew he would never be able to use his hands again.

And was that not fitting? His hands—during his stasis, they alone had been free. They had not touched the succubus because she did not exist; she was a phantasm. Yet hands had touched *him*—and what hands could these have been except his own? He had touched his own lips, poked his finger in his own mouth, and stroked his own body under the guise of flailing at the apparition. He had manipulated and stimulated his own member in a desperate effort to refute his demoniac castration. His own hands were the instruments of his attempted pollution; they had now paid the Churchly penalty.

The scribe-witness held his quill ready. "We will record your recantation now," Brother Thomas said.

Brother Paul suffered a lucid moment. "Shove it up your ass," he said delicately.

"The mouth must pay the penalty for blasphemy," Brother Thomas said sadly. Now he inserted the metal choking-pear into Brother Paul's mouth, and rotated the handle so that the two halves of it pressed pitilessly apart, forcing open the mouth until the hinge of the jaw broke. The temperomandibular joint. He could no longer even scream effectively—

Yet out of his mouth he had spoken heresy, supporting the gross impertinence of the Waldenses. He had uttered the sacrilegious interpretations of the Tarot and demeaned the Holy imperatives of the loving Mother Church. Thus the mouth that had so gravely transgressed was indeed punished: an eye for an eye, a tooth for a tooth—

No! he cried internally. *I may be a sinner, but the Waldenses are good people and the Tarot is valid. I cannot betray them!*

Brother Paul woke in sweat. It had been a nightmare—a demon of sleep. His hands were whole, his jaw hinged.

As he lay there and let his sweat dissipate, he realized that the signs of nightmare had been evident all along. The succubus had looked like Yvette—like Amaranth. That meant she was a creation from his memory, rather than an external character of the Animation. Real women did not act like that, which was why men had to make do with the guilty dreams. And the torture instruments—the hand-press and choking-pear—these had been levered by threaded metal screws. They were more sophisticated devices, more technologically progressed; they existed in the later centuries of the Inquisition, not here in the 14th century.

The whole thing had been a Freudian dream-within-a-dream, a mechanism of double censorship showing him the lusts and fears his own mind balked at admitting. Now he had reverted to the more general dream, which was this Animation—itself a vision sponsored by Satan in the original Animation. Now that he had seen what was buried within the triple prison—

Well, what about it? So he had lusts! So he feared pain! Weren't these natural feelings? The dream had only shown up the foolishness of his secrets!

Still, the local tortures were fully sufficient to the need. If he were tortured at *this* level of reality, he would surely yield up his information and betray his friends. Only in the exaggerated dream state was he bold enough to tell the Inquisition to shove anything, anywhere. No one could withstand such savage physical coercion indefinitely! Thus he could only hurt himself by holding out.

Yvette opened the door and stood there a moment, a lamp in her hand, like the succubus she had seemed to be. She glided in. "Juggler—I came in haste before dawn, lest we both suffer. You acted precipitously by walking out on the King. But I convinced him you had a sudden call of nature and fled lest you disgrace yourself in his presence like old Blowhard in the dining room. Charles is so fascinated by the notion of the magic cards he is willing to forgive your indiscretion if you return to him immediately." She stood over him, an ethereal female spirit, breathtakingly lovely. If he were to draw her down now, remove her dress, would she perform, after all, like the succubus? He suffered abrupt, savage temptation, yet did not act. "I beg of you, friend," she continued. "Come with me before the Holy Office takes you below. Once the torture starts even the King will not intercede, lest he suffer excommunication by Pope Clement."

Excommunication by the Pope! The Church knew no limits to its abuses! On top of that, Clement was known historically as an antipope, though his election had been no more political than that of a number of authorized popes. Perhaps his major crime was that he did not reside in Rome. The Church forced complete compliance with its dictates, yet could not even agree on its

Pope, or that the Office was more important than the residence. Suddenly Brother Paul decided. "I will come with you."

"You will?" she asked, amazed.

Her surprise made him pause. *What was he doing?* He knew that giving the cards to the King would be the same as confessing to Brother Thomas. In either case the Waldenses in France, the Holy Roman Empire, and perhaps even in Italy itself would be routed out by the Inquisition. They would be tortured and perhaps exterminated, as the Albigensians had been.

Yet there was no way he could hold out against the tender persuasions of the Church. It was not a choice between right and wrong, but between obvious wrong and subtle wrong. The only question was whether he would yield up the information before or after suffering dislocation of his arms or destruction of his fingers. Since he was bound to capitulate, he might as well do it comfortably, feasting at the King's table and dallying with the King's mistress.

Shame! Yet what better course was there? His sense of personal dignity, the last of the qualities in himself he valued, had been beaten down. He had been degraded by this Hell stage by stage, until he could not maintain his pride intact any longer. So he would do what he had to do—if only he knew what that was.

Well, he could run away. They could not watch him *all* the time, and in time his health should improve, and if he started out describing unimportant cards of the deck he might get a chance to make his break before the key cards came up. By accepting King Charles' offer, he was buying time and leeway—

No! He would not bargain in bad faith. If he gave his word to produce the cards for the Mad King, he would have to do the job. His pride had not yet descended below that level.

Though the originators of the Tarot suffered their special genocide in consequence? What kind of pride was that?

Yvette was leading him on, in more senses than one, out of the silent monastery into the hooded chariot away from the place of torture. The eastern horizon was brightening. He wished he could see the sunrise!

She paused to kiss him. "I'm so glad you have come to your senses! Everything is ready. I shall introduce you to the artist immediately."

"Artist?"

"The one who will paint the cards as you direct. His name is Jacquemin Gringonneur. It is imperative that the work proceed quickly, for the King is impatient and already just a bit wroth with you. He is a young man, not yet twenty-five years of age, but let that not deceive you. He is capable of truly mad acts."

"I'm sure he is," Brother Paul agreed, thinking of the historical Charles VI who assumed the throne as a boy of twelve and became insane at age twenty-four—and of Therion now playing that part. But he was more concerned with his own problem. It seemed the only practical and honorable way remaining to him to save himself from torture and to save the Waldenses from destruction—was suicide. That must have been hovering somewhere in his secret mind when he agreed to come to the palace. So long as the Juggler lived, in any form, the Waldenses were not safe, and the Tarot itself was in danger of obliteration. That last was especially ironic: the rendering of the Tarot in a beautiful court edition, publicizing it—would destroy it because of the extermination of its originators. It would cease to have meaning and become—just another pack of cards.

Did he have the courage to sacrifice himself? Was this the pass that prior investigators of the Animation phenomenon had come to? Very soon he would find out!

The chariot stopped. Yvette led him this time to a garden within the palace estate concealed from outside by a stone wall. "Wait here," she said. "I will fetch the artist."

As she spoke, the dawn sun emerged from behind clouds to shine brilliantly over the wall into the garden. Its first beam struck a sundial set on a pedestal. Tall flowers waved in the morning breeze; were they sunflowers so early in the season? Yet he could not know precisely what season it was; he had assumed spring, but it might be fall. The sun was so brilliant the beams of it speared out in sixteen directions, quartering the quarter circles, illuminating all the world.

Brother Paul stood there, holding Yvette's hand, loath to let her go despite his judgment of her nature. After all, she was doing it for him; she could have seduced King Charles without bothering with any Tarot deck. By her morality, she was doing right. It was wrong to condemn her merely because her values differed somewhat from his own. And somehow it was easier to forgive a lovely woman.

Suddenly, in an incandescence rivaling that of the sun, he had his revelation. *He had another alternative*—one that would satisfy all parties, hurting none—except perhaps the Inquisition itself.

"Let me tell you of the first card I shall describe to the court artist," he said to her. "This one is dedicated to you, my pretty minionette."

"For me?" She smiled, flattered.

"For you, child of the garden. It is a scene of this very place at dawn with the wall and the flowers—and two young people, virtually children before the glories of creation, naked as it were like Adam and Eve—"

"Sir?" she inquired archly.

"Clothed, then," he said with a smile. He had visualized the card of the Holy Order of Vision Tarot, but of course that was anachronistic. "Bathed in the brilliant light of the golden disk. And the name of this picture is—The Sun."

"The Sun!" she repeated, pleased.

Her pleasure was no less than his own. For now he knew his course. He would create a Tarot for the King—but not precisely the Tarot of the Waldenses. He would truncate it, eliminating certain cards of the Triumphs so that the Inquisition would never be able to divine the full meaning of the deck. Some cards the Dominicans already knew about, so these Brother Paul had to retain, though he would delete key symbols so as to render the meanings obscure. Since the pictures were already designed to be interpreted on two levels, the genuine and the superficial, this part was easy; he would never betray the true nature of any picture. And if he could eliminate entirely as many as eight Triumphs and abolish in one bold stroke the whole of the key suit of Spirit—

He smiled again, still holding her hand as they stood before the wall. Mad King Charles VI would never know the difference; he cared only for the beauty of the cards (or the beauty of the lady who sold him on the project) and their supposedly magic properties. Brother Thomas would not realize that the deck was incomplete for some time because he had not had an opportunity to count the cards of the full deck, and Brother Paul would present the cards in mixed order. He would retain the first half-dozen of the Waldens' order intact just in case. Given the time it would take the artist to complete each one, especially if Brother Paul arranged to be picky about details—so that the King might have the very *best* deck of course—it could be months before the deck was done. By then, who could say for sure whether it was complete or which items might be missing? Lee would know, but as Brother Thomas he would not be able to prove it—not by the rules of this game.

Brother Paul would in fact create a new Tarot, consisting of a score or so of Triumphs, and four suits of thirteen cards each—well, maybe fourteen, no harm in that. A full deck of around 75 to 80 cards, each with its superficial title and interpretation concealing the real message. The Inquisition could play with copies of this deck as long as it chose; it would only waste its effort. The Waldenses would not long be fooled by a "Juggler" who never spoke of the Ghost, or Nature, or Vision, or the Lady of Expression, or the Two of Aura. Or who, for that matter, failed to discuss the underlying meaning of the Triumph known popularly as The Sun.

For the Waldenses interpretation of that last card was—

Triumph.

VI

Reason: 25

The slime rose up to criticize the work of art. "There you sit," it said, "serene and content in your ebony gloss—yet utterly useless. You think you are beautiful, but you are only a molded husk. You are glazed, but you are brittle and shallow. Where is there any softness in you? Where is that fine slippery resiliency that is the heritage of the commonest blob of grease? Where is the rippling undulation of fluid motion, the flexibility and warmth of dishwater? You lack the variety of size and shape and color that glorifies the contents of every garbage can. You cannot take flight in the soft air in the free manner known to every particle of dust swept from the floor. You cannot appreciate the refractive art of the dirty window pane in the sunlight. You can never immortalize your substance by leaving a pretty stain on the wall. And never, never will you bring that worthy satisfaction of a job well done that every human being obtains from cleaning up rubbish like me."

"You are not beautiful—you are a monstrosity."

The work of art listened and was ashamed. It fell off the antique table and shattered on the *floor. The slime looked on as the housewife swept up the myriad fragments, all shapes and colors and sizes, and dumped them sadly into the wastebasket.*

"Now you are beautiful," said the slime, and it vanished down the drain.

"Well," Satan said, "are you satisfied about the origin and nature of Tarot?"

"Yes," Brother Paul agreed. "It was some lesson. But how did I acquit myself in the matter of the wish?"

"You passed," Satan said frankly. "I thought I had you there for a while, caught between sin and torture, but you threaded the needle. Of course you compromised yourself somewhat by consciously misleading the Inquisition—but the point of the dilemma was that you were left not with a choice between good and evil—"

"But with a choice between evils," Brother Paul filled in. "That was the Hell of it."

"Precisely. Anyone can tell good from evil if he wants to in a limited situation; not everyone can comprehend evil well enough to deal with it sensibly. You did an excellent job, and I fear you are not destined to reside in Hell—but there remain two wishes. Often a person who surmounts the most devastating challenge succumbs to the minor one. Shall we proceed?"

What use was there in waiting? Brother Paul wanted to be through with this awful examination! "Proceed," he said, buoyed by his triumph. What could be worse than the medieval Hell he had just been through?

"Name your second wish."

"I wish to know the evolution and future of Tarot."

Satan flicked his tail with a snap like that of a whip. "So shall it be—"

"But not in physical incorporation!" Brother Paul cried. "I just want to *perceive* it, not *live* it!" Would Satan accept the modification? One physical experience of history had been more than enough!

"Very well. Bye-bye," Satan said, making a little

wave with four fingers. That gesture, by any other entity, would have seemed effeminate.

Brother Paul felt himself rising. He looked down —and there was his body, standing in Satan's office. Satan and the furniture remained in place. As Brother Paul continued to rise, he saw the secretary's office too—she was cleaning her nails in the timeless manner of the type—and the surrounding rooms. He could see through the walls, focusing on any portion he wished, seeing that portion clearly: a variable X-ray vision.

So this was what soul travel was like! His aura had detached from the host body and was now traveling and perceiving by itself. He had, as it were, become one with the fifth suit of Tarot.

There were scores of offices—hundreds—thousands —too many to count. Each was a mere cell in the total, connected to its neighbors by vessels, forming cohesive larger organs. "And each in the cell of himself is almost convinced of his freedom," he thought, remembering the words of the poet Auden. The whole mass formed into a monstrous building thousands of stories tall, irregular in outline, supported by two massive round columns—the shape of Satan Himself.

Then on up, out, he viewed the environs of Hell with its own myriad cells, each with its special tortures. And finally he burst into the bright day of the world. He was out of Hell at last—but only by the spirit.

Now he coasted to the continent of medieval Europe, aware of the date without knowing how, and to the city of Paris. Still he had no chance to look at it, for he phased in to the bedroom of the King. Charles VI was abating his melancholy by playing with his Gringonneur Tarot. The deck was pretty much as Brother Paul had edited it: twenty-two Triumphs, four suits, seventy-eight cards in all. The mere shadow of True Tarot, but a private victory for Brother Paul!

Because Charles liked companions for his gaming, he impressed his courtiers into Tarot playing sessions. It was fun for them; they became adept at inventing new interpretations for given cards and given spreads that catered to the King's ego. Soon more decks were made, and it became fashionable to play Tarocchi all over France, and Europe, wherever they could be afforded. Tarot became a status symbol. Quickly variations appeared, associated with special locales or interests. Some decks had as many as forty-one Triumphs—the word soon simplified to Trumps—consisting of the "basics" Brother Paul had retained plus twelve signs of the astrological zodiac, plus the four "elements" (he really had succeeded in eliminating the fifth one!), and certain Virtues. Some decks had eight suits. But none restored the particular cards Brother Paul had hidden: eight Triumphs and the entire suit of Aura.

The Waldenses, of course, knew the truth—but they never made it public. And so they survived despite persecutions and plagues, eventually surfacing as a legitimate Christian sect with branches all over the world, even in America. In later centuries, when heresy became respectable under the name of Protestantism, the secret could have been safely told—but by then it was no longer important enough to recall. Persecution had made the original Tarot what it was; in the absence of persecution, it faded. The truncated Tarot became a virtual property of the Gypsies and other fringe elements of society who used it primarily for fortune telling. And so the secret remained, forgotten at last even by the Waldenses themselves.

The development of printing at the end of the fifteenth century brought playing cards to the masses. But many people found the full deck too cumbersome. As the cards sifted down from the nobles and the rich to the poor, full pictures were too expensive. More cards were dropped until the deck returned almost to the original form that the Waldenses had hidden their illustrated lecture in. Of all the Trumps only the Fool remained, now called the Joker. Sometimes a blank replacement card was also provided, the manufacturer's unwitting ghost of the Ghost. The Knights were banished, reducing each suit to thirteen cards. Thus the peasant deck came to rest at fifty-three cards—the number of weeks in the year plus one for the fraction left over. The symbols of the suits metamorphosed to the peasant level too: Swords converted to Bells, Pomegranates, or Parakeets, and then to Spades (Tarot really did beat its swords into plowshares!), Cups to Roses and to Hearts, Wands to Acorns to Clovers later called Clubs, and Coins to Leaves and to Diamonds. German cards of 1437 depicted hunting scenes, with suits of Ducks, Falcons, Stags, and Dogs. A later deck had sixteen suit signs: Suns, Moons, Stars, Shields, Crowns, Fish, Scorpions, Cats, Birds, Serpents, and others. People played games called Trappola, Hazard, Bassett, and Flush; and they gambled avidly. The cards had come of age—at the lowest common denominator.

But the "complete" Tarot continued as a subgenre with a strong appeal to persons interested in the occult. In Italy, Philippo Maria Visconti, Duke of Milan, loved cards and commissioned for a small fortune several expensive sets, including an elegant heraldic deck to commemorate the union of his daughter with the scion of Sforza in 1441. "Ah yes, the most beautiful of the classic decks," Brother Paul murmured soundlessly as he hovered, contemplating the cards in their original splendor. There was the Cardinal Virtue Justice pictured by a lady robed in a dress of spun silver, holding sword and scales, and in the background a knight galloping his charger. There was the Moon held by a lady's right hand while her left tugged at the cord securing her skirt: if the lunar symbol was too obscure for the viewer, the left hand made the female mystique somewhat more evident. Ah, woman: where would she be without her hinted secrets? And the card of the World, showing a walled city suspended between sky and sea. Cardinal Virtue Fortitude, showing a burly Hercules beating a lion with a club. Skeletal Death with his giant longbow. And Time with a bright blue cloak over a yellow tunic, hourglass in hand.

But Brother Paul could not stay. He had to move on, tracing the Tarot wherever it might lead. He saw a simplified, almost cartoon-figure Tarot emerge in Italy; this was easier for the peasants to understand, and it became very popular among the lowest classes. It was soon copied in France and called the Marseilles Tarot. Further variants developed over the decades, culminating in the famous Swiss Tarot classic of the eighteenth century. Unfortunately, the symbolism had suffered further degregation over the centuries, much of it by "iconographic transformation"—the misreading of the pictures and revised interpretation based on those misreadings. Time lost his hourglass and became the Hermit with a lamp, and the Hercules of Fortitude became a lady gently controlling the lion, the card labeled Strength.

Experts came along, vowing to restore the Tarot to its pristine state—but though the Inquisition had passed, they did not discover the missing cards. Count de Gebelin decided the Tarot was of ancient Egyptian origin, based on sevens: twice seven cards in each suit, three times seven Trumps (plus the numberless Fool; eleven times seven total (plus Fool). The name itself, he said, derived from the Egyptian *tar*, meaning "road," and *ro*, meaning "royal." Therefore, Tarot translated as the "Royal Road of Life."

Brother Paul shook his head invisibly and moved on. He encountered a disciple of Gebelin called Aliette, a wigmaker by profession, who decided that the origin of Tarot dated back almost four thousand years to the general time of the Deluge. He reversed his name and used it to entitle his deck, adding a modest description of its worth: the Grand Etteila. Here the Lady Pope became the Lady Consultant, a lovely nude woman standing within a whirlwind; that card also bore his name, Etteila. The Kings and Queens became professional men and social ladies, and the Fool was Folly or Madness. The deck was well illustrated and very pretty—but Brother Paul was not inclined to linger.

Next he found Alphonse Louis Constant, who under the *nom de plume* Eliphas Levi traced Tarot back further yet to Enoch, the Biblical son of Cain. He tied it in with the Jewish Qabalah, aligning the Trumps to correspond to paths along the Qabalistic Tree of Life. Then Brother Paul saw Gerhard Encausse, who under the name of Papus aligned the Trumps to the twenty-two letters of the Hebrew alphabet. "Abraham the Jew would have loved that!" Brother Paul commented and moved on.

At last he approached the twentieth century. There was the Order of the Golden Dawn, and there was Arthur Edward Waite, designing yet another "corrected" Tarot. Waite made the Fool into a saintly figure with the dog a prancing pet instead of a seat-biting menace, and the notorious Lady Pope became a virginal High Priestess. He converted one of the Devil's imps into a full-breasted nude woman suggestive of Eve, and he dabbled generally with the symbolism like an editor blue penciling a manuscript he did not understand. And of course he failed to restore the Hermit to Time. Paul Foster Case, another *Dawn* member, refined the images, retaining all Waite's errors for his B.O.T.A. (Builders of the Adytum) deck, and Brother Paul's own Holy Order of Vision further refined the Case variant for its private Tarot.

But Brother Paul now discovered he could no longer accept the Vision Tarot. It had only partial relation to the truth as he now saw it. "Oh, Satan—you have divested me of something I valued," he said. "I was satisfied with the Vision Tarot, believing it to be the most refined and authentic deck available—until I went to Hell."

Nevertheless, he moved on. Aleister Crowley was another *Dawn* member who had to dabble. He converted Fortitude to Lust with the nude woman voluptuously bestriding the multi-headed beast, one of her hands resting on the animal's penis while the other supported a cup like a filling womb against a background of sperm and egg cells. His Devil most resembled a monstrous phallus with a buck goat superimposed. Justice became Adjustment, Temperance became Art, Judgment became Aeon, the Hanged Man was castrate (Brother Paul suffered a sudden shock of empathy), and the Hermit—remained the Hermit. Brother Paul threw up his invisible hands and moved on. Now he knew the theoretical identity of his Bad Companion and wasn't sure he cared to know more.

Yet the Tarot variations multiplied. One group used mediums and a ouija board to derive a "New" Tarot quite different from all prior decks. There was also a military Tarot, and an animal Tarot, and a nude-woman Tarot and a Star Maiden Cosmic Tarot and even a Devil's Tarot—

"Enough, Satan!" Brother Paul cried soundlessly. "They are all variants of the meaningless deck I foisted on the world, interpreted to destruction by idiots! Let me center on something meaningful, not this interminable proliferation! And let me interact at least a *little*!" If this was the life of a ghost or traveling soul, it was frustrating enough to be another version of Hell. In assimilating the world's knowledge, the ghost also assimilated its follies—and could do nothing to abate them.

"So shall it be," Satan agreed. The cards flew up, exploding from their packs to fill the scene with multiple pictures like the conclusion to the story *Alice in Wonderland*, spinning about him with increasing rapidity until their images blurred and he was in a wash of confusion.

Help!

Was it his own cry? No, he knew he was in the power of Satan and needed no other assistance; the cry had come from elsewhere, perhaps telepathically. In his aural state he might be receptive to such a message.

Brother Paul tried to orient on the soundless plea, but he remained in chaos. Colors swirled about him, yielding no fixed forms. It was as though he floated through a waterless ocean, unbreathing, for his traveling aura had no lungs. Disembodied yet sentient, he was unable to control his whereabouts without Satan's imperative.

My soul drifts free, he thought.

But not without purpose. Someone had called for help, and Brother Paul had received that plea and was drawn by that need.

Am I dead?

It was a flashing of light, the meaning in the flow. A spirit newly freed of its mortality, a soul rising toward

Nirvana or sinking toward Hell. If he could only reach it, help guide it—

I am a fool! it flashed.

Brother Paul began to learn how to navigate in this chaotic state. He oriented on the flashing voice. Of course this person was a fool—the Fool of Tarot. *Every* person was. Brother Paul moved along a corridor that opened ahead, not a special avenue exactly but a—

The person screamed. The Fool must have stepped off the precipice! That was the nature of Fools. So noble, idealistic, well intentioned—the epitome of the finest expectations of civilization. Yet also supremely impractical. Fools tended to get bitten in the posterior by unruly canines: anal sadism to gratify the spectators. Especially when practiced on an individual of lofty aspirations.

The journey was amazingly far, though not precisely long. He moved at impossible velocity through a veil he could not quite define. At last he saw the person who had summoned him. Flashing for help, it was no human being at all, yet not a creature like Antares either. This was a hideous animate disk harrow. A savagely ringed worm with laser lenses.

I need a guide! it flashed.

Brother Paul was taken aback. He had somehow anticipated a human being, not this flashing slash thing. Yet it seemed this *was* a creature in need. How could he refuse? "I will be your guide," he said almost before the thought was complete. Yet how could he guide when he was lost himself?

As he spoke, his setting filled in about him: the Station of the Holy Order of Vision with its important windmill turning behind him. His last conscious contact with the elements of nature and Tarot before he had been summoned to this unique quest, what seemed thousands of years ago. It was good to feel firm ground beneath his feet again; chaos really did not appeal.

Could he simply walk back into his former life at the Station, leaving all Hell behind him now? He was tempted to try! But first he had to help this entity who was in need, if he could.

What mode of thing are you? the creature demanded,

just as though it were the normal entity and he the weird monster. Well, its viewpoint was no doubt valid for it—and after what Brother Paul had learned about himself, he could well understand how monstrous he might seem to another sapience.

He suddenly realized that this was no part of his own framework, but that of the summoning creature. His setting of the Order Station was merely a bit of mocked-up background to make him seem more natural, much as a specimen in a modern zoo might be placed in a cage painted to resemble its home milieu. This was in fact—the future! He had traveled forward through time to a period far beyond his own mortal termination.

"No thing am I, though once a thing I was," Brother Paul said with a smile. He, like the Roman poet Vergil, author of the *Aeneid*, had been brought forward in time to assist one who knew of him. No wonder he had been so conscious of the Triumph of Time in the Tarot! "I lived on Planet Earth, circa 2000, in the time of the Fool emigration program that depleted our planet." He explained his origin in more detail, knowing it would be difficult for this entity to credit.

Sibling Paul of Tarot! the creature interrupted him. *The Patriarch of the Temple!*

Well, these confusions had to be expected. "No, I am merely Brother Paul, a humble human creature. No patriarch, no temple—the Holy Order of Vision is not that type. But I will help you all I can since you seem to be in need and have called, and I have heard, and this is my purpose in life—and it seems in death also. But I shall be able to help you better once I am oriented. Of what species, region, and time are you that you thus invoke me?"

To you, your repute may seem minor, the thing flashed. *But to me, a Slash of Andromeda 2,500 years of Sol after your time, there is no greater name than Sib—than Brother Paul. You are the creator of the Cluster Tarot, one of the great forces in the shaping of the contemporary scene.*

Cluster Tarot? Brother Paul did not place that one. Surely some misunderstanding there. For the moment, another matter was more pressing: the time span. Two thousand five hundred years after his time? That would be about the year 4,500! And this was a sapient creature of another galaxy, Andromeda! What a jump he had taken! "But who are you, friend? I can't just call you Slash, can I?"

I am Herald the Healer—though I am in sore need of healing myself!

"Ah, heraldry," Brother Paul said. "I have often admired the herald's art, though I supposed that would be forgotten in your century, if indeed it can really be known in Andromeda."

It survives, it flourishes, Herald flashed. *Especially in your Cluster Tarot.*

Brother Paul shook off the misplaced reference again. "No matter. Come, creature of the future: let us explore together. Where are we, and what is our purpose?"

And the Andromedan explained: he had been injured during a visit to the Planet Mars of System Sol in Segment Etamin in Galaxy Milky Way of the Cluster—injured by a laser strike from an enemy spaceship. He had been dug out of the rubble and taken to something called a Tarot Temple where they practiced Animation Therapy to reconstitute minds. Herald had conjured Brother Paul from the distant past to aid in this reorientation.

Did that mean that Herald of Andromeda was the real person while Brother Paul himself was a figment of the imagination of an entity 2,500 years yet uncreated? That was a difficult concept to accept completely! "I suffer from some confusion," Brother Paul said, feeling dizzy.

The Andromedan flashed a laser beam on him, and Brother Paul abruptly felt more secure. Apparently he could exist in this framework so long as his companion believed in him. After all, he had visited the human colony in the Hyades, in Sphere Nath, three hundred years after his time; this was merely a greater extension of that mechanism. *What do you wish to know, Sibling Patriarch?*

"Just call me Brother, if you don't mind." Brother Paul cast about for a suitable starting point to enable him to relate to this alien properly. "Let's start with this: why did you conjure a human being instead of a creature of your own type?" What did he really wish to know? *Everything*—but it was obviously not his purpose here to aggrandize his personal curiosity. Not directly at any rate. He had been on a quest for the future of Tarot, but that had to wait; his human conscience would not allow him to neglect an entity in need.

I loved a female of your species, the creature confessed.

This absolute alien loved a human girl? How was this possible? But Brother Paul concealed his confusion. "So did I, so did I! There is nothing like a sweet, pretty girl is there!"

Nothing in the Cluster! Herald agreed. *I was in Solarian host, and she*—

Solarian—that would be a creature associated with the star Sol—or a human being. And host—but better not to make assumptions. The way of Antares might not be that of Andromeda. "Let's start just a little further back," Brother Paul said. "This matter of—Solarian hosts?"

After your time, Herald said. *Naturally you have not encountered it. Today we shift from body to body, since our identities are incarnate in our auras. Transfer the aura—perhaps you call it soul—and*—

Confirmation! "The soul! You *can* move souls from body to body?"

We can. We do, Brother. Though I am a Slash of Andromeda, I can inhabit the body of one of your kind. In that form, I naturally react in the manner of—

"Ah, yes. As a human being, you could take an interest in a human girl. Sorry I was slow to grasp your meaning. No doubt if I were to occupy a Slash body, I would pay similar respects to Slash females." That seemed impossible; he could not at the moment imagine an animate light-emitting disk harrow with sex appeal. But intellectually he could concede the validity of the concept. "Yet you *are* of completely different species, so no lasting emotion exists—"

On the contrary! Aural love is absolute.

"Love is the Law—Love under Will," Brother Paul agreed—then paused, realizing that that was what Therion liked to say. Was Herald the Slash another manifestation of Therion ready to lead him into yet another aspect of Hell? Alien miscegenation, Slash breeding with Human?

No, it did not matter. Brother Paul had survived this much of Hell and perhaps been somewhat cleansed. He was not about to be led into further compromise. He would do what was right *because* it was right. If Herald were an aspect of Therion—well, who needed help more than Therion did? In fact, with the retrospect of several thousand years, he could not even call Therion evil; in the fourteenth century roles had been reversed with Lee playing the persecutor and Therion the persecutee. How did that little saying go? "There's so much good in the worst of us, and bad in the best of us, it ill behooves the most of us to talk about the rest of us." Whoever had said that had really understood human nature. Therion had a lot of good in him, many admirable qualities despite some appalling lapses. And surely Satan was cauterizing out those lapses by forcing him to play the role of an insane king. . . .

With that reconciliation of attitude, Brother Paul felt an exhilaration akin to Redemption. He *had* learned something by his experience in Hell. He had learned caution in judging, lest he be judged himself. Maybe in time he would master the art of forgiveness that he preached.

Love is the Law—Love under Will, Herald echoed in pretty flashes. *I do not know whether that is a universal truth, but it is true for me. I suffer grievously the loss of my Solarian bride. Life means little to me without her.*

"Tell me more about this," Brother Paul urged. "I do not know how I can help, but I will do what I can."

I cannot face it directly, yet.

"Approach it obliquely," Brother Paul said. "You summoned me—"

Yes. I was flashing through the Cluster Tarot Triumphs in order, in the standard reorientation program, and—

There it was again. Maybe he *was* here to learn the future of Tarot. If his own quest related to Herald's problem, he should check it out. "I am familiar with a number of versions of the Tarot deck, but not this 'Cluster' you mention. Does it most nearly relate to the Waite, or Thoth, or Light, or—?"

I know nothing of these names. It is the one you created on Planet Tarot. Don't you remember?

Brother Paul shook his head. "I have created no deck, except in the sense that I may have expurgated the original Waldens' deck to protect—"

Perhaps you called it by another name. It may be that it was termed Cluster after your death.

Brother Paul thought about that. He had not yet finished his life; he could not speak for what he might do in later years if he survived the Animation sequence. He *was* dissatisfied with conventional Tarot decks, including that of the Holy Order of Vision. Only the original Waldens deck suited him now, and that one had been lost to the world since 1392, though there was no longer any reason for it to be hidden.

It burst upon him like the Vision of Saint Paul: *he* could restore the Waldens deck and give it back to the world! He could undo the damage he had done, now that the world was safe for genuine Tarot. "That so-called Cluster deck—does it have five suits?"

Certainly.

"And thirty Triumphs? One hundred cards in all?"

You remember it now! That is the one. And the Ghost has fifteen alternate faces, for those who require forty-four Triumphs or an extra suit.

Fifteen faces for the Ghost card? *That* did not match the Waldens' deck! Still, the puzzle seemed to have been partly solved. "I believe what happened was that I restored the original Tarot, and later generations elaborated and retitled it. I deserve no credit for creating it; that belongs to the anonymous people six hundred years before my time. And I have nothing to do with any temple."

My knowledge of ancient history in alien Spheres is

inexact, Herald said diplomatically. *But I am certain you are the Founder*.

And who could say what might be attributed to him after his death when he could not protest? Pointless to discuss it further. "I came here to assist in your problem, not mine. What is most meaningful to you?"

There was some confusion, but in due course the Andromedan nerved himself to respond. *You ask what is meaningful to me? It is my Solarian child bride, burned for possession, though innocent—*

"Possession? Of what? A proscribed drug?"

Of alien aura.

"Oh. You said it was possible to transfer the soul from one body to another." This would have made very little sense if he hadn't interviewed Antares! "And some souls—some auras are not permitted in some bodies—some hosts? So they punish—"

Abruptly Herald projected the image of a castle: a medieval edifice of Earth complete with turrets and a moat as big as a lake. It was very like the structure Brother Paul had sought in the first Animation. This one was under siege with strange wheeled creatures driving along a gravel ramp or fill extending from one shore across the water toward the outer wall.

"The Tower of Truth!" Brother Paul breathed. "Or is it the Dungeon of Wrong?"

The Slash did not respond directly. The view expanded. The effect was of flying across the lake and into the forbidding island fortress. More soul travel!

In the central courtyard was a great bonfire—and in that fire, suspended from a bar, was a lovely nude young girl. The flames were leaping up around her legs which she vainly tried to lift out of the heat.

Her skin was an alien tint of green or blue, but her features were immediately familiar. "Carolyn!" Brother Paul gasped in sudden anguish. His daughter!

Herald flashed at him questioningly, and Brother Paul realized that the Slash did not perceive the same identity. The girl was not, could not be, the original Carolyn; she would have lived and died in the twenty-

first century. Yet this was her surrogate, perhaps her far
future descendent, his Daughter-image, the innocent
child. Here she had grown to early nubility—as well she
might in twenty-five centuries!—and she was beautiful.
If her character matched what Brother Paul had known,
it was no wonder Herald had loved her. To know her
was to love her, whatever the situation! Brother Paul
himself loved her—but that was not competitive with
Herald's love; it was the natural complement.

But such conjecture was a waste of thought in the
present crisis. "This was real?" Brother Paul demanded, appalled by the flames, the obvious and
horrible torture. *Carolyn—in the flames of Hell!* Had
Satan lied to him, sparing her from the sacrificial knife
at the Black Mass only to claim her in this far worse
fashion? "In this far future, this age of intergalactic empire and the concourse of myriad sapient species via the
miracle of the transfer of auras, this happens?" Yet obviously it did.

Oh, help me, Patriarch! She is my beloved!

The image disappeared, perhaps abolished by Brother
Paul's own revulsion. Patriarch? If he were sure that
any descendant of his would perish barbarically,
chained in flames, he would never beget the line! "In
the face of such a loss, there is little I can offer except
my own grief." But that would not solve anything! He
tried to continue: "Though I hope there is some feasible
way for you to find relief." How utterly, inanely callous
he sounded—yet if he had spoken the way he felt, it
would have been a cry of simple pain and horror: *oh,
Satan, you saved your worst torture until last!*

Then show it me! the creature flashed. *This Healer
needs healing!*

Show him—yet what *was* there? How could death
itself be negated? Especially when Brother Paul was
only visiting this time as an incorporeal aura. "Perhaps
a Tarot reading would help."

*This is the Temple of Tarot. But no mere Animation
can satisfy me long. I need reality, not illusion.*

An interesting comment in this situation. Brother
Paul had traversed so many levels of illusion he was not

sure whether he would ever recover reality. Still, he had to believe that some things were constant, and the Andromedan had a good, solid orientation. "The Tarot reveals reality. Shall we try a spread?"

The Cluster Satellite Spread is best.

"I haven't heard of that one. Suppose you describe it, and I'll lay it out." Brother Paul found a deck of cards in his hand. He shuffled them, resisting the temptation to look at their faces. What was important was that they related to Herald's need, and he was sure they did.

Deal them into five piles, the Slash flashed. *The piles signify DO, THINK, FEEL, HAVE and BE.*

Brother Paul dealt them out face down. What an interesting set of representations! Surely they matched the five suits, which in the Waldens deck stood for WORK, TROUBLE, LOVE, MONEY, and SPIRIT. In the popularized version, anyway, that matched the superficial titles. The fundamental meanings were much closer to those Herald had listed. He had seen how they also equated to the medieval elements of society: Peasant, Soldier, Priest, Merchant, and the whole class of rootless people like entertainers, gypsies (who had not actually come on the European scene by 1392), and criminals. It was an intellectual challenge to line things up by fives. The Rhine experiments had used five symbols; did these also match the Tarot suits? Square, circle, cross, star, and wavy lines. The wavy lines obviously stood for water or the suit of Cups; the circle was a disk or Coin; the cross would be a Sword. But the square, now—well, four sticks, clubs, or scepters could form a square, so that might be the suit of Wands. And the star, like the Star of Bethlehem, signaling the location of the holy spirit of Jesus—that would be Aura. Somewhat forced, maybe, but still—

He had come to the end of the cards. Now they were in five piles, twenty cards to a pile. The mode of this new layout came to him. "Your Significator, the card that most nearly represents you—that should be the King of Aura." For he was abruptly aware that Herald the Healer had a phenomenal aura; he could feel it impinging on his own. Not since Jesus Christ had he experienced its like. Perhaps that was what had really reached out across the millennia to summon him. "We must locate that card."

You are of equivalent aura yourself—as of course you would be, the Andromedan flashed.

Antares had said the same. Extremely high aura—that notion jogged something. Something highly significant. There must be a fundamental connection between aura and Animation—

Then the card came up, breaking the chain of thought. "Here it is in Pile Two: THINK. In my terms, TROUBLE or MAGIC, that I'm sure has metamorphosed in your day to SCIENCE."

But my problem is FEEL, Herald protested.

"Perhaps the Tarot is telling you that the solution lies in your thinking rather than in your emotion. We can at least explore the possibilities." But privately he doubted. What mode of thinking could justify the burning of an innocent young woman? "Now how does this 'Cluster' spread go?"

Following Herald's directions, Brother Paul formed the layout. He started with the Significator, crossed it with Definition, and followed with cards to the South, West, North, and East, forming a cross. "Past, Present, Future, and Destiny," Brother Paul murmured, appreciating the simplicity of it. "Modified Celtic layout."

Celtic? the Andromedan flashed, perplexed.

"A spread of my day, having little if anything to do with the historical Celts. This spread of yours seems to be oriented on fives, and it rather appeals to me. The spreads of my day may have been less precise." But again he was dubious; how could five cards define a problem as aptly as ten or twenty cards?

Brother Paul considered the cards he had dealt. The Significator was crossed by the Three of Aura, labeled Perspective or Experience. Because it was sidewise, he could not tell which aspect dominated; probably both applied. Regardless, it was relevant. The card in the PAST location was—

Brother Paul paused, amazed and gratified. "Ah, the

vanity of the flesh!'' For the card was Vision, eighteenth
Triumph in the Waldenses' deck, and it was illustrated by
the scene he had visited from *The Vision of Piers
Plowman*. He must have had a hand in this, for though
that classic was contemporary with the Waldenses in the
fourteenth century, the Waldens' Tarot had not used
this particular illustration. He could not remember now
what they *had* used, but not this. He must have successfully re-created the deck, drawing at least to some
extent on his own experiences.

Half bemused by his growing awareness of his own
complicity in the shaping of this deck, Brother Paul
moved on through the Cluster Satellite Spread, tracing
Herald's problem. Yet revealing as the messages of the
cards might be to the Andromedan, they spoke with
perhaps even greater eloquence to Brother Paul himself.
For these cards were not as a rule illustrated by medieval
scenes; the court cards were alien creatures and the
Triumphs—

He was unable to grasp or retain the whole of the
illustrations for the Triumphs. Many related to concepts
that seemed not to exist in his own framework, though
they obviously derived from the basic notions of the
Waldenses. Here in Animation the cards became mind-
stretching aspects of the future universe, and all he
could do was absorb as much of it as possible without
critical examination. His assimilation came in diverse
gouts, but the overall picture was roughly this:

After the Fool period of mankind's history the expansion of Sphere Sol slowed, stabilizing at a radius of
about a hundred light years. The farthest human settlement was Planet Outworld whose people were green;
the King of Swords had a picture of Flint of Outworld, a
high-aura native of this facet. But the Tarot in its
multiple variations continued to expand explosively,
knowing no Spherical or species boundaries. The
Animation effect of Planet Tarot was exported to other
planets, though it was proscribed by Sphere Sol. The
Tarot symbols took on four dimensional attributes that
multiplied the effectiveness of divinatory readings.
Alien missionaries carried Animation Tarot across the

Milky Way Galaxy. Most Spheres adopted variations of the 100 card Cluster deck, but some used the 78 card decks or other sizes. Temples of Tarot were established among the wheeled Polarians (78 cards), and the swimming Spicans (100 cards), and the musical Mintakans (114 cards, counting the variations of the Ghost). In just a few short centuries Tarot ranged thousands of light years, coming to dominate the culture of the great conglomeration of species that formed the mighty interstellar empire called Segment Qaval, whose dominant sapients resembled nothing so much as vertical crocodiles. Then Tarot leaped a million light years to Galaxy Andromeda and Galaxy Pinwheel. Sophisticated interstellar organizations drew on Tarot for symbols, such as the Society of Hosts whose card was Temperance: the soul or aura being transferred from the living vessel of one host to another. Indeed, the proper designation for that card was Transfer. In a devious but compelling sense, Tarot helped organize the entire local Cluster of galaxies.

Brother Paul saw a fleet of huge spaceships, each one to two kilometers in diameter, each one shaped like the symbol for one of the Tarot suits. Ships like Swords battled with ships like Scepters and Cups and Disks and Atoms. It seemed the suit of Aura was variously known as Lamps, Plasma, and Atoms; in fact the variations of Tarot among alien creatures dwarfed in number and imagination those Brother Paul had surveyed on Earth. This did not mean the medieval Tarot decks of Earth were forgotten; quite the opposite. The aliens gleefully adapted *all* the old cards to new purposes, filling out each deck to a hundred cards and overflowing into the Ghost. Every Tarot deck that had ever existed anywhere was, by the definition of the Temple of Tarot, valid.

Concurrently, every deity that had ever related to Tarot was also considered valid. Thus the God of Tarot was a composite of every conceived and conceivable deity in all time and space. "All Gods are valid," became a common saying.

The shortage of energy caused galaxy to war against galaxy. Only the phenomenal efforts of Tarot-inspired heroes prevented horrendous destruction. The Solarian Flint of Outwarld, spying his enemy by a Tarot reading and neutralizing her; Melody of Mintaka, herself an expert Tarotist; and Herald the Healer, laboring to save the entire Cluster from the threat of alien conquest and destruction—

And *this* was the Tarot spread that might motivate Herald to achieve his vital mission. And Brother Paul was the guide. He shook his head, bemused again. "I have come from Hell to help you," he murmured.

I do not comprehend.

"It is not comprehendable. Perhaps the whole of my life and death has been for no other purpose than to facilitate your mission. On the other hand, this could be an incredible delusion of grandeur. Regardless, I shall do what I can." Brother Paul looked at the final card of the reading. "Here is Destiny—but it is the Ghost, the great Unknown. The reading cannot end here!"

The spread can be augmented, Herald flashed. Actually, this exchange occurred somewhere during Brother Paul's series of revelations about the future history of Tarot; everything was mixed hopelessly together, but it did not matter.

Lo, they dealt a satellite spread, modifying and clarifying the main layout. Somewhere here or elsewhere the cards augmented his knowledge of the Ancients, those creatures whose civilization had spanned the entire Cluster, three million years ago. Their technology had been well beyond anything known even in the modern, Solarian-year-4500 Cluster. Yet they had vanished completely. Now an alien invader known only as the Amoeba was attacking with technology that seemed to approach the Ancient level. The only hope of repelling the Amoeba was to discover Ancient technology—in a hurry.

How was a Tarot reading guided by a man two and a half millennia out of date to accomplish such a thing? Tarot could evoke only what was already in the mind of the querent—and Animation was much the same. Yet what could he do but go on?

Still, something nagged at his awareness. An-

cients—Animation—Amoeba . . . there was some
critical connection of such overwhelming importance
that . . . but he could not quite get his thought around it,
and the revelation escaped.

They formed a second satellite spread. This one
animated—the Daughter figure again. She was in the
fire as before, writhing in silent but devastatingly
evocative agony, trying to draw her slender legs out of
it, then resigning herself to her doom. As Jesus resigned
himself to his doom on the cross—

"No—I forbid this!" Brother Paul cried. "There is
no way this torture can promote the welfare of your
culture! I have felt the fires of Hell myself; do not do
this to her again!"

She is my wife, the Page of Swords! Herald flashed,
and his agony was a terrible thing in its brilliance. His
love was in the flame, and his sanity was breaking. *Suffer as I suffer! She burns, she burns!*

It was Herald's vision, not Brother Paul's. But it was
the Page of Disks he saw more than the Page of Swords.
Carolyn. His child. Or the child of his child, a hundred
generations removed. One card of the Tarot for each
generation. But the connection—absolute. There was no
way he could tolerate the infliction of such horror on
her.

Brother Paul aspired to be a peaceful man, but now
he had to fight. "I sub-define!" he cried, slapping down
another satellite card. "The Eight of Aura—Conscience!" Maybe in this distant future the card no
longer represented this concept, but he willed it so regardless.

Carolyn did not fade. Her anguished mouth opened,
and she cried: "Herald forgive them—they know not
what they do!"

As Jesus had cried. Now Brother Paul's own descendant begged the same reprieve for her tormentors. In
this moment her aura was like that of Christ; he could
feel the gentle power of it like none other in the universe. Yet Christ's sacrifice had not purified the erring
populace, had not expunged evil from the world. In-

stead evil had infiltrated Christ's own Church and
prospered as never before. The tears of Jesus—

Now another innocent was being sacrificed, as it
were, progressing from the incarceration of a sealed-in
chamber in a wall to the dancing flames. Her lovely hair
puffed into a blaze, shriveling with horrible speed into a
black mass.

Herald charged the fire, but this was useless; even in
the Andromedan's own framework, this was only a
memory vision. Brother Paul slammed down another
card, not knowing what it was, only praying that
somehow this recurring wrong could be righted.

Time froze. This card was blank, for he had not selected any, and in this Animation there was no random
manifestation. He had to choose, consciously or sub-
consciously. What *did* he want?

"Oh, God, I want her safe, unburned," Brother Paul
whispered.

God did not answer. And why should He? It was not
God's way to interfere directly in the affairs of living
species. That was Satan's business.

"Then what do You offer, Satan?" Brother Paul
asked.

The response was instant: *Vengeance.*

God was distant, aloof; Satan was near and relevant.
Suddenly it was easy to appreciate why a man like
Therion would prefer to worship the Horned God. The
promises of God were nebulous and often postponed
until their completion became pointless; justice delayed,
justice denied. Satan operated on a much more direct,
responsive basis. Satan was a businessman; He set a
price on what He offered—but He damn well delivered.
He never cheated, not directly; He used any conceivable
loophole to make His gifts more costly than any person
would voluntarily pay, but He abided by His infernal
rules. He had shown Brother Paul the origin and purpose of Tarot and also the evolution and future of
Tarot; now He was angling for that fateful third wish.

To make that bargain would be in effect to worship
Satan. Yet there was much that was worthy in Satan.

Perhaps Brother Paul had spent his life seeking the wrong deity.

But he could not make this bargain. Not quite. "No! I want her alive!"

"*Vengeance—and life,*" Satan replied, right on top of the situation. To bargain with God was an exercise in futility; Satan was the one in control.

Brother Paul looked again at the awful flame. "I'll take it!" Carolyn had prayed for forgiveness of her persecutors. Instead Brother Paul was bringing vengeance. Surely Jesus' tears were flowing yet!

The card he had chosen manifested as the Tower—the House of God—and of the Devil. It was the Tower of Truth, and the Dungeon of Wrong, and this very castle. From the sky a bolt of energy came—and everything was a blinding brilliance.

Revelation! The vision retreated, and he saw the roiling fireball of an atomic explosion. This was the vengeance sponsored by Satan: fiery destruction of the entire castle. All those who had perpetrated the atrocity of burning Carolyn had been hoist by their own petard. All had died in fire.

Now Satan guided him on a kaleidoscopic tour of the Cluster, showing him the war with the alien Amoeba. This was the Age of Aura; the soul of Carolyn, known to Herald as Psyche, was captive in the Transfer network of the Ancients. As this network was restored, that soul was freed.

Carolyn/Psyche had lost her lovely human host, but she lived eternally in other hosts. She and Herald were happy. She was no longer Brother Paul's little girl in either body or spirit. She had found her own life. And that was the way it had to be.

Satan had granted the third wish—and Brother Paul knew he had expended it in a selfish manner. When the final test of his conscience had come, he had sacrificed his personal honor for this. It was the measure of his nature that he was not sorry.

And do you know the verdict on your soul? Satan inquired from the swirling chaos of the void.

"In the final crisis, I yielded to my baser instincts,"

Brother Paul said. "I am, after all, a worshipper of the Horned God."

What fate awaits you now?

"I am doomed to Hell," Brother Paul answered, knowing that his unworthiness only reflected that of mankind. Man was not yet ready to meet God—not in Brother Paul's time, not in the forty-fifth century, perhaps never. Satan had brought him at last to reason. "I am ready."

So shall it be!

Abruptly chaos vanished. Brother Paul found himself standing on the green turf of Planet Tarot. Scattered about within a half-kilometer radius were Lee, Therion, Amaranth, and Carolyn.

Brother Paul looked about, realizing that the third and final Animation was over. All five of them had survived it. He himself stood restored in health and sanity, uncastrate.

With increasing amazement and horror he grasped the reason.

VII

Decision: 26

The Devil is the father of all misunderstood geniuses. It is he who induces us to try new paths; he begets originality of thought and deed. He tempts us to venture out boldly into unknown seas for the discovery of new ways to the wealth of distant Indies. He makes us dream of and hope for more prosperity and greater happiness. He is the spirit of discontent that embitters our hearts, but in the end often leads to a better arrangement of affairs. In truth, he is a very useful servant of the Almighty, and all the heinous features of his character disappear when we consider the fact that he is necessary in the economy of nature as a wholesome stimulant to action and as the power of resistance that evokes the noblest efforts of living beings.

God, being the All in All, regarded as the ultimate authority for conduct, is neither evil itself nor goodness itself; but, nevertheless, he is in the good, and he is in the evil. He encompasses good and evil. God is in the growth and in the decay; he reveals himself in life, and he reveals himself in death. He will be found in the storm, he will be found in the calm. He lives in good aspirations and in the bliss resting upon moral endeavors; but *he lives also in the visitations that follow evil actions. It is his voice that speaks in the guilty conscience, and he, too, is in the curse of sin, and in this sense he is present even in the evil itself. Even evil, temptation, and sin elicit the good: they teach man. He who has eyes to see, ears to hear, and a mind to perceive, will read a lesson out of the very existence of Evil, a lesson which, in spite of the terror it inspires, is certainly not less impressive, nor less divine, than the sublimity of a holy life; and thus it becomes apparent that the existence of Satan is part and parcel of the divine dispensation. Indeed we must grant that the Devil is the most indispensable and faithful helpmate of God. To speak mystically, even the existence of the Devil is filled with the presence of God.*

—Paul Carus: *The History of the Devil and the Idea of Evil*, New York, Land's End Press, 1969 rpt. of 1900 ed.

"I can see you have the answer at last," the Reverend Siltz said.

"No, no answer. I fear it was an impossible mission," Brother Paul said, chewing on the good bread his host provided. It was not as interesting as the dishes of Charles VI's palace, but it was satisfying. "I went to Hell—but I learned about Tarot, not God."

"Tomorrow we shall see," Siltz said confidently. "I observed your face as you emerged from Animation and the faces of the others. It was as if you were of a single family, transfigured. We shall have the truth from you."

"The truth is hardly relevant," Brother Paul said. "I learned of the original Tarot, which has thirty Triumphs, each with a pseudo-meaning and a genuine meaning. Together, these Triumphs represent the life of Jesus which is also the life of Everyman, beginning in nothingness, developing through childhood and adolescence to maturity, then undergoing the vicissitudes of chance, error, trial, punishment, and transformation to another status where his real education begins. In the end he is subject to the final judgment and perhaps salvation. The minor cards offer spot guidance along the way—five suits, each covering a fundamental aspect of life, each card with two versions of the basic message. A most sophisticated deck of cards—yet so much more than that. All religious history is reflected in the Tarot!''

"So it would seem," Siltz agreed. "Perhaps you should record this special deck before it fades from your memory.''-

Brother Paul nodded. "Yes—I destroyed it; I must restore it. Humanity deserves the true Tarot! And I must give the world the Cluster Satellite Spread too—or would that be stealing from the future?''

"That must certainly have been a remarkable Animation," Siltz observed. "I become most curious. What were the meanings of the cards of this extra suit?''

"That would be the suit of Aura. The ace is titled BE, and the symbol is an oil lamp in the shape of a cosmic lemniscate." He made a figure with his finger in the air: ∞ . "In the future they will render it as a broken atom, a proton-neutron nucleus surrounded by a spiral electron shell. He made another figure: ∞."It also resembles a galaxy, by no coincidence." He smiled. "Iconographic transformation. The cultures of the Cluster draw from any variants that please them, just as they do with measurements. In Etamin they use miles instead of kilometers—" He caught himself. "I'm drifting! The deuce is illustrated by an outline of the human aura, and its interpretations are SOUL or SELF, depending on the way it falls. The trey covers PERSPECTIVE or EX-PERIENCE—''

"Here, write it down, write it down!" Siltz said. "I am most intrigued by your dream deck! A symbol for each small card?''

"Yes. All symbols in a suit relate to the suit theme, and of course each suit is color coded. This is the suit of Art, coded violet—''

"I thought you termed it the suit of Aura.''

"Merely alternate aspects. Aura, Art, Spirit, Plasma, Atoms—''

"All one suit?" Siltz inquired, frowning.

"Yes. Each suit has many interpretations, depending on the frame of reference. It is like the function key on a calculator. The cards look the same, but a shift of function makes them perform in a different manner. That way the usefulness of a single deck is multiplied. Instead of one hundred or two hundred aspects, there are a thousand or more, each fairly specific. When the reference is the classical elements, we call the suits FIRE, AIR, WATER, EARTH, and AURA. When it is the endeavors of man, we call them NATURE, SCIENCE, FAITH, TRADE, and ART. In medieval times that second suit was MAGIC rather than SCIENCE, but the meaning hasn't changed."

Siltz laughed. "I dare say it has not!"

"When the reference is popularized divination, the suits are WORK, TROUBLE, LOVE, MONEY, and SPIRIT. When it is the states of matter they are ENERGY, GAS, LIQUID, SOLID, and PLASMA. When—"

"Plasma?"

"In physics that is the compressed state that occurs in the hearts of superdense stars where the pressure is so great that the normal nucleus-electron structure breaks down—"

"Oh, I comprehend. The broken atom! The squashed galaxy. Write it down, write it down! You do not want to have to go into Animation for what you forget. Make a table for your titles and numbers and symbols." He drew lines on the paper, making boxes. "Now your five aces stand for—"

"DO, THINK, FEEL, HAVE, and BE," Brother Paul said, filling them in. "With symbols of Scepter, Sword, Cup, Coin, and—"

A knock on the door interrupted him. "Come in, girl," Siltz called without removing his eyes from the developing chart. Privately to Brother Paul, he muttered: "I thought she'd never relent! It has been several days and not a night at my house!"

Jeanette entered. She was almost beautiful in a surprisingly feminine dress, her hair set just so, her legs well exposed and well formed. "You—how did you know—?"

"Brother Paul's hundred-proof Animation Tarot informed me that mischief was afoot. Your business has to do with work, trouble, love, money, and spirit."

"Not with money!" she snapped. Then, abruptly shy, she dropped to one knee before him. "Reverend Siltz of the Church of Communism, I beg permission to marry your son."

Siltz pointed his finger at her pert nose. "Two grandchildren!"

"The first two children shall be raised in your faith," she said grimly. "*Only* the first two!"

Siltz smiled with crocodilian victory. "I am a reasonable man, though at times it pains me. I grant permission."

Jeanette's reserve crumbled. "Oh, Reverend, I thank you!" she exclaimed, jumping up and flinging her arms about him.

"Please, daughter—you will scatter Brother Paul's valuable cards, flaunting your pretty skirt about like that."

"Never mind my cards," Brother Paul said quickly. "I'm sure you two have details to negotiate about the wedding and such. I'll take a walk." He moved to the door.

Neither of them seemed to hear him. "You called me 'daughter'!" Jeanette exclaimed. "How sweet!"

"Just you take good care of my son," Siltz grumbled. "He is not used to marriage. He will not know what to do."

"He has a fair idea how to start," she said, flushing passingly.

Brother Paul emerged from the house. He was touched by the reconciliation, but it reminded him strongly of his own problems. He, too, wanted a daughter—but the daughter he had in mind belonged to another man, and he had no wife. In any event he would soon be mattermitting back to Earth—and the others could not go. Above all, he did not have the answer he had come to find. Not any answer he was prepared to present to the colonists! How could he stand before the community tomorrow and disappoint them?

It was dark. Light spilled from the cabin windows, helping him make his way, but beyond the village he had to depend on starlight. He wondered whether any of the stars of the entities he had learned about were visible now: Etamin, Mintaka, Spika, Polaris, or the galaxy Andromeda. And where would the galaxy called Pinwheel be? He had never heard of that one! Here in the night, those alien civilized Spheres seemed both very close and painfully distant in time and space. He wished—but that was futile. He had used up his three wishes, and now he was in Hell where he belonged.

He proceeded toward Northole, aware that he was taking a foolish risk by departing the village stockade alone and unarmed, but he did not care. He had seen and lost the universe; what did he have to lose now? What beast of prey could be worse than what he had already faced in Hell?

Ahead he spied the flashes of the nova-bugs. There was the place to walk! But one foot snagged on something. He dragged it violently forward, recovering his balance. There was a series of faint pops. Tarot bubbles—he had walked through a cluster of them nestled in a hollow of the ground. A nova bug flashed brightly right before him, illuminating the shriveling Bubble remains.

Triggered by that, something illuminated in Brother Paul's mind. "Animation!" he exclaimed aloud. "The source of Animation! Now at last I understand!"

He concentrated. Light flared—no nova-bug this time, but illumination Brother Paul had willed. Yet he was not yet in the Animation area. "I control it," he said. "I have solved the problem of Animation!" Then, more slowly, "But I have not solved the problem of God."

He stood for some time in thought, working out the presentation he would make to the colonists. "Animation," he said. "The Ancients. Aura. It all ties together as I almost discovered two thousand five hundred years hence in Herald the Healer's vision." Then

he set about gathering Tarot Bubbles with which to
decorate tomorrow's stage.

Brother Paul stood at the apex of the wood pile. "I
came here to identify the God of Tarot," he said. "The
question was whether God is behind the Animation effect, and if so, what God he is. I now have an answer—but it is not one that pleases me or will please
you. I could tell you that Animation tells me that *all*
Gods are valid—" But as he had guessed, they were
shaking their heads. They could not accept that answer.
They wanted a single, dominant God, not a compromise
philosophy.

He paused, trying to phrase his decision in a manner
that would not be as painful for this group as he feared
it would be. Yet what point was there in balking, after
he had passed through Hell? But he found that he could
not state his conclusion baldly; he had to lead up to it.
"Much of the data on which I base my opinion is
suspect because it derives from Animation which is the
thing being studied. Animation is a tangible composite
of the imaginations of the participants. A shared dream,
if you will. It seems that the dream was principally
mine, and I am an imperfect vessel—how imperfect I
never properly appreciated until I had this experience!
So you may reject my conclusion if you will."

All were watching him in silence. Deacon Brown of
the Church of Lemuria, eyes downcast, yet watching: an
eerie effect! Minister Malcolm of the Nation of Islam.
Mrs. Ellend of the Church of Christ: Scientist, perhaps
the oldest member of this audience. Pastor Runford, the
Jehovah's Witness. Jeanette, sitting closely beside the
Reverend Siltz: Scientology and Communist united at
last. But not the Swami, who remained unconscious.

"Three million years ago there existed a species of
creature we know only as 'The Ancients.' They were not
human; rather they were part of an alien culture embracing the several galaxies of this Cluster: Milky Way,
Andromeda, Pinwheel, and assorted lesser structures.
They were highly sophisticated creatures whose
technology has never been matched elsewhere. One of

their many avenues of exploration related to the expression of Art as controlled by sapient consciousness. They were much concerned with the mechanisms of imagination and sought ways to make Art more direct. Why go through the tedium of painting a picture or molding a sculpture if the mind can create the images direct without the intercession of material things? Not only would such dream art be more convenient, occurring virtually instantaneously, but it would be far more versatile than any prior medium. Thus the Ancients created Animation."

Brother Paul paused. He was oversimplifying, for he knew that much of the joy in art lay in the doing of it. But he had a problem of timing. The sun was beating down warmly now. Most of the pretty Tarot Bubbles had popped. It was time.

"This," Brother Paul said, lifting and spreading his arms, "is Animation."

Abruptly the world turned purple. The wood, the ground, the people—all were shades of purple. They looked about and stared at each other, amazed.

Then they turned green. And black. Stygian darkness closed about them—until nova bugs flashed, restoring intermittent light.

The effects faded. All was as before. "The nova bugs make their light by Animation," Brother Paul said. "That is why their physical light-making apparatus has baffled science. The mechanism is not physical at all. It is imaginative—literally. I dare say many other unusual features of this planet's life will become explicable by the application of this insight."

Reverend Siltz, as baffled as the rest, faced Brother Paul. "How—?"

"I am coming to that, Reverend Communist," Brother Paul said. "Let's relax with something pretty while I cover the dreary details." The village houses vanished, replaced by lovely flowering trees. A sparkling stream coursed in a meandering path between people, arriving at a central conic fountain. Brother Paul stood at the apex of the fountain. "As you see, Animation can make images appear where there is nothing or conceal what is actually present. It can also produce sounds to a lesser extent; but most meaningful speech has to be spoken by a living person. It affects touch, but usually only to the extent of modifying existing surfaces. In short, there is normally a physical basis for a structure of Animation—but the basis and the appearance need not correspond very closely. Animation can produce the sensations of water—'' and here the fountain spread out to become a rising lake surrounding the colonists, wetting them— "but it can not actually drown you unless you fall into *real* water. You might suffocate because you believe you are underwater, but that would not be the direct result of Animation." The water was above waist level, swirling ever higher as the colonists stood, causing considerable alarm. "But I do not mean to torture you, only to show you how it is possible to die in Animation without actually being killed by it." The water dropped, forming back into the fountain.

"Note that this is not mass hypnosis," Brother Paul continued. "I have shown you rather than told you of these effects. All living creatures have an intangible force about them we call Aura. An aspect of it has been photographed by the Kirlian process—but this appears to be only a refraction caused by water vapor associated with our type of life. The original aura can be detected only by extremely sophisticated equipment which our human species will not develop for several centuries yet. Some would call it the Soul—the ultimate essence of individuality, independent of body. In fact, some alien cultures can transfer that soul to other bodies, in effect giving their people the chance to travel on other worlds in other hosts.

"As will be discovered, the auras of individual entities vary widely in type and intensity; most are near 'Sapient Norm' which is coded by the numeral 1; some are more intense, coded by higher numbers. *Every* aura is unique and wonderful—but the extremely intense auras are spectacular in special ways." He paused, and the fountain turned bright yellow and developed a ring of green eyes at the base.

"Still no verbal suggestion," Brother Paul said with a smile. "Yet obviously my will is being communicated to you! Have no concern for your sanity; each of you perceives the same impossibility. I possess one of the most intense auras found among our species. I do not claim this makes me a superior man; far from it! I am an imperfect vessel with extremely human failings. Chance bestowed this gift on me. Until I came to this planet I was not even aware of it, and until last night I did not appreciate it. But it turns out that aura controls the Animations—and so this is my power." The yellow water solidified into a yellow monster that quivered and roared, supporting Brother Paul on its tongue.

"When we went into Animation, my aura extended out, interacting with the weaker auras of the others, informing them of my will. And so they saw what I saw and spoke as I would have them speak, in a general way. It resembles telepathy, but it is not direct mind-to-mind rapport. Since Animation does not affect the mind directly, only the perceptions, they actually interpreted their parts rather freely—but the play was always mine."

"But what makes it happen?" Reverend Siltz cried, staring at the monster. "Why does Animation only happen here on Planet Tarot? Surely other people on Earth have auras."

The monster dissolved into a pile of yellow rubble with a ring of green jewels. "The Ancients used their sophisticated science to create a special life form whose purpose was to facilitate the communication of auras," Brother Paul said. "This unique creature generates a—I suppose you'd call it a kind of gas that somehow enhances the overlapping of auras so that much improved contact occurs. A catalyst. Ordinarily auras are discrete, maintaining their separateness even when these auras overlap. Some creatures like to associate in close physical proximity so that their auras form something like a common pool, while others prefer to stay apart. This substance nullifies that separateness of aura to a certain extent, making the auras permeable, merging them. In a rather fundamental respect, groups of people in the vicinity of this gas join together, sharing themselves. Animation may be the ultimate tool for unity.''

"But some Animations are nightmares!" Pastor Runford cried.

"Yes, indeed!" Brother Paul agreed. "Because the average person is not ready for unity. He has enough trouble with his own nightmares, which Animation makes starkly tangible, without sharing those of others. Those of us who participated in this experiment suffered horrors that only we could imagine. Others before us have actually died. It is dangerous to loose the untamed horrors of the mind, especially when they have been so long suppressed. The Swami Kundalini tried to warn me of this." He paused, reflecting. "Fortunately we were a fairly balanced group with our horrors canceling each other out as much as they augmented each other. We experienced a kind of composite that became largely independent of the will of any one of us, including myself. The application of Tarot images helped, for the Tarot is a refined body of imagery and philosophy with roots deep in human experience and symbolism. Without that to lean on, to structure our creations, we could have been in very bad trouble. In the future, the Temple of Tarot will integrate Tarot with Animation with potent but precisely controlled effect, spreading its system safely across the Galactic Cluster." He smiled. "Everywhere but in Sphere Sol. The human government will ban such use of Animation, and thereby fall behind other Spheres in this respect, ironically."

Jeanette's brow had furrowed during this speech. Now she jogged Siltz's arm and leaned closer to whisper in his ear. How rapidly she had assumed proprietary rights, advertising them to the entire community! She could have spoken for herself, but now preferred to have the Reverend speak for her. She showed her power not so much by marrying young Ivan—who it seemed was not even attending this meeting—but by her proximity to Ivan's father, the head of the family. She had become one of the family, and in her public deferral she claimed her victory.

Siltz listened gravely, as a man listens to his daughter, then spoke aloud. "You have not answered, Brother Paul. Where *are* these Animation creatures? Can you show us one?"

Ah, yes; he had drifted from the subject, as was his wont. "Everywhere. They are the Tarot Bubbles."

"The Bubbles!" several others exclaimed.

"Correct. These innocuous fragments of froth that generate in the night and pop by day. They are a form of life—whether plant or animal or fungus or germ or some alien type I can't say. But I suspect the last, as things seem to fall naturally into divisions of five here, like the Tarot suits. They multiply and grow and feed and seek to survive—"

"But they just sit there or float about!"

"They sit there in the shade," Brother Paul explained. "When they pop, they release their hallucinogenic agent and some spores so that new ones can grow when favorable conditions return."

"But why bother with the Animation effect, then? *They* don't need it!"

"They did not evolve naturally. They were created or modified by the science of a culture whose motives and abilities were incredibly sophisticated. But Animation may be a survival mechanism after all. It may protect the Bubbles from molestation by evoking distractions culled from the minds of the marauders. And the desire that most sapient species seem to have for hallucinogenic experience may cause them to spread the Bubbles all across the Cluster, much as they spread fruit-producing plants or sweets-producing insects or useful animals. I also suspect controlled Animation can serve as a natural painkiller and as an excellent teaching tool. Thus specialists of various types will find uses for it. To control Animation they need the Bubbles. I believe the survival of the species is assured." Brother Paul frowned. "However, I am less sanguine about the prospects for our own human species, whose madness may be aggravated. Many quite beneficial drugs have been sorely abused in the past such as morphine and mnem. What will happen to Earth when Animation arrives there? Obviously the repercussions will be sufficient to cause Animation to be banned.''

The yellow monster faded out. Brother Paul was back on the pile of wood in the center of the village. ''The gas seems to have dissipated,'' he said. ''When the threshold of Animation passes, the effect disappears rapidly like a candle going out. I brought a number of ripe Bubbles here last night, but they were not enough to maintain the effect for long. In the depression of Northole, where conditions are better for them, Animation is much more persistent, except when storms move the gas elsewhere. But I trust I have made my point.''

''You have made your point,'' Reverend Siltz said. ''But what is your answer? Who is the God of Tarot?''

''That is the difficult answer since you declined to accept the one I proffered,'' Brother Paul said slowly. This was the part he hated! ''All the manifestations of Animation turn out to have a physical explanation. The variables of the Bubbles and individual auras made that explanation difficult to come by, but I believe independent investigation will corroborate my conjectures. Thus we do not need to assume the direct participation of a deity.''

There was a moment of silence. ''There is no God?'' Siltz asked slowly. He seemed to have become the spokesman for the community. Brother Paul was not sure from the way the man spoke whether this, to him, represented defeat or victory. Many humanists believed in the spirit of Man, not God; what was the stand of the Church of Communism?

''I—can not say that,'' Brother Paul said. ''I can only say that God did not make Himself manifest to me through Animation. Therefore, I can not identify the God of Tarot—because I have no concrete evidence there *is* a God of Tarot.''

''Yet there *is* a God,'' Siltz persisted. ''And that God is found within the human heart. And Animation makes manifest what is in the human heart. You were questing for that truth. Surely you found *something*.''

"No," Brother Paul said heavily. "I am no longer sure there is a God. I looked for Him as hard as I could, yet was invariably turned aside, and found only the debunking of my most cherished beliefs. The closest I came to God's presence was, through the irony of precession, when I was questing in quite another direction."

There was no cry of outrage. The assembled villagers of diverse faiths looked at him with regret and compassion. "Surely you retain your faith in your prophet, Jesus Christ," Reverend Siltz said. "We asked you to choose among our Gods, not to renounce your own."

"I am not sure I do retain that faith," Brother Paul said. "What Jesus did can be accounted for by the presence of aura. He could have been an ordinary man, even a—a mutilated one, with an extremely intense aura. Aura can sponsor visions; aura can heal. In the future there will be entities who make a business of healing through aura, attributing no religious significance to it." *Herald the Healer, where are you now?* "God—I find it difficult to discover an objective rationale for the existence of a Supreme Being in the face of what I now know of Animation and aura."

"But this is not negation!" Siltz insisted. "These things may prove only that God operates through such tools as Ancients and aura. There are unknowns we can not explain; there are rights and wrongs. There must be Divine inspiration, a Guiding Force—and you must have had some hint as to the identity of that Force."

"Perhaps," Brother Paul agreed reluctantly. He knew what Siltz was trying to do: rescue Planet Tarot from the depression and chaos that a negative decision could mean. Better a foreign God than anarchy. This colony needed to unite, at least politically, about a single deity—*any* deity. "Yet I am not certain, now, what is right and what is wrong or whether there is in fact any distinction between them. One concept is meaningless without the other, much as the black markings we call writing are meaningless without the white background of the paper. Black and white must work together to form meaning; it is foolish to call either color God. Right and wrong exist only as companions, as extremes of perspective; God may be in both or in neither, but God can not be taken *as* one or the other. Yet I would not presume on the basis of such subjective evidence—"

"It is not presumption! Five of you participated in the Animations; all contributed to the visions. In that group effort, some consensus must have developed or you would have destroyed each other. You emerged unified—it shows in each one of you, even the child. As a group you have agreed, even if you have not consciously understood the rationale of that agreement. If as diverse a group as you five can unify, so can our colony—about the same deity. As a group, *you have identified God!*"

Brother Paul looked at Lee, and at Therion, and Amaranth and Carolyn, all sitting on the wood behind him. Slowly, each nodded. Yet he resisted. "What we experienced," Brother Paul said, "this was a special situation probably not applicable to the outside world. You would not be able to accept—"

"Must we direct the question to the Watchers?" Siltz inquired.

Brother Paul did not reply.

"We require an answer," Siltz insisted. "Mormon—your credibility is unblemished. We know you will not mislead us, though your own faith be forfeit. Who is the God of Tarot?" But Lee shook his head in negation, refusing to answer.

Siltz turned on Amaranth. "Abraxis? You were not scheduled to be a Watcher, but by your survival of three Animations you have proven yourself. Who?" But Amaranth also declined.

The Reverend's gaze now fixed on Carolyn. "Child, the Nine Unknown Men will not be pleased if you do not reveal what you agreed to Watch. Who is God?"

The girl tried to resist, but under the group's uncompromising cynosure she wilted and broke. "S-sa'n," she whispered.

"I did not hear," Siltz said sternly. "Speak clearly!"

Carolyn tried again. "Sa—Satan is the God of Tarot."

Now Therion, who had held himself impassive, smiled. "Otherwise known as the Horned God," he said. "Returned after thousands of years to claim His own. From me you would not have believed it, but from these others you *must* believe it." He turned to address the other Watchers and Brother Paul. "Who here denies it?"

No one denied it. Brother Paul felt a special agony of faith. What had he done, when he yielded to his baser nature in making his third wish? He had been relegated to Hell—and this was now Hell. Satan was the God of Hell.

"Humanity belongs to the Devil," Therion said triumphantly. "And the world of the living is but an aspect of Hell. We failed to find grace in Animation—yea, even the Mormon, even the child, even Brother Paul of Vision!—and so Satan returned us to His realm. We have the truth at last."

And the congregation was silent.

VIII

Wisdom: 27

Time is running out on the laisser-faire or 'mad dog' phase of human exploitation of the earth, owing to the mathematical increase of the human population on the one hand, and, on the other, the increasing pollution of both the land and sea masses by human beings, through chemical and biological poisons used as insecticides, or created by energy producers ('nuclear reactors'), and weapons of war. Despite all the tendentious propaganda being spread about, the earth can very easily feed all its animal and human population, for many hundreds of years to come, especially if—as Victor Hugo demanded in Les Misérables *a century ago, in 1862—human feces cease to be poured into the rivers and the seas, as at present, and are reprocessed and used as fertilizer, instead of the pollutive insecticides and chemical fertilizers now being used. For the paradox is:* It is shit that is clean, and the 'pure white powders' that pollute! *As it appears, however, that this rational course will not be followed, and that* lasser-faire *capitalistic exploitation of both the earth and all the other planets will remain in force and be enlarged, the*

*terrestrial food-supply, as we know it, is doomed.
The ocean being increasingly polluted already, it
will probably be a mere bacteriological and
radiological swamp, impossible to 'farm,' by the
time the population/food balance becomes
dramatically skewed. Sea-borne foods, such as
algae, fish, and plankton—on which such
delusory hopes are now being pinned—will long
since all have disappeared owing to the pollution
of their viable space.*

—G. Legman: *Rationale of the Dirty Joke:
Second Series,* New York, Breaking Point, Inc.,
1975.

Therion was leading several villagers in solemn
prayer:

*Our Father, Who art in Hell, Damned be Thy Name
Thy Kingdom come, Thy Will be done, on Earth as
   it is in Hell.*

"This *is* Hell," Brother Paul muttered. And thought
with sudden hope: had his failure in the trial of the third
wish really brought the entire planet to this, doomed by
himself as imperfect Everyman? Or was this merely
another Animation masquerading as reality, as the air-
port scene had been? It was difficult to be certain
anymore. So maybe—

No. If this were *not* reality, then he could never in his
life be sure of the distinction between reality and
Animation. Assuming it was what it seemed to be, it was
still Hellish. How would Satan answer the prayers of his
new constituents? Surely only in such a fashion as to
make them regret it!

"Oh, Swami," he murmured. "You were so right in
your warning! I unlocked the secret of Animation—and
loosed Satan upon us all!"

Yet Satan had honored His bargains with Brother
Paul. Satan had answered when God stood aloof. Satan
was honest and responsive. Perhaps Satan was indeed
more worthy of worship.

"Sad, isn't it," a man said beside him. Brother Paul
turned. It was Deacon Brown, the Lemurian.

"Not for me, really," Brother Paul said insincerely.
"I'm leaving soon."

"For *him*," the Deacon said, indicating Therion.
"He has been granted what he thought he wanted—and
that's Hell."

"But he's happy, isn't he?"

"Not at all. Listen to him."

Brother Paul listened. Therion, it seemed, was now
telling a dirty joke, ". . . so he went on down to Hell. 'I
was bored up there,' he said to Satan. 'No liquor, no
women, no parties.' Satan waved his hoof, and there
was a roomful of drunken, naked, eager, beautiful
women. So Prufrock dived in amongst them. But in a
moment he cried, 'Hey, these gals have no holes!'
'That's right,' Satan replied. 'This is Hell.' "

The reaction of the congregation was less than en-
thusiastic. "You see, now he has responsibility," the
Deacon said. "He has to guide them and entertain
them, and their values don't coincide with his. He's
trying to get through to them, to shrive himself by
making them react with laughter or horror or anger, and
they aren't reacting. That leaves him the obvious
butt—and that's Hell for him. His own refuse is bouncing back in his face."

"Yes . . . " Brother Paul said, seeing it. "But surely
he should have anticipated this sort of thing when he
took the Horned God as his deity."

"He did not choose the Horned God; that was thrust
upon him. Back on Earth he married the most beautiful
and intellectual woman he found—then she turned out
to be a lesbian, using him only as a cover."

"She had no hole!" Brother Paul exclaimed, catching
on.

"None he could use. She two-timed him with a female
lover. That sort of thing is Hell-on-Earth for a normal
man—and perhaps worse for an abnormal one, strongly
sexed but afraid of the opposite sex."

"The Gorgon," Brother Paul said. "The castration
complex. He has it with a vengeance! In the
Animations—" But he decided he didn't want to talk
about his own castration; he now saw that it was no

more a product of his own desire than the soul-as-excrement concept had been. "She put horns on him—without another man, really complicating his complexes. So he adopted the Horned God!"

"That's why he distrusts all women now and seeks to defile them," the Deacon agreed. "He's afraid anyone he loves will betray him."

"Seeks to defile women . . ." Brother Paul repeated, again reminded of his disaster of the Seven Cups, and Satan's clarification of it. Excrement in the face of the female! The Black Mass too—the attempt to have a young female killed on the body of a mature one. Much was coming clear now. "Yet if he found one that *wasn't* lesbian—how would he know? By rejecting *all* women, he makes his own Hell."

"Precisely," the Deacon agreed. "And what woman would attempt to break through his defense and abate that Hell? A thankless task!"

Brother Paul shook his head. "He is a man of many qualities. I believe his attitudes suffered fundamental changes in Animation, and he is ready to accept normal heterosexual relations. Perhaps one day some hardy woman will perceive those qualities and make the effort."

Meanwhile, Therion was still trying, almost pitiful in the new perspective. "Now let me tell you about the Sleeve Job. This man had tried every conceivable kind of sexual experience and wanted something really different. So . . . ."

Brother Paul walked away, leaving Therion, leaving Deacon Brown. His mission here was over. Now he was only waiting for the return of his capsule to Earth. This had been pre-scheduled when this mission had first been instituted; the capsule would return at its appointed time with or without him. Certain Planet Tarot artifacts would be shipped back, including a sealed terrarium containing Tarot Bubble spores, as a supplement to his report. All Brother Paul had to do was wrap up his personal affairs. No easy task!

First he had to settle with Amaranth. She had expressed serious interest in him between Animations as well as during them, but despite temptation he had found his own emotion falling short. She had a marvelous body and a willing nature—but somehow he could not envision himself married to a perpetual temptress, a Lilith figure. There were other things in his life besides sex. So even if it had been possible for him to take her back to Earth with him, he would not have done so. The roles the two of them played in life were too different. Had she been more like Sister Beth and less like a minionette of Satan—

The problem was, how could he tell her that? She had, by her definitions, done everything right. She had undressed herself frequently and to advantage and had not bothered him with intellectual discussion. Her notion of the ideal woman. He knew from her prior discussion about nature and the Breaker that she had more depth than that; the shallowness was merely a role she played. She would make a good wife—for the right man. It just happened that he was not that man.

He found that he could not tell her that. Not directly. So he retired to Reverend Siltz's house and pondered his Tarot chart—and it came to him. Therion's demon Thoth Tarot was adaptable to this purpose!

In the end he found he had written a poem titled "Four Swords"—in the Thoth Tarot, the Four of Swords signified Truce. He would give her this Tarot poem message, explaining about the problem of roles, and perhaps she would understand. This was also his farewell to the Thoth Tarot, and to all other four-suit Tarot decks; henceforth, he would devote his energies to restoring and perfecting the five suit Tarot of the Waldenses. Satan had given him this, and he could not let it go. Perhaps he was, after all, a worshiper of—

There was a knock on the door. Brother Paul went to open it—and there stood Amaranth.

"I'm sorry," she said. "I can't go with you, Brother Paul. I thought you were the one for me, I really did, but those Animations showed me things—I really got to know myself better, playing those roles, and I saw how dumb some of them were. That's not what I really want to be."

"I understand," Brother Paul said. How well he did!

"I—have a greater affinity for another man," she continued. "One I wouldn't have looked at before Animation. I prayed to Satan to solve my dilemma, and He sent me—"

"Therion!" Brother Paul exclaimed.

"Yes. He—he's really more my type. He likes my body, and I like his mind. In the Animations—it worked out pretty well. Actually. When he was King Charles. He does with gusto what you resist, and I—I need to be gustoed."

"Yes," Brother Paul agreed.

"He's not really bisexual or whatever. He just never got close to a female woman before, despite all his talk. He has very broad horizons. Broader than mine. So he can show me new avenues, and I *need* those avenues because I can't stand dullness. It never would have worked out between you and me, Paul. I was never Sister Beth, or the Virgin Mary, or any of those lovely pure women that turn you on. I'm a creature of indulgence, uninhibited. I want a man foaming at the lips to get at my secrets, tearing the clothes off me—"

She broke off. "But I know it bothers you, my just telling you this. You never tore clothing off anybody. Even in the middle of the act, you just lay there without responding."

In the middle of the act? She was referring to his dream within a dream, being ravished by a succubus, unable to respond because he was paralyzed and castrate. That really had been her playing that part!

"So—farewell." She turned and walked away.

Brother Paul looked down at the paper in his hand. He had never even given her the poem. He *had* been unresponsive!

Should he destroy the poem? It had had only one purpose, and that was now passed. No—he did not believe in book burning or anything that smacked of it. He would file it away; maybe future scholars of the Temple of Tarot would find it in his papers and wonder what it meant. It was about as anonymous as a poem could be; he didn't even know the proper name of its addressee. With luck, he would never know.

Yet, now that it was over, he felt a letdown. It might
have been fun Amaranth's way. Tearing the clothes off
her. She was the creature for which man's lust had been
designed, and he was after all a man. Too bad the fourteenth century Animation had cut off before they had
gotten into the Palace affair; she might have discovered
that he was not always paralyzed.

He shook his head. Therion's Satan, perhaps in His
jealousy, had made sure Brother Paul could not climax
anything with Amaranth in that sequence. And there
were other matters.

Now he had to settle with Carolyn. His love for her
was stronger than anything he had felt for Amaranth, if
of a different nature. He would have to explain to her
that even if he could take another person home with him
(which he could not), he could not take a child away
from her natural father. What had been in Animation—could not be in life.

This was Hell all right.

He walked slowly to the Swami's house. Reverend
Siltz had mentioned that the Swami had finally
recovered consciousness, perhaps in response to Mrs.
Ellend's ministrations, so Carolyn was moving back in
with him. Most of the villagers were out about their
work in field and forest; the rigorous climate of this
planet did not permit much time off from chores. There
was the sound of hammering, momentarily sending a
chill through him until he realized it was from the shop
of the stove-smith. The man was laboring to convert the
first units to body heating rather than space heating.
Several fisherpeople were trawling a net through
Eastlake, harvesting waterlife for drying and salting for
winter. What would happen if Lee passed by in his
Christ-visage and said "Rise, follow me, and I will
make you fishers of men"? Probably nothing, for Satan
ruled here. One man was working on his roof, thatching
an annex with freshly cured broadleaves. The main section remained turf, but evidently in summer other
roofing could make do. Everywhere were reminders that
this was but the summer interstice; the rest of the year
was—Hell.

Therion was concluding his service: "Satan is my Shepherd; I shall not be satisfied . . . ." Brother Paul hurried on. He had brought this answer to this colony, but he could not accept it. Satan might have commendable qualities, but surely . . . .

The Swami's house was empty. Then where was Carolyn? She was not yet required to work, and the village school was not in session this day because the community had not yet agreed on the necessary revisions of texts to reflect the revealed reality of the God of Tarot. She must be taking a walk in the countryside, sorting out her own feelings. She knew she had to make a life of her own here, even if she could not accept it. He would find her.

She was not in the village. That meant she was out in the country. That bothered him; the wilderness was unsafe at best for any lone person and worse for a troubled child. Why had she risked herself so foolishly?

Why, indeed! Her whole life was in crisis; what did one extra hazard matter? Somehow he had to convince her that life was worthwhile . . . even life in Hell. Sure.

He found her in the afternoon on the steep eastern slope of Southmount, as the wind was stirring. He saw her small body on a ledge, the feet dangling over and swinging idly in little girl fashion. Suicide? No, she was not the type; she was merely comfortable there. But clouds were boiling up in the north, presaging another storm. These tempests seemed to be an almost daily occurrence, and they moved and spread rapidly—and brought unwanted Animation. Carolyn had to get off that mountain in the next few minutes!

Brother Paul ran to the foot of the nearer cone, getting pleasantly winded. He had neglected his exercises here on Planet Tarot!

The storm, racing him, loomed horrendously. Brother Paul could see the thunderhead of it shoving high into the sky, challengingly, a great black knob like the head of Satan, rotating its eyeless visage to bear upon this newly liberated settlement. Below, the shifting vapors showed the turbulence folding in on itself in living layers. This was a bad one!

"Get down from there!" he cried, doubting she could hear him from this distance over the swish of the fringe wind. But Carolyn looked down, her eyes bearing on him as the air tugged at her dress. Now she was aware of the threat. She scrambled onto the flat of the ledge, then started down, running fleetly along its broken slopes, hurdling the crevices with an agility that seemed foolhardy.

The wind stiffened. The first splats of rain struck the slope. This storm was straight from Northole; it would be carrying a full charge of Animation. Carolyn had to make it down before the effect distorted her perceptions. She could take a fatal fall!

Abruptly she stopped on a ledge about ten meters above Brother Paul's level. She screamed.

"Don't be frightened!" Brother Paul called. "Come down carefully, and we'll talk. Watch out for slippery rock where it's wet. I can control the visions—"

But she was pointing over his head. Alarmed, Brother Paul turned.

There was Bigfoot as huge and hairy as before.

"Stay up there!" Brother Paul cried to Carolyn. "I'll stop it from climbing." For there was no question of the monster's objective; it was heading not for Brother Paul, but for the nearest ramp ledge leading from the base toward Carolyn's perch. It was after her!

Brother Paul charged. He had no illusions after his prior encounter with this creature about his ability to beat it in physical combat. He had bested the Breaker, and the Breaker had balked Bigfoot—but it was also possible that Bigfoot had finally realized that Amaranth was not the woman it sought to kill, so had given up the attack. At any rate, Bigfoot's terrible mass and power would tell; judo could go far to equalize the imbalance, but at best the match was chancy. Brother Paul, in challenging this thing, was undertaking the fight of his life.

But he had to do it. Bigfoot had reached the foot of the cone and was starting up the ledge. Carolyn's frightened face poked over the edge, staring down. Bigfoot saw her and made that soul-chilling scream, and her face disappeared. All children of the human species had imaginary monsters that terrified them in the dark; Carolyn had a *real* one.

The wind intensified, buffeting the rock; Brother Paul hoped the child was bracing herself securely in some alcove so that she could not be dislodged. Bigfoot was not the only threat here!

He reached the ledge and ran up it. Bigfoot, quite agile, was negotiating the first bend. Brother Paul caught up, reaching for the creature's massive arm.

Bigfoot turned to face him, making that terrible swipe. But Brother Paul had anticipated this. He ducked under, caught that arm with both his own, and tried to heave the monster over his shoulder and off the face of the mountain.

Tried. For heave as he might, he could not budge Bigfoot. Despite the slick-smooth surface of the rock, the creature seemed to be rooted. What weight the thing must have to balk a throw of this power!

But if he didn't throw it now, he would be in Bigfoot's power, for he could not match its strength. Brother Paul threw his weight forward, his right arm extended in the *uchi makikomi* or inside wraparound throw. His own weight was leaning over the ledge, over a drop of about two meters, hauling Bigfoot's weight behind. This was one of the most powerful techniques in judo; the fall could knock the victim unconscious. Yet still Bigfoot resisted.

Brother Paul made his final effort. He twisted violently to the left, balanced on his left foot, and swept his right foot back against Bigfoot's leg in a *hane* motion. This should have lifted the creature right off the ledge and hurled the two of them to the ground below—but it didn't.

Now Bigfoot's hairy arms closed about him, squeezing. Brother Paul was lifted into the air, his feet dangling.

He jammed one elbow back, hard. It bounced off solid hide. He bent one knee and stomped backwards with his heel. The strike should have crushed tender anatomy—but it too bounced off harmlessly. He clutched at one of the hairy hands that pressed against his chest, seeking to hook one finger and bend it backwards until pain made the creature go—but the fingers were each like iron rods, immovable. He tried to shove his own two arms up and forward, forcing the enclosing arms apart so that he could drop free, but he could not get purchase. Bigfoot seemed invulnerable!

Now Brother Paul felt the breath of the monster on his neck. The thing was going to bite him!

Suddenly he had the inspiration of desperation. He could not overcome this thing physically—but maybe he could use Animation!

Brother Paul concentrated. He made himself resemble the Breaker.

Bigfoot reacted immediately, hurling away this dread infighter. Brother Paul sailed out over the ledge, oriented himself, and landed fairly neatly on his feet. It was a bone-shaking impact, but not a destructive one. Brother Paul absorbed the shock in his legs, fell forward, and took a rolling break-fall. This was not comfortable on this hard terrain—but a lot better than what Bigfoot had had in mind for him. As his back struck with a rolling impact it was cushioned by a cluster of Tarot Bubbles that skidded by; they popped all about him, releasing their gas.

He lurched back to his feet and looked for Bigfoot. The creature had resumed its climb, hugging the face of the rock so as to keep out of the buffeting wind. The rain remained light. Soon Bigfoot would reach Carolyn's ledge; then—

Brother Paul concentrated. The path in front of the monster became a void, dropping into an immeasurably deep chasm. Bigfoot halted, as well it might.

Now was the test: was this a stupid beast or a smart one? If the former, Brother Paul had it beaten—so long as the Animation effect lasted. He could show it a ledge that would drop it off the mountain. If the latter, Bigfoot would soon see through the ruse. That would mean real trouble.

The monster put one foot forward cautiously, one

paw sliding along the cliff wall. The continuing ledge might be invisible to it, even unfeelable to it, but the substance was there and so there was no fall. So—Bigfoot was too smart to be fooled by illusion more than momentarily. That was bad. Still, its progress had been greatly impeded.

Could he conjure a sword and hurl it at the monster? The conjurations of the men at the mess hall, back at the outset, had been solid. But Brother Paul realized now that those would have been converted objects of the table, wooden bowls and such, rather than constructs of air. Anything solid in Animation had to have some solid basis; otherwise it was no more than an illusion that would have no substance when touched. Illusory knives would not faze Bigfoot much longer than the illusory void had.

Still, it was necessary to try. Brother Paul conjured a huge black winged hawk. The bird of prey dived on Bigfoot. But the monster ignored it. Such hawks were not native to this planet, so were obviously fabrications. No luck there; the monster had human cunning.

How was he to stop Bigfoot? The thing was now halfway up the slope toward Carolyn, and once it got its paws on her, no illusion would help her. The Animations were losing their effect, and Brother Paul could not handle the creature physically. There were no convenient rocks here to throw, no suitable weapons. Nothing to adapt! Yet he could not let the thing get at Carolyn!

Only one thing seemed to offer a chance: Brother Paul had to fight it again—masking his location and intent by means of Animation. If Bigfoot could navigate a treacherous slope in a storm while under attack by an invisible enemy, then nothing could stop it.

One other notion. Brother Paul conjured an airplane towing a sky sign: HELP—SOUTHMOUNT. He sent it flying toward the village. If that Animation lasted, if the effect extended to the village, someone would see it, and then an armed party would have to investigate. They probably would not arrive in time, but at least it was a chance.

Now he conjured a group of Breakers. One by one they closed—and had no physical effect. Bigfoot had been fooled the first time; now it ignored Breakers. But one among that charging line was no phantom; it was Brother Paul in disguise. If he could get between the monster and the wall and shove outward, striking suddenly and by surprise—

Bigfoot was almost to Carolyn's ledge when Brother Paul caught up. The girl was cowering at the far edge of a level area; from there it was necessary either to climb up a meter—or down ten meters. The rock faces were slick with rain, and the wind was still gusting powerfully; it would be suicidal for her to attempt that route.

Before, she had foiled Bigfoot herself by making an Animation river the monster couldn't cross. This time she was too frightened to think of that—and the monster was not about to be fooled that way again anyway. It knew she was trapped.

The moment Brother Paul touched Bigfoot physically, the monster would recognize him—and that would be the end. Bigfoot was just too strong for him! Yet the thing's progress was inexorable—and now its eyes were fixed on the girl. No mock gulf or barrier would stop it, and she couldn't run. What to do?

Brother Paul concentrated. A wall of dancing yellow flames sprang up between monster and child. Bigfoot hesitated, then pushed through. Beyond—was nothing. The girl was gone.

Bigfoot paused, momentarily baffled—then made a human-sounding chuckle. It had caught on; Carolyn was there—but now she was invisible. Brother Paul had blotted her out via Animation. The monster cocked its head, listening.

Behind it, Brother Paul breathed hard, trying to drown out the sound of Carolyn's respiration. He hadn't learned how to control sounds yet. But that gave *him* away; now Bigfoot knew there was another person on the ledge. Brother Paul in his haste was making errors as fast as good moves. And time was running out.

There was a cry from below. It was Lee from the

village. "What's going on up there? There's a storm breaking!"

"Bigfoot's after Carolyn!" Brother Paul cried. "I can't stop it!"

"I'm coming up there!" Lee cried.

"No! There isn't time! Find a weapon, rocks, anything!" But in his agony of indecision, Brother Paul had let his Animation fade. Carolyn reappeared.

Bigfoot uttered a harsh scream of victory. It charged.

Brother Paul charged after it, concentrating again. A second Carolyn appeared beside the first, then a third. "Move about!" he cried to her. "So it can't tell which one is you." But she was frozen by terror.

Bigfoot closed on the real one. One hairy arm went out, catching the girl, lifting her up. "Daddy!" she screamed despairingly.

Brother Paul struck. Headfirst, he butted Bigfoot in the belly. All his weight was behind it; the monster was shoved backward one step, two. Brother Paul assumed a new form as he straightened up within the grasp of Bigfoot, reaching for the child.

Bigfoot stared in almost human dismay. Then its rear foot, seeking the ledge, came down on nothing.

Brother Paul wrenched Carolyn from the monster's grasp as it fell. Bigfoot windmilled its arms but could not recover balance. It fell—ten meters to the base of the cliff.

Lee arrived on the ledge. He came to look down on the still monster. "My God!" he exclaimed. "It's the Swami!"

Brother Paul stared. It *was* the Swami—and he looked dead.

Carolyn had cried "Daddy!" Brother Paul had misunderstood the reference. She had recognized her natural father at the last moment. And so had Brother Paul, unconsciously; only the Swami's power of *ki* or *kundalini* could account for the strength Bigfoot had. The last form Brother Paul had assumed had been that of the Swami himself. Bigfoot, seeing its alter ego, had been amazed—and had made that one careless misstep that had doomed it.

Brother Paul had killed Carolyn's real father.

"Come away from here, dear," Lee murmured, putting his arm around Carolyn. Her face a dry-eyed mask, she yielded. Dully, Brother Paul watched them go, experiencing *déjà vu*. This had happened before, this departure of man and girl from horror—at the gate of Hell.

And this was Hell too—and this was real.

Brother Paul paced alone in Reverend Siltz's cabin, waiting for his honor guard to accompany him to the mattermission capsule station. His mission here was over, his personal entanglements abated—but his depression had not lifted. If only he had achieved the wisdom of experience sooner, before he killed his daughter's true father! The signals had been there had he had the wit to interpret them correctly. The Swami, a serious man, intolerant of other religions, possessing strong psychic power, was unable to accept his wife's refusal to convert to his own faith. At the Animation fringe his savage and bestial rage had assumed physical shape—perhaps the result of intensive positive feedback. Anger, guilt, madness: Animation could be a destructive drug like heroine, cocaine, LSD, or mnem, abolishing the human mind's natural curbs and loosing monsters. How right the Swami had been in his initial warning: there was special danger in Animation. The Swami had known whereof he spoke first hand.

Yet Brother Paul could not believe the man had been evil. The Swami had evidently taken good care of Carolyn during his human phase; had his transformation into Bigfoot been conscious? Probably not. Had the Swami been a criminal, he would not have needed the assistance of Animation to kill his wife and daughter. Animation might seem to lend a special ability, as with Therion and his judo skill when he played the monster Apollyon, but that had really been Brother Paul's doing; he had credited Therion with a talent the man actually lacked, and played along governed by the role. The skill that the Swami had had, in contrast, had been genuine. Bigfoot's enormous size and mass were of course Animation enhanced, but the *ki* that had balked Brother Paul's attacks was inherent. Had the Swami's psychic power been directed in the area of aura, as Brother Paul's was, the Swami could have been a similar magician in Animation. But he had focused on one thing only: Bigfoot. This had been the man's private war between the conscious and unconscious minds, Dr. Jekyll and Mr. Hyde, two irreconcilable attitudes. Schizophrenia. Satan only knew how deep religious currents ran in some individuals! Brother Paul knew he would never understand the full nature of the Swami's motivation. To seek to kill one's own offspring—!

Now the child was doubly orphaned. Her mother had been killed, her natural father had become a monster, and her Animation adopted father a murderer. Justifiable homicide, legally, or self defense; Lee had been witness to Brother Paul's good intent. But in the eyes of Carolyn—

There was a measured knock on the door. Time to go. Brother Paul opened it—and there stood Lee. "Oh—I thought it would be—"

"Soon, not yet," Lee replied gravely. "I regret bracing you with a personal concern at this time, but I have no choice."

"Come in, sit down!" Brother Paul said heartily. "I am in the depths of a depression and need distraction though I may not deserve it. I failed my mission, wreaked religious havoc on this colony, and orphaned an innocent child. Planet Tarot deserved better!"

Lee faced him squarely. He was a handsome man whose strong character showed in his manner. He did indeed seem Christlike. "Who in Hell do you think you're fooling?" he asked evenly.

Brother Paul almost laughed at the incongruity. Yet in the context of the Animations, Christ and Hell were compatible. "I hope to fool nobody. I will make an honest report, buttressed by the holographic recording I was required to make, and then return to my Order of Vision station to seek what respite I am able from my conscience. I would apologize to you and the others of this Planet, if that were not ludicrously insufficient."

Lee shook his head. "I sent myself to Hell, and I deserved to go. You brought me out by showing me the error of my thinking, acquainting me with my true sin and exorcising it. Now it seems you have sent yourself to Hell—and it falls on me to return the favor. Paul, you succeeded in your mission, brought this colony the answer it demanded and deserved, and released a wonderful girl from certain death. I saw you in Hell and came to know you as well as a stranger can. You are determined and true, a great and good man, the closest approach to a living saint I know."

This time Brother Paul did laugh. "Hyperbole will get you nowhere! I daresay the truth is somewhere between the extremes we two have described. I once heard it said that truth is a shade of gray."

Lee smiled. "Or of brown. I will never forget what you did for me. You broadened my perspective and restored my faith when I doubted it sorely. Because of you, I questioned tenets of my religion I had never thought to question before and learned that Jesus would not have acted as I had. In fact, through you I came to understand Jesus Christ in a deep and personal manner. He will always be with me, henceforth; I bear the stigmata of his presence. I know now that a man's soul cannot be judged by his race—and I will exercise such powers as I can muster to have that doctrine of my Church revised. Yea, I will preach even the Parable of the Good Nigger—for you are that man."

"Thank you," Brother Paul said, uncertain whether to smile or frown. Just as the derogatory term "black" had come in the mid-twentieth century to be a mark of pride for those affected, so had the term "nigger" by the turn of the century. The same thing had happened earlier with the "Quakers" and no doubt would happen in future centuries too. Perhaps one day "Hell" would be an analogy for spiritual enlightenment. Perhaps that had already happened.

"And that brings me to my immediate business with you," Lee continued. "Your daughter necessarily also has black ancestry—"

"Carolyn? She is not my daughter; in reality she has *red* ancestry. The Swami was Amerind, not Asiaind."

"Oh?" Lee said, surprised. "The Mormons have compassion for Amerinds, who are the descendants of the early Israelite colonies of America. But this is irrelevant. I do this neither to show my freedom from the racial bias I carried into Hell nor to test it; I mention it only to clarify that without your intercession I would have been unable to consider it."

"Consider what?" Brother Paul asked, confused.

"The merging of the races of man."

"I must be of slow wit this morning. I don't follow—"

"She has no father now but you, and so it is to you I must, according to the custom of this Planet, make petition for—"

"Please stop!" Brother Paul said, pained. "I have no authority of any kind over Carolyn! Even her name is a construct of my ignorance; she must assume her own name. I am about to leave this planet."

"Yes. That is why I had to ask you now, for she is as yet underage and of a foreign faith. I would not change that faith, but will compromise in the manner shown by Reverend Siltz and—"

Brother Paul's brows furrowed. "Underage for *what*?"

"Sir," Lee said formally. "I humbly request permission to take your daughter's hand in matrimony."

Stunned, Brother Paul could only stutter. "You—you—"

"I was, among other roles, Herald the Healer of the far future. She was Psyche. Suddenly I knew that I loved her, and that love had been growing from the time of her act of courage in becoming a Watcher of the Animations, and that I had to have her though Hell itself bar the union. When I saw Bigfoot about to kill her—"

Still overwhelmed by the chaos of his emotions, Brother Paul lurched to his feet and stumbled outside.

Carolyn stood there, as he had somehow expected. She wore a sleek white dress, and her hair was elegantly braided and looped like a diadem. She resembled a fairy princess—no longer a child. For an instant Brother Paul saw Psyche, writhing in the terrible flame, the sacrificial child bride: a soul-searing image, yet indicative of the new reality. Little girls did grow up, and the jump from age twelve to age thirteen could be a giant one.

"Daddy!" she cried and flung herself into his arms in much the way Jeanette had gone to the Reverend Siltz. Child yesterday—woman tomorrow.

"Yes!" he cried, hugging her close, joy bursting upon him like the light of a nova. "Yes, Carolyn, yes—marry him! There is not a finer man on the planet! You will never burn, you will never suffer fear again, you will never be alone! You will make your own family, needing no other!"

She kissed him gently and disengaged. Through the blur of his tears Brother Paul saw Lee standing beside them. He caught Lee's hand—and saw the spot, the mark of the puncture of the nail. The stigmata of Christ. Only a scar, yet—

He set Carolyn's hand in Lee's, aware of his own intense relief. Now he knew she would be well cared for! "With my blessing," he said, squeezing their hands together.

There was a smattering of applause. Brother Paul blinked—and saw Reverend Siltz and his wife, and beside them Jeanette and a young man who favored Siltz in a meek way, and Therion and Amaranth and the rest of the villagers.

"It is time to march to the mattermitter," Siltz said.

"Bless you all," Brother Paul said, his depression abating.

Alone in the mattermission capsule, Brother Paul laid down his mock-up Animation Tarot cards on the crate of Bubbles in a game of Accordion. Each card had only its Triumph or suit and number designation notes; there were no illustrations. This makeshift deck was not pretty, but it satisfied his present purpose. In his mind's eye he saw the symbols as they had been in the Waldens deck, and as they would be in the Cluster deck.

He was playing this game because otherwise the sudden loneliness would overwhelm him. What he had experienced here, in person and in Animation—forever finished.

The Ghost Triumph came up. From its blank surface a film spread out and up, solidifying in air. It swelled, extending a pseudopod to touch the floor. Soon a substantial mass of protoplasm rested there. "Salutation, human friend," it signaled.

"Hello, Antares," Brother Paul said. "Good to meet you again."

"It was an intriguing adventure, much relief of tedium," Antares said. "This is a marvelous deck of concepts you are living."

"The Animation Tarot? Did you really participate?"

"In Animation, yes. Your aura made this possible. And your imagination. Perhaps there was an affinity of effects because both aura enhancement and Animation derive ultimately from the science of the Ancients. But you were the one who reunified them. Do you realize that this experience relates most closely to your deck of concepts?"

"My experience?"

"Your world sets the stage with its folly of matter-mission. The other cards follow in sequence, right until this present aspect of your wisdom. You have become a savant, more experienced in this unique area than others of your kind. Now you go forward toward Completion."

"You mean I did not discover the Original Tarot?" Brother Paul asked, troubled. "I merely translated my own life into the cards?"

"Not at all. Your life *reflects* the original Tarot, as all lives do. But for you it has been more dramatic than usual and more artistic. Even the five suits have direct force as segments of your adventure. This Tarot of yours will spread across the Cluster, affecting many alien civilizations and finally saving the Cluster itself from disaster."

Brother Paul smiled. "So the Animation suggested. But we have no way of knowing such a thing, alien friend. It was merely our imaginations functioning."

"I confess that much of the futuristic detail was my doing," Antares replied. "The culture of Sphere Nath, for example. But not all of it. There was an element that cannot be accounted for by rational means."

"Meaning this was all one big fantasy," Brother Paul said. "Yet I would never trade the experience for another. My life has been marked by what passed on Planet Tarot." Lee wore his stigmata on his body; Brother Paul wore his on his soul.

"I'm sure it has. But I do not believe it was fantasy. I prefer to call that unknown element the handiwork of God in whatever manner He may choose to manifest. In fact I am inclined to agree with the thesis of the Tarot Temple that *all* forms of God and all faiths are valid."

"The Tarot Temple . . ." Brother Paul repeated. Could he really be about to found anything like that? Surely not!

"When I was Herald the Healer, sharing the role with your son-in-law, I learned the history record of your life. You were quite famous as an ancient figure, in the forty-fifth century of the birth of your Jesus of Christ. You popularized the Cluster Tarot and the notion that true belief, rather than its particular form, was the essence of faith and that no religion should question the mode or precepts of any other. The Temple of Tarot was formed in your name, perhaps after your death, and every novice had to experience the Animation record of your adventure on Planet Tarot. You were called the Patriarch of Tarot."

"Over my dead body," Brother Paul said tolerantly. "Does your imaginative memory of my future also tell you what happened to my little girl in the airline terminal?"

Antares considered. "No, that detail was lost to history. But I am certain no bad thing happened to her, for she grew up to illustrate the Animation cards most prettily. I conjecture that the normal prediction of that vision was interrupted by the role player's imposition of her own concerns so that the sequence became invalid at that point. Probably the *real* Carolyn remained with you throughout, and the two of you returned to your wife, her mother, without further event.''

What wife? "That is a comfort to know," Brother Paul said. "Tell me, friend—since you manifest only in Animation or mattermission, will I ever meet you again? I don't expect to make any more such trips.''

"This is unknown," Antares responded. "But since you are conveying a sample of the Animation Bubbles to Earth, you may experience the effect again, and if you think of me at that time I shall be with you.''

"But how will I know it is *you*, and not just a wish fulfillment?''

There was no answer. Brother Paul found himself looking at his Ghost card—the symbol of the unknown. The trip was over.

Yet the significance remained, which the colonists had rejected but, it seemed, future civilization accepted: *All faiths were valid*. If that were so, why not his faith in his friend, the alien Antares?

IX

Completion: 28

I can hear the ministers, the priests, the rabbis, now screaming in their God-given robes that God can demand the life of any man, that we must all give our lives to God, offer ourselves up to His trust, do what He tells us to do in the "Good" books, which strangely enough are all written in the language of men. . . . But if we smash God in the grinning face, slip out of the way of that religiously swinging knife, trip Him and slip away to live for a few more days, escape again and again, cunningly slide from His grasp and disappear from His view, slip around Him, over Him, under Him, hanging onto our lives at all costs, then when He finally does get us, and He will, for everything is so much mightier than one thing, then He will have the sacrifice of a worthy opponent, a man who never asked for pity, who succumbed at the end in spite of himself, and lingering on in the absence of a body will be the gigantic spirit of one man's effort to belong to no one but himself, whole and complete, memorable even in defeat, distinguished even in death, leaving the ghostly presence of his pride, his will to be, his hatred of death and all ends, and this Holy Ghost

*will give the future such a forceful start it will be
off and running before God can kill it again.*
   —James Drought: *The Secret*, Norwalk, Conn.
Skylight Press, 1963.

Brother Paul expected complications of debriefing,
but these were few. Bored clerks took his recording
equipment, and a physician checked his vital signs.
"You have suffered some physical regression, Father,
but it is not serious. Get a few good nights sleep, exercise a little, eat well and you'll be back to norm quickly
enough."

He was dressed and on his way to the next office
before it registered. *Father*? He must have misheard.

"We are through with you," the clerk said. "The
computer is analyzing your holographic record now; we
will be in touch if any clarification is required." Obviously neither clerk nor computer had any notion what
was in that record; to them, this was mere routine.
Brother Paul wanted to get out of here and into the hin-
terland before anyone was disabused! "Where will we
be able to reach you?"

"I will report first to my superior, the Right Reverend
Father Crowder of the Holy Order of Vision," Brother
Paul said. "His address is in your records. Then I expect
to return to my own Station and start catching up on
backlogged chores. They must be just about out of
wood by now." But the clerk did not smile; he was
hardly paying attention. He was making his notes on a
slip of paper. Brother Paul was reminded of the old
definition of lecturing: a system whereby the material
passed from the notes of the instructor to the notes of
the student without going through the mind of either.
"You will be able to reach me through the Right
Reverend."

"Good enough," the clerk agreed, marking "RR" on
his slip. He smiled. "Good luck, Father."

Was he back in Animation? Brother Paul shook his
head, accepted the travel voucher, caught the electric
bus, and in four hours was met by the Right Reverend

himself. "Welcome back to Earth, Father Paul. I trust you are well?"

"I seem to be having some difficulty readjusting to reality. By what title did you address me, Reverend?"

"I shall clarify the situation succinctly," Rt. Rev. Crowder said briskly. "The Holy Order of Vision is expanding rapidly. It seems that the accelerating deceleration of our culture resulting from the colonization program creates an insatiable need for our type of ministry. No doubt the tide of social history will turn in due course, and we shall have to contract again, but at the moment we are desperately in need of competent organizers for new Stations. We must provide service where service is needed; that has always been our mission. In certain cases we have been forced to waive normal requirements. You have excellent recommendations, and your performance on this extraterrestrial mission did not diminish your prospects. You have suffered promotion, Father Paul."

"My performance!" Father (what a strange ring to that word; he was not sure he liked it) Paul exclaimed. "How would you know of that?"

"Mere survival would have been sufficient; the promotion was in the works before you departed this planet. But since we are the parent institution for this project, we received an immediate computer statement, unedited," Rt. Rev. Crowder explained. "In only four hours I could not of course do more than skim it—but that sampling was enough to convince me that you are a remarkable man. You have, it appears, identified God."

"No!" Father Paul cried. "I cannot accept that!"

"Oh, the holographs are quite specific, and so are the supplementary data. You might be interested to know that the technicians ran a check on the mattermission circuitry and discovered an imbalance corresponding to the postulated 'aura' of the alien visitor who brought to Earth the secret of mattermission. And the Extraterrestrial Chemistry Laboratory has been locked into absolute security by your sample of 'Tarot Bubbles.' Thus, to the extent we can verify it, your experience has objective bases. I am convinced that you did encounter Satan.''

Father Paul was afraid to ask how much of that holographic record would be made available to outsiders. He opposed censorship, but in this case he was tempted. ''But I went in search of God, not Satan!''

''There is no question Satan answered the prayers of the colonists,'' the Rt. Rev. Crowder continued. ''They wanted relief from the rigors of the planetary climate. They shall have it now. Planet Tarot is about to be declared proscribed; the Colonization Computer has declared Animation to be too dangerous for human use. All people there are to be resettled on other planets. The bureaucracy can move rapidly when it has to.''

''They're destroying the colony?'' Brother Paul asked, aghast. ''All the people in all the villages of the planet?''

''Satan does not pussyfoot, as you well know.''

''But this was not necessary to—''

''Do not be so shocked, Paul. There is no sacrilege here. Satan is but the nether face of God.''

''The nether face of God!'' Father Paul exclaimed.

''There is and can be only one God—but He has many aspects. For those people who are unready to face Him in His Heavenly phase, He makes available one for their level. There need be no mystery about this. In fact, Christianity draws its dualism from the Gnostics: the belief that all things are dual. Black versus white, good versus bad, God versus Satan. Just as two sexes facilitate the evolution of species, it seems that two facets of deity facilitate the evolution of conscience. Through this constant interaction we are tested and improved until we are more than we might have been. Just as women complement men, to their confusion and advantage, Satan complements God.''

''But everything had a rational explanation! There was nothing to show that the intercession of any Higher Power was necessary or that there was really any distinction between good and evil. In the framework of the intergalactic civilization of the Ancients—''

The Rt. Reverend looked at him shrewdly. ''You do

not regard these factors as products of your imagination?''

"I—" Father Paul hesitated, trying to marshal his mixture of thought and emotion. "You said yourself there is objective evidence for the existence of Antares in the—"

"I did indeed. I believe in the authenticity of your vision, Paul. I merely am verifying whether you believe in it yourself."

Again Father Paul hesitated. "I do believe—though it led me to Satan or to the renunciation of any concept of deity. I realize that makes me unfit for the promotion you have proffered or for any place in the Holy Order of Vision, and I regret intensely failing you in this way. But I must act on what I believe."

"And can you inform me what science or technology makes possible a divinatory look into the future?" the Rt. Reverend inquired.

"I—"

"And when you met Satan and were physically picked up by Him and consumed—what planetary reality accounted for that?"

"I cannot explain these things," Father Paul admitted. "I can only affirm that I believe in them."

"And so does your holograph—and the Colonization Computer, and a growing army of technicians," the Rt. Reverend said. "I believe them too. How would you explain the fantastic coincidence of the single man with the most potent aura among this species—being the one assigned to the planet where aura controls Animation?"

"I—" Father Paul began, baffled.

"I submit to you that there is only one agency that can reasonably account for the totality of your experience. What name would you put on that Great Unknown?"

"Why, that could only be—" The concept dwarfed his ability to express it. "I—saw God?" Father Paul asked numbly. Suddenly things were falling into place. Could all that precession have guided him accurately after all? "But God would not destroy the entire colony!"

"I offer a rationale," the Rt. Rev. Crowder said. "Let us surmise that, for the benefit of the Universe or at least the Galactic Cluster, it is necessary to educate a series of sapient entities in a very special way. High-Kirlian-Aura creatures to be suitable tools, perhaps fashioned from imperfect clay, yet tailored to the need. Call them Herald the Healer, or Melody of Mintaka, or Flint of Outworld—or Paul of Tarot. Perhaps even Jesus of Christ. Assume that these entities, properly prepared, will set in motion currents that will in the course of several millennia preserve the entire Cluster from needless and ironic destruction. As by devising or reconstituting a deck of cards whose images evoke key understandings on critical occasions—"

"Ridiculous!" Father Paul snapped.

The Rt. Reverend smiled. "No doubt. I certainly will not repeat such fancies to others. But were such a thing conceivably the case—would not the viability of a single colony planet be a trifling price to pay? We question God's purposes at our peril."

Father Paul put his hand to the pocket where he carried his mocked-up Animation Tarot deck. Could such a thing be true? "In that case," he said, awed, "God does exist—and this is His will."

"Is it not better to believe that—than to renounce your prior faith in Him?"

"Yes!" Father Paul exclaimed, as his balked belief was undammed. Undamned. Suddenly he felt whole again.

The Rt. Rev. Father smiled again. "Rest assured that neither this discussion nor the holographic record will be put into general circulation. The Colonization Computer, I am sure, is even now classifying the whole matter Absolute Satanic Secret, and I expect my copy of the holograph to be confiscated shortly. I only want you to know that I believe it was God's will that you be subjected to this experience, this tempering of your spirit in Hell, and that you surely acquitted yourself in a manner satisfactory to Him. It is easy to be noble and chaste when one is not subjected to stress and temptation and alteration of consciousness. You were Everyman; you

were flawed, yet survived. Thereby, you justify the
species and perhaps the form that life has taken in this
segment of the Universe. Life with aura.''

"Thank you," Father Paul murmured, not feeling
noble or chaste.

Rt. Rev. Crowder made a gesture of subject
dismissal. "There is another matter. The Holy Order of
Vision is, as I mentioned, expanding. This is not from
any missionary zeal on our part, but because we appear
to answer a need of the contemporary society in crisis.
But I repeat myself, I fear. My point is that it is important for attrition of our competent officers to be
minimized."

"Of course," Father Paul agreed, uncertain where
this was leading.

"I trust you will agree that the Reverend Mother
Mary is competent."

The relevance became uncomfortably clear. "Yes!
She helped lead me out of the darkness of my prior
ignorance. But she would never leave—"

Rt. Rev. Crowder shook his head. "She has given
notice."

Father Paul was shocked. "Her faith in God is absolute, not subject to vacillation like mine! She—"

"She wishes to leave the Holy Order of Vision. She is
carrying on only until we arrange a replacement for her
Station. It occurred to me that you might have some insight into her problem."

"I? No, I—" Father Paul broke off, dismayed. "You
didn't promote *me* to take her job!"

"No, no, of course not! Not directly at any rate. She
was due for rotation to a new Station anyway, so your
assumption of the office at the familiar Station is appropriate for your first assignment. But since you know
her better than I do, I thought it would be appropriate if
you spoke to her before she left. I hardly need to stress
the importance of persuading her to remain with us. She
has been one of the very finest of our young officers,
but I am thinking not merely of the welfare of the Order, but of Mary herself. I do not believe she would be
happy in another occupation."

"No, she would not," Father Paul agreed. "The Order is her whole life. This—this is not like her!" He shook his head, troubled. "I had looked forward to working with her again. Do you have any hint why she—?"

The Rt. Rev. Crowder frowned. "Her personal file is available to me, of course, as is yours. I am aware of the manner you came to the Holy Order of Vision. I know you were converted by Sister Beth before she—"

"I killed her," Father Paul said. "You know this, yet you promote me—"

"You, like her, were a victim of circumstance. All of us have enough sin on our consciences without exaggerating the significance of events beyond our control. My point is this: we of the Holy Order of Vision know our members rather well, particularly those in whom we see special promise. Most of our people are rather literally from the gutter. *I* am. I have blood on my hands, and a micro-lobotomy scar on my brain. Like you, I failed my final test; but it was society, not Satan, that brought me to justice. It is a cruel world we live in. Hell, in fact. But it is Hell, not Heaven, that most needs social workers. Therefore, your own past history does not surprise or shock me. What matters is your *present* state—which I believe is the point you made to the Mormon. Mary was a similar convert."

"This I can not believe!"

"Your naivete becomes you, Paul. You have spent all your life in Hell and have hardly seen it. I shall not betray the details of Mary's prior existence or how she came to us. You have seen what a jewel she became. I only want to clarify that had she been allowed to undertake the Planet Tarot mission, the Animations would have been no more comfortable for her than they were for you."

"*Allowed?* You mean she—"

"Mary volunteered for the mission, yes. We forbade it because we felt she lacked the physical stamina necessary. And so we subjected her to the double indignity of assigning you instead."

"She—she suspected what it would be like?"

"Yes. And I rather think she suffers from guilt for sending you—much as you suffered guilt for releasing Sister Beth to the police. Fortunately you survived, vindicating my judgment—and I think if you were to talk to Mary—"

"Yes! Yes, of course," Father Paul agreed. "She need feel no guilt on my account!"

"I was sure you would understand," the Right Reverend Father Crowder said. But his smile was enigmatic.

Brother Paul's route home differed from his one to the mattermitter so long ago in experience. This too was Order policy: to seek new territory even when only passing through, rather than retrace steps. Thus he found himself one night at the Tribe of the Picts. Whether they really resembled the original Gaelics or Celts of Europe was questionable, but he was too diplomatic to evince skepticism.

Their Chief was naked, his torso stained blue and green and horrendously tattooed: obviously a matter of great pride. "Seldom have I encountered such handsome art," Father Paul said tactfully.

"Welcome to our hospitality," the naked artist said appreciatively. "But Father, if you would—my child is sick—"

"I am not a doctor—" Father Paul said cautiously.

"We have doctors; they have been unable to help. They say she needs a hospital, X-rays, blood transfusion, diagnostics, drugs—" He faced Father Paul. "It is a long ride to civilization. She will die before we can get her to such help!"

"I will look at her," Father Paul said. One problem with this retreating technology was the return of ancient killers, increasing child mortality. Diseases of inattention and malsanitation and ignorance. The Picts *were* far from civilization—in a number of ways.

The child lay on a cot in a dark hut. As he came to her, Father Paul had another siege of *déjà vu*. Had he been here before? Not in this century surely!

She was certainly sick. She was about ten, her face wizened by pain, the rind of old vomit at the corners of her mouth. Malnutrition was probably a complicating factor, as it had been in medieval times. He reminded himself again that this was not intentional child neglect; primitives simply didn't *know* what good diet was or what a healthy environment was. Probably the doctors had tried to tell the Chief—but there was only so much any person could say in such a situation if he wished to keep his own health. Father Paul would make a prescription that might balance her intake somewhat if he were able to help her through this crisis; *if* he helped her, her father might pay attention.

Her skin was pale, almost translucent. She needed light and attention—and love. Where was her mother? Someone to hold her and tell her stories and listen to her little joys and tribulations. True primitives centered their lives around their children, but these modern regressed people hadn't put it all together yet. Their families were likely to be destroyed along with their prior livelihoods. Different people regressed at different rates in different ways. It was Hell on marriages. He would have to make a prescription in that area too.

Yet it would all be academic if she were too far gone. First he had to catch his rabbit.

He sat beside her, taking one burning little hand. "Pretty child, I love you. Your father loves you. God loves you. Wake and be well." He put his other hand on her forehead and prayed silently: *God, help this child. Bring her out of Hell.*

His aura flowed through her body—that aura others said was one of the strongest known. This was not Animation of external appearances, but attempted animation of something more important: the will to live. He had to form a new self-image within her to make her believe that her illness was an illusion to be banished, that she, like the Christian Scientists, could conquer—if she had faith.

And—she healed. Her fever dropped, her tension eased, and she woke. He felt her consciousness rising through her modest aura, drawing strength from his strength, his love. Her eyes opened, bright blue. She smiled.

"From this day forward," the Chief said from behind Father Paul, his voice trembling with emotion, "this Tribe worships your God."

"My God is Love," Father Paul said.

Then the reaction struck him. *He had healed her!* He had touched her, willed her to live, called on God, and used his aura in a new way to make this child well—just as Herald the Healer had done in the far future and Jesus Christ in the near past.

The ability he had realized in Animation—remained with him in life. He was now a Healer.

The Station was poignantly familiar with its windmill and conservative buildings. Father Paul had to remind himself that he had been away only a fortnight or so, though he had roamed back and forth through some five thousand years in that interim. From the Buddha to the Amoeba!

Brother Peter emerged from the kitchen as he passed. "Congratulations, Father!" he exclaimed. "Go right on to the Reverend's office; she's expecting you."

Father Paul lingered a moment over the handshake. "Brother—how is she? I have heard she is not well."

Brother Peter glanced down at their merged hands. "There is something about you—some power—"

"The power of a renewed faith in God," Father Paul said. He did not care to explain about the aura at this time. "But about the Reverend—"

"Father, I'm sure you can handle it." And that was all Brother Peter would say.

Father Paul went to the office, though he was somewhat grimy from the trek. This was where his mission had started a world and time ago; it was appropriate that it also terminate here. He paused at the door, nervously rehearsing his arguments: how she could do so much more good within the Order than without it; how she had done him no disfavor by sending him to Planet Tarot, but instead had greatly facilitated his self-discovery; how the Right Reverend Father had spoken well of her performance in office; and how the Order needed her services now more than ever in this crisis of its expansion. He would not mention what he had learned of her pre-Order past of course; that would not be diplomatic, though it provided her with a human dimension in his mind that she had lacked before. Instead of an angel, she was an angelic woman: a significant distinction. But he would try his best to persuade her to remain. Yes.

He opened the door and stepped into the small office as he had before. She was standing by her desk, facing away from him, a stunningly forlorn figure. *What had happened to her?*

"Mary," he said, experiencing a rush of strange emotion. That had not been what he meant to say!

"Paul, I know what case you mean to make," she said, her voice partly muffled. "But my decision has been made. I only want to explain the mechanisms of the office and to congratulate you on—"

Something about her—the Animation scene of Dante's *Paradiso*, where—"Mary, face me," he said gently.

Slowly she turned about, not bothering to dab the tears from her cheeks. "You are safe. God bless you."

God bless you. Father Paul studied her face, recognizing only now what he had been unable to see before. *She* was the angel he had been questing for all through the Animations! No wonder he had never really acquiesced to Amaranth's advances. Amaranth had been at best a surrogate figure, standing in lieu of the woman he really loved. During his whole adventure in Animation he had been searching for—what he had left behind. The girl next door. Yet he had not dared, even in imagination, to hope that this ideal woman could ever be his.

And what made him suppose anything had changed? She had never given any hint of romantic interest in him; she had always been completely proper as befitted her position. It was difficult to believe that her pre-Order history could have been as checkered as his; she had to be of a higher plane. Now, upset at what she thought had been a bad decision on her part, did she propose to return to that lesser prior life?

He wanted to cry out his suddenly discovered love, but could not. What a fool he would be to suppose that this angel would ever consider his suit! To speak it would be to invite a polite, gentle, half-apologetic demurral: her attempt to set him straight without hurting his feelings. Despite her own pressing problem, she would make this effort out of the decency in her heart. To touch her would be to destroy her as he had destroyed Sister Beth—even if he only touched her with a word. He had no right!

Yet—why was she crying? He had never seen her in such open distress, such loss of equilibrium; he had never known there were tears in her. If it had been concern for him while on the dangerous mission she had been denied, she was now absolved. He had survived, he had grown, he had returned! If it was her sadness at resigning the Order, why was she *doing* it? There had to be something else.

"Mary, will you tell me what grieves you?" he asked. "If it is the loss of your Station here, I will gladly renounce the office. I know I can not measure up to the standard you have maintained. I will go away from here—"

Her voice was now normal, controlled, in contrast to her eyes. "Do not do that, Paul. I am glad for your success. I apologize for losing control; it ill becomes the occasion." She paused. Then: "You have seen God."

And she had not? She was not the type to envy him that! Still there was something unclear here, yet vital.

He thought of his new Tarot. Could it help him? No, he had to work this out alone. He had made the wrong decision with Sister Beth, a girl he hardly knew. How much more critical was *this* decision! Should he risk all by professing his love for Mary openly—or by concealing it? He could not bear to see her this way, so inexplicably tearful—yet he could not afford to aggravate the situation by making another error.

There was only one thing to do. Father Paul dropped
to his knees to pray to God for the answer.

Opposite him, the Reverend Mother Mary did the
same.

*God of Tarot, God of Earth, God of my experi-
ence—show me the way!* he prayed in silence.

God did not speak to him. God never had—not this
way. Should he pray instead to Satan? The Devil was
always responsive!

No! God and Satan might be one, and there might be
no such thing as Evil—but he had to orient on the aspect
he believed in. The God of Good, of Right, of Love.
Thy Will be done.

Mary spoke. "I see you are troubled, Paul. It is not
right to conceal my concern from you; God tells me
that. I will tell it simply. I—had visions relating to you
during your absence. It was at times as though I was
a—a siren, a harlot, a temptress, as once I was before I
found God. An evil creature, luring you into error in
thought and action. Your heart and eye were fixed on
God, but I was the agent of Satan, leading you to Hell
itself, balking at nothing, using strange Tarot cards—"
She hesitated, weeping. "I never suspected such depths
of depravity remained in me. I must get out of your life
forever. May God forgive me my sin against you!"

Father Paul opened his eyes and stared across the gulf
that separated him from Mary. Her eyes remained
closed, and her face was now in repose, hauntingly
familiar in a new way. She had made her confession—without comprehending its true nature. *She
had suffered a psychic linkage with him during his
Animations!* She thought Amaranth's mischief and
Therion's stemmed from her own imagination and will.
She could not know that what was false to her was,
paradoxically, true to him. She had seen Satan—and he
recognized it as God.

What quirk could have linked their minds across the
light years? No known force could explain it, other than
God's will—expressed through the force of love.

She loved him!

He studied her face with new understanding. Mary had shared his experience. He would need to keep no secrets from her, hide no shame. She had seen him at his worst—and tried to absorb the evil to herself.

"And did you also stand before the Cross as Jesus was crucified?" he inquired gently. "And in the Tenth Heaven of Paradiso?"

"That too," she agreed, not comprehending. How blessed was her innocence!

In this calm pose she reminded him strangely of—

Like another nova burst, it came to him. *Of Carolyn!* His daughter of Animation! Not to the child actress, now bound with her fiancee for some distant colony planet where religion would not be so bad a problem and Animation would be no problem at all. Rather, to the one he had accompanied on the airplane, revisiting his old college, ten years hence. To the one he had struggled to save from death in the fourteenth century. His *real* daughter—or daughter-to-be.

This was the mother of that child.

Father Paul reached across and took Mary's hand, letting his aura heal her.

The God of Tarot had answered.

Appendix

ANIMATION TAROT

The Animation Tarot deck of concepts as recreated by Brother Paul of the Holy Order of Vision consists of thirty Triumphs roughly equivalent to the twenty-two Trumps of contemporary conventional Tarot decks, together with five variously tilted suits roughly equivalent to the four conventional suits plus Aura. Each suit is numbered from one through ten, with the addition of four "Court" cards. The thirty Triumphs are represented by the table of contents of this novel, and keys to their complex meanings and derivations are to be found within the applicable chapters. For convenience the Triumphs are represented below, followed by a tabular representation of the suits, with their meanings or sets of meanings (for upright and reversed fall of the cards); the symbols are described by the italicized words. Since the suits are more than mere collections of concepts, five essays relating to their fundamental nature follow the chart.

No Animation Tarot deck exists in published form at present. Brother Paul used a pack of three-by-five-inch file cards to represent the one hundred concepts, simply writing the meanings on each card and sketching the symbols himself, together with any other notes he found pertinent. These were not as pretty or convenient as published cards, but were satisfactory for divination,

study, entertainment, business and meditation a
required. A full discussion of each card and the specia
conventions relating to the Animation deck would b
too complicated to cover here, but those who wish t
make up their own decks and use them should discove
revelations of their own. According to Brother Paul'
vision of the future, this deck will eventually b
published, perhaps in both archaic (Waldens) an
future (Cluster) forms, utilizing in the first cas
medieval images and in the second case images draw
from the myriad cultures of the Galactic Cluster, circ
4500 A.D. It hardly seems worthwhile for interested per
sons to wait for that.

TRIUMPHS

 0 Folly (Fool)
 1 Skill (Magician)
 2 Memory (High Priestess)
∞ Unknown (Ghost)
 3 Action (Empress)
 4 Power (Emperor)
 5 Intuition (Hierophant)
 6 Choice (Lovers)
 7 Precession (Chariot)
 8 Emotion (Desire)
 9 Discipline (Strength)
10 Nature (Family)
11 Chance (Wheel of Fortune)
12 Time (Sphinx)
13 Reflection (Past)
14 Will (Future)
15 Honor (Justice)
16 Sacrifice (Hanged Man)
17 Change (Death)
18 Vision (Imagination)
19 Transfer (Temperance)
20 Violence (Devil)
21 Revelation (Lightning-Struck Tower)
22 Hope/Fear (Star)
23 Deception (Moon)
24 Triumph (Sun)
25 Reason (Thought)
26 Decision (Judgment)
27 Wisdom (Savant)
28 Completion (Universe)

SUIT CARDS

	NATURE	SCIENCE	FAITH	TRADE	ART
1	Do *Scepter*	Think *Sword*	Feel *Cup*	Have *Coin*	Be *Lemniscate*
2	Ambition Drive *Torch*	Health Sickness *Scalpel*	Quest Dream *Grail*	Inclusion Exclusion *Ring*	Soul Self *Aura*
3	Grow Shrink *Tree*	Intelligence Curiosity *Maze*	Bounty Windfall *Cornucopia*	Gain Loss *Wheel*	Perspective Experience *Holograph*
4	Leverage Travel *Lever*	Decision Commitment *Pen*	Joy Sorrow *Pandora's Box*	Investment Inheritance *Gears*	Information Literacy *Book*
5	Innovation Suspicion *Hand of Glory*	Equilibrium Stasis *Kite*	Security Confinement *Lock*	Permanence Evanescence *Pentacle*	Balance Judgment *Scales*
6	Advance Retreat *Bridge*	Freedom Restraint *Balloon*	Temptation Guilt *Bottle*	Gift Theft *Package*	Change Stagnation *Möbius Strip*
7	Effort Error *Ladder*	Peace War *Plow*	Promise Threat *Ship*	Defense Vulnerability *Shield*	Beauty Ugliness *Face*
8	Power Impotence *Rocket*	Victory Defeat *Flag*	Satisfaction Disappointment *Mirror*	Success Failure *Crown*	Conscience Ruthlessness *Yin-Yang*
9	Accomplishment Conservation *Trophy*	Truth Error *Key*	Love Hate *Klein Bottle*	Wealth Poverty *Money*	Light Dark *Lamp*

SUIT CARDS (Continued)

	NATURE	SCIENCE	FAITH	TRADE	ART
10	Hunger *Phallus*	Survival *Seed*	Reproduction *Womb*	Dignity *Egg*	Image *Compost*
	ENERGY	GAS	LIQUID	SOLID	PLASMA

COURT CARDS

	NATURE	SCIENCE	FAITH	TRADE	ART
PAGE	Child of Fire	Child of Air	Child of Water	Child of Earth	Child of Aura
KNIGHT	Youth of Work	Youth of Trouble	Youth of Love	Youth of Money	Youth of Spirit
QUEEN	Lady of Activity	Lady of Conflict	Lady of Emotion	Lady of Status	Lady of Expression
KING	Man of Nature	Man of Science	Man of Faith	Man of Trade	Man of Art
	ENERGY	GAS	LIQUID	SOLID	PLASMA

NATURE

The Goddess of Fertility was popular in spring. Primitive peoples believed in sympathetic magic: that the examples of men affect the processes of nature— that human sexuality makes the plants more fruitful. To make sure nature got the message, they set up the Tree of Life, which was a giant phallus, twice the height of a man, pointing stiffly into the sky. Nubile young women capered about it, singing and wrapping it with bright ribbons. This celebration settled on the first day of May, and so was called May Day, and the phallus was called the Maypole. The modern promotion of May Day by Communist countries has led to its decline in the Western world, but its underlying principle remains strong. The Maypole is the same Tree of Life found in the Garden of Eden, and is represented in the Tarot deck of cards as the symbol for the Suit of Nature: an upright rod formed of living, often sprouting wood. This suit is variously titled Wands, Staffs, Scepters, Batons, or, in conventional cards, Clubs. Life permeates it; it is the male principle, always ready to grow and plant its seed. It also relates to the classic "element" of Fire, and associates with all manner of firearms, rockets, and explosives. In religion, this rod becomes the scepter or crozier, and it can also be considered the measuring rod of faith, the "canon."

FAITH

The true source of the multiple legends of the Grail is unknown. Perhaps this famous chalice was originally a female symbol used in pagan fertility rites, a counterpart to the phallic Maypole. But it is best known in Christian mythology as the goblet formed from a single large emerald, from which Jesus Christ drank at the Last Supper. It was stolen by a servant of Pontius Pilate, who washed his hands from it when the case of the presumptuous King of the Jews came before him. When Christ was crucified, a rich Jew, who had been afraid before to confess his belief, used this cup to catch some of the blood that flowed from Jesus's wounds. This man Joseph deposited Jesus's body in his own tomb, from which Jesus was resurrected a few days later. But Joseph himself was punished; he was imprisoned for years without proper care. He received food, drink and spiritual sustenance from the Grail, which he retained, so that he survived. When he was released, he took the Grail to England, where he settled in 63 A.D. He began the conversion of that region to Christianity. The Grail was handed to his successors from generation to generation until it came at last to Sir Galahad of King Arthur's Round Table. Only the chaste were able even to perceive it. The Grail may also relate to the Cornucopia, or Horn of Plenty, the ancient sym-

bol of the bounty of growing things. It is the cup of love
and faith and fruitfulness, the container of the classic
"element" of water, and the symbol of the essential
female nature (i.e., the womb) represented in the Suit of
Cups of the Tarot.

TRADE

It is intriguing to conjecture which of the human instincts is strongest. Many people assume it is sex, the reproductive urge—but an interesting experiment seems to refute that. A group of volunteers including several married couples was systematically starved. As hunger intensified, the pin-up pictures of girls were replaced by pictures of food. The sex impulse decreased, and some couples broke up. Food dominated the conversation. This suggests that hunger is stronger than sex. Similarly, survival—the instinct of self-preservation—seems stronger than hunger, for a starving person will not eat food he knows is poisoned, or drink salt water when dehydrating on a raft in the ocean. This hierarchy of instincts seems reasonable, for any species must secure its survival before it can successfully reproduce its kind. Yet there may be an even more fundamental instinct than these. When the Jews were confined brutally in Nazi concentration death-camps, they co-operated with each other as well as they could, sharing their belongings and scraps of food in a civilized manner. There, the last thing to go was personal dignity. The Nazis did their utmost to destroy the dignity of the captives, for people who retained their pride had not been truly conquered. Thus dignity, or status, or the perception of self-worth, may be the strongest human instinct. It is represented in the Tarot as the Suit of Disks, or Pentacles, or Coins, and associates with the "element" Earth, and with money (the ignorant person's status), and business or trade. Probably the original symbol was the blank disk of the Sun (gold) or Moon (silver).

MAGIC

In the Garden of Eden, Adam and Eve were tempted by the Serpent to eat of the fruit of the Tree of Knowledge of Good and Evil. The fruit is unidentified; popularly it is said to be the apple (i.e., breast), but was more probably the banana (i.e., phallus). Obviously the forbidden knowledge was sexual. There was a second special Tree in the Garden: the Tree of Life, which seems to have been related. Since the human couple's acquisition of sexual knowledge and shame caused them to be expelled from Eden and subject to the mortality of Earthly existence, they had to be provided an alternate means to preserve their kind. This was pro-creation—linked punitively to their sexual trans-gression. Thus the fruit of "knowledge" led to the fruit of "life," forever tainted by the Original Sin.

Naturally the couple would have escaped this fate if they could, by sneaking back into Eden. To prevent re-entry to the Garden, God set a flaming sword in the way. This was perhaps the origin of the symbol of the Suit of Swords of the Tarot, representing the "element" of air. The Sword associates with violence (war), and with science (scalpel) and intellect (intangible): God's manifest masculinity. Yet this vengeful if versatile weapon was transformed in Christian tradition into the symbol of Salvation: the Crucifix, in turn transformed by the bending of its extremities into the Nazi Swastika. And so as man proceeds from the ancient faith of Magic to the modern speculation of Science, the Sword proceeds inevitably from the Garden of Eden . . . to Hell.

ART

Man is frightened and fascinated by the unknown. He seeks in diverse ways to fathom what he does not comprehend, and when it is beyond his power to do this, he invents some rationale to serve in lieu of the truth. Perhaps the religious urge can be accounted for in this way, and also man's progress into civilization: man's insatiable curiosity driving him to the ultimate reaches of experience. Yet there remain secrets: the origin of the universe, the smallest unit of matter, the nature of God, and a number of odd phenomena. Do psychics really commune with the dead? How does water dowsing work? Is telepathy possible? What about faith healing? Casting out demons? Love at first contact? Divination? Ghosts?

Many of these inexplicable phenomena become explicable through the concept of aura. If the spirit or soul of man is a patterned force permeating the body and extending out from it with diminishing intensity, the proximity of two or more people would cause their surrounding auras to interpenetrate. They could thus become aware of each other on more than a physical basis. They might pick up each other's thoughts or feelings, much as an electronic receiver picks up broadcasts or the coil of a magnetic transformer picks up power. A dowser might feel his aura interacting with water deep in the ground, and so know the water's location. A person with a strong aura might touch one who was ill, and the strong aura could recharge the weak one and help the ill person recover the will to live. A man and a woman might find they had highly compatible auras, and be strongly attracted to each other. An evil aura might impinge on a person, and have to be exorcised. And after the physical death of the body, or host, an aura might float free, a spirit or ghost, able to communicate only with specially receptive individuals, or mediums.

In short, the concept of aura or spirit can make much of the supernatural become natural. It is represented in the Animation Tarot deck as the Suit of Aura, symbolized in medieval times by a lamp and in modern times by a lemniscate (infinity symbol: ∞), and embracing a fifth major human instinct or drive: art, or expression. Only man, of all the living creatures on Earth, cares about the esthetic nature of things. Only man appreciates painting, and sculpture, and music, and dancing, and literature, and mathematical harmonies, and ethical proprieties, and all the other forms and variants of artistic expression. Where man exists, these things exist—and when man passes on, these thing remain as evidence of his unique nature. Man's soul, symbolized as art, distinguishes him from the animals.